UNCLOTHED AND UNASHAMED

Rosellen's heart beat against her chest. Slow, hard, sure. Cason kept the gun pointed straight at her as she rose from the windowsill. He was ___ ___ man. Powerful and dangerous.

He didn't move to pull ___ ___ with the sheet.

She knew he wanted h ___ up her spine.

With deliberate slowness she let her gaze travel down his strong neck, over his broad, muscular shoulders and chest, then lower to his firm, flat stomach and lean, narrow hips.

"Are you through looking me over?" he asked. "I can stand here longer if you need more time."

She lightly cleared her throat before attempting to speak. "I have three older brothers. I've seen the male body."

"But you haven't seen *me* before."

"That sounds like a challenge."

"Then it must be." He dropped his gun to his side.

Without conscious effort her gaze followed the movement of his hand to the lower part of his body. She saw curly, dark golden blond hair and—*big*.

Her body responded with excitement, but she said, "You all look alike."

An attractive grin lifted one corner of his mouth. "Liar."

EVERYONE LOVES THE ROMANCES OF GLORIA DALE SKINNER

CASSANDRA

"Once you pick up *Cassandra*, you can't put it down."
—Joan Johnston, author of *The Bodyguard*

"*Cassandra* will captivate and steal your heart. A warm-hearted, tender tale of love lost and found. . . . A delightful read!"
—Millie Criswell, national bestselling author of *Dangerous*

"Great characters, great setting, great romance."
—Patricia Potter, author of *Starcatcher*

"An entertaining, enlightened, and endearing romance. This one will brand your heart and touch your soul!"
—Pamela James, *The Literary Times*

"Gloria has written one of my favorite kinds of books—a real 'heart fuzzy.' It's warm and tender with just a touch of spice. . . . Way to go, Ms. Skinner!"
—Denise Smith, Aunt Dee's Book Bag

"*Cassandra* [captures] the West as we love it. Good guys and bad, action and adventure, romance and passion. A rip-roaring good read."
—Yvonne Zalinski, Paperback Outlet

"Ms. Skinner brings the reader a dramatic, inspiring story of the western frontier and how two people made it work with their love."
—Celia Davis, Bell, Book & Candle

"[A] moving story. . . . Emotions run high and you are riveted with Cass' feelings of rejection and hurt. I really enjoyed this book."
—Becky Rotz, *Old Book Barn Gazette*

"Great action, terrific love story, [a] one-day read—and well worth it!"
—Dawn Acosta, Cover to Cover

JULIANA

"This wonderfully emotional novel is a delicious blend of suspense, exciting characters, and smooth narration. *Juliana* is a touching love story readers won't soon forget. Get ready for a great adventure!"

—*Rendezvous*

"Fast-paced and warmhearted, this story carries readers into a world of justice and love."

—Anne Black, *Romantic Times*

"A rousing, action-packed adventure that will thrill fans of the Americana romance. Characters so very well developed that they feel like next-door neighbors. This glorious novel is worth reading."

—*Painted Rock Reviews* (online)

"Gloria Dale Skinner is superb in *Juliana*. A deeply touching story to share with others. Four and a half bells!"

—Donita Lawrence, Bell, Book & Candle

RANSOM

"A tale full of passion, humor, and adventure that readers will treasure. This finely crafted story shows Ms. Skinner's writing at its best. Superb!"

—*Rendezvous*

"An action-packed, fast-paced adventure with a feisty heroine and a macho hero."

—*Romantic Times*

"The authentic western dialect and spicy love scenes tickled the senses."

—*Rawhide & Lace*

Books by Gloria Dale Skinner

Ransom
Juliana
Cassandra
Hellion

Published by POCKET BOOKS

GLORIA DALE SKINNER

HELLION

POCKET STAR BOOKS

New York   London   Toronto   Sydney   Tokyo   Singapore

This book is a work of fiction. Names, characters, places and incidents are products of the author's imagination or are used fictitiously. Any resemblance to actual events or locales or persons, living or dead, is entirely coincidental.

An *Original* Publication of POCKET BOOKS

A Pocket Star Book published by
POCKET BOOKS, a division of Simon & Schuster Inc.
1230 Avenue of the Americas, New York, NY 10020

Copyright © 1998 by Gloria Dale Skinner

ISBN: 1-4165-0303-X

This Pocket Books paperback printing May 2004

10 9 8 7 6 5 4 3 2 1

POCKET STAR BOOKS and colophon are registered trademarks of Simon & Schuster Inc.

Cover art by Kam Mak

Printed in the U.S.A.

HELLION

Chapter

→ 1 ←

Poppy, Colorado

Rosellen Lattimer stopped outside the batwing doors of the Silver Nugget Saloon and looked down one side of the street and up the other. From where she stood on the boardwalk she could see the length of Main Street and most of its weathered buildings.

Satisfied it was a quiet afternoon in Poppy, Colorado, Rosellen flipped her hat off and let it fall to the back of her neck, then shouldered her way through the batwing doors of the town's most popular watering hole. Afternoon sunshine spilled in behind her. Pausing just inside the doorway for a moment, she let her eyes adjust. The saloon was hot, dark, and quiet. The stifling scent of stale tobacco and rank whiskey hovered like a foggy cloud in the windowless room.

"You're late."

At the sound of the feminine voice, Rosellen's gaze swept the area behind the bar. She recognized the woman who'd spoken as Delta. Rosellen had seen the soiled dove in town, shopping for fancy fabrics, lace, and scented water at the general store.

She didn't like being reprimanded but decided to hold her tongue until she knew why she'd been summoned to the saloon on this summer afternoon. The only thing Rosellen could think of was that it had to do with her wanting to be the new sheriff of Poppy.

The whole town was in an uproar over it.

"A woman sheriff?" people said. "What in the blue blazes is she thinking?" "A sheriff named Rosellen? What an an outrageous idea!"

"Gayla's other guest has already arrived," Delta said in a slow purring voice.

Rosellen hid her surprise at hearing she wasn't the only one who'd received the request for a visit with the aging madam.

Movement at the far side of the room caught Rosellen's attention. A tall, powerful-looking man stepped out of the shadows and into a slice of hazy sunlight. All of her senses went on alert.

Sandy brown hair fell loose across his forehead. He stood straight, proud. Slender masculine fingers held a new black Stetson with a fancy braided hatband.

Rosellen made it her business to know everyone in town. A quick assessment told her this man was a stranger, and instinct told her he was no ordinary cowboy. He looked too confident, too much at ease with his surroundings. She stepped closer and watched his dark brown eyes size her up the way a gunfighter might study his opponent before he drew his gun. He was definitely giving her a close once-over.

For a heartbeat, Rosellen's stomach fluttered. But with three older brothers she'd learned the hard way not to let any man intimidate her. She squared her shoulders and subjected the powerful-looking stranger to the same intense scrutiny he was giving her.

She couldn't distinguish his features clearly but saw

enough to know he would send most women into a swoon. She took note of a clean-shaven face with a strong jawline. The bridge of his nose flared slightly, and his cheekbones were well defined.

He wore black trousers and a white banded-collar shirt. The sleeves were rolled up just past his elbows, showing muscular forearms. His wide-strap gun belt rode low over slim hips. The ivory handle of his revolver looked expensive—and worn.

An uncomfortable feeling skittered up Rosellen's spine, but she tamped it down. If she wanted to be sheriff she couldn't allow herself to be spooked by every dangerous-looking man who rode into town.

She walked farther into the saloon and nodded once to the stranger. He barely returned the greeting, but she refused to be intimidated by his unfriendly manner.

Giving her attention back to Delta, Rosellen said, "I'm here now. Where do we go?"

Delta cut her eyes around to the man and slowly stroked her lips with the tip of her tongue before saying, "Follow me."

The young woman pushed away from the bar and sashayed toward a door at the back of the room. Her rounded hips swayed suggestively beneath the pink satin robe that clung to her contours.

The heels of Rosellen's new mule-ear boots clicked on the wide-plank floor as she strode past the bar and the unoccupied gaming tables. Rosellen didn't know if it was out of respect for the Lord's day or if the men just wanted to spend more time with their families, but the saloons didn't get much business on Sunday afternoons anymore.

Years ago when her father was first elected sheriff of Poppy, no time of day or night was respected in the town. The saloons were always open. She'd heard her father say many times that when morality showed up in a mining town, the bawdy houses were the first establishments to shut down.

Out of habit she let her right arm swing loose at her side as she walked, occasionally brushing the carved wooden handle of her old army-issue Colt. Her father had bought the rare short-barreled gun from a traveling salesman as a gift for Rosellen when she was sixteen.

Delta halted and braced herself against the door-jamb, rolling her back from shoulder to shoulder against the wood while keeping her sights on the stranger. "Gayla's room is down the hallway. Last door on the right. It's open. Go on in."

Rosellen stopped and turned around, nearly bumping into the stranger. She had to look up at him for their eyes to meet. It surprised her that he had his gaze on her and not on the cleavage Delta proudly displayed for his attention.

His chin was softly rounded with the tiniest hint of a cleft in its center. Full, attractively shaped lips fell slightly parted. The rhythm of Rosellen's heartbeat increased.

"I don't like having a stranger at my back," she snapped, suddenly confused by the way she felt.

A reckless smile flashed across his face. "Name's Cason Murdock. Does that help?"

The name sounded vaguely familiar, but Rosellen couldn't bring anything immediately to mind. She'd probably seen his name and his face on a wanted poster over at the jail. He looked like an outlaw and probably was one. Again forcing down her apprehension about him, she turned and headed for the room.

She'd learned all she could about being a sheriff from her father. Now she had to allow instinct to take over and let her know whether she was just being jumpy or if she truly needed to be cautious.

Rosellen stepped through the doorway, and the

4

heavy mixed scents of sweet perfume and rich tobacco smoke hit her like a blast of tepid air. She saw a pretty woman with gray-streaked strawberry blond hair flowing in soft waves over her shoulders. Long, dark lashes framed big blue eyes that stared with interest at Rosellen.

Gossip in town said Gayla was dying, but if that was true it didn't show on the well-groomed woman. She lay propped up in bed against fluffy satin-covered pillows in varying shades of light purple. A gentle breeze from an open window ruffled lace sheers, which were bracketed by lavender velvet draperies. An oil lamp on the short chest by the bed gave the room a golden glow.

The woman motioned to her. "Come on in. Don't be shy. I won't bite." A soft, husky chuckle floated on the air. "Besides, I feel like I know you, even though we've never been properly introduced."

Everyone knew the owner of the Silver Nugget Saloon. Twenty years ago when Poppy, Colorado, was a lawless boom town Gayla had been the most sought-after madam in the area. She was beautiful and refined. She understood men and knew how to treat them. She entertained most of the important men who had cause to visit Poppy.

According to gossip, she considered herself an intimate friend to the wealthy and the powerful as well as grubstaker for needy prospectors. The Silver Nugget had always been the busiest saloon in the small tent city that had eventually become an established mining town.

Gayla hired pretty young girls, and it was said that she never cheated them out of their wages. She forced the girls to save money so that when she decided they were too old for the sporting life they'd be able to start over in another town. Seldom did any of Gayla's girls fall victim to the overuse of opium or whiskey, which had sent more than a few prostitutes to an early grave.

At least once or twice a week Gayla would call for drinks on the house, making her saloon a favorite place for both locals and travelers.

"Come closer. I've seen you in town many times, although we've never spoken," Gayla said.

Rosellen continued on into the room but remained quiet. She was waiting to find out what this invitation was about.

"I can't understand why your father allowed you to run after your brothers like you did or follow him around the streets at night. I always thought it was too dangerous for a young woman to be that free."

"I most certainly could take care of myself then— and now," Rosellen said defensively.

Suddenly the woman drew forward. Her aging face glowed with remembrance as the stranger walked in behind Rosellen. A sweet, sympathetic smile curved her painted lips.

"Cason. I'd know you anywhere." Tears pooled in her eyes, and she sniffed quietly. "I didn't expect you to look so much like your father. Maybe you're a bit taller and stronger, but, oh, he was so handsome. Just like you."

Gayla's voice was husky and deep with emotion. That confused Rosellen. What did this stranger and Gayla's reaction to him have to do with her?

At the mention of the man's father a muscle twitched in the stranger's cheek. His fingers tightened on the brim of his hat. "My father's been dead for fifteen years. I'm not the person you want to talk to."

"Yes, you are. I remember very well the day Frank Murdock was killed. I saw you come running into town, breathless, tears streaming down your face. I wanted to help you, but I didn't know how. And I didn't know the whole story then, either."

"I don't talk about my father with anyone." Cason slammed his hat on his head and turned to walk out.

"Not even someone who can clear his name?" Gayla asked.

Cason stopped cold in the doorway, then turned to face Gayla.

Frank Murdock. Rosellen knew *that* name.

No wonder Cason looked like a fast gun to her. His father had been a murdering outlaw. He'd ridden into town in broad daylight, robbed the bank, and killed a teller. As sheriff, her father had hunted Frank Murdock down and shot him dead.

A protective impulse toward the people of Poppy surged inside her. Rosellen barged in front of Cason. "What are you doing in my town?"

"Right now I have business with this woman. If you want to talk to me, stand in line." He brushed Rosellen aside with a strong arm and strode over to the bed.

Rosellen's temper flared. She had spent too much time fighting with her brothers to let any man get away with ignoring her, especially one who already had her attention. Moving in between Cason and the bed, Rosellen glared up at him. Most of his face was shadowed by his hat, but she saw annoyance smoldering in his eyes.

"Who the hell do you think you're pushing around?" she asked.

"You. You're in my way. Now, stay out of this."

"Don't talk to me as if I were a child you could order around."

"Then don't act like one by butting in where you don't have any business."

"If I didn't have a reason to be here, Gayla wouldn't have sent for me."

"Stop this!" Gayla cried, beating on her fluffy bed-covers with a round satin pillow. "I brought you two here to listen to me, not to argue with each other like temperamental children."

Cason glared at the woman on the bed. "If you have something to say to me, start talking."

Gayla huffed. "I can see I'm going to have to get right to the point. Very well." She tossed the pillow aside and wiped the corners of her eyes with long, yellow-stained fingers. "I knew and loved both of your fathers."

Rosellen stiffened. The last thing she had expected to hear was anything connecting her father intimately to the town's infamous madam. She backed away. "What's going on? I don't want to hear this. I thought you asked me to come here because you wanted to talk about me running for sheriff."

A scowling wrinkle formed between Gayla's eyes. "You can listen to what I have to say now or later. It doesn't matter to me. I plan to tell this story, and it concerns your father."

Something in the tone of Gayla's voice stopped Rosellen from leaving. Gayla reached over to the chest by her bed and picked up a rolled cigarette from a stack of about fifteen.

The sulfur scent of the lit match floated past Rosellen as Gayla settled back against her pillows and took a deep draw on the cigarette before exhaling. Rosellen had smoked off and on since she was about thirteen, but that was one of the many things she'd given up in order to be a more respectable citizen of the town.

"You should remember everything clearly, Cason. You were thirteen or fourteen years old, but, Rosellen, you were only six at the time."

"Get to the point. I don't have all day," Rosellen said.

Gayla smiled smugly at Rosellen, then turned to Cason. "Your father was innocent, Cason. He had nothing to do with the bank robbery that happened fifteen years ago or with the murder of the bank teller."

Rosellen saw the man beside her tense. His breathing became shallow, but his expression never changed. Gayla had his attention.

"What the hell do you know that I don't?" he demanded quietly.

Gayla breathed the smoke deep into her lungs. "The whole story."

"What does any of this have to do with me?"

Gayla turned a serious face to Rosellen. "Your father was the bank robber—and the killer."

Rosellen gasped in outrage. How dare this woman tell such a despicable lie? She wanted to jump on the bed and wrestle Gayla to the floor as if the woman were one of her brothers and force her to take back those damning words.

But Rosellen suppressed the urge. For the past year she'd been trying hard to redeem herself. She'd been doing a good job of not settling her differences by cussing or fighting.

"That's a damn lie," she said immediately breaking her vow to stop cussing. "I don't care if you are sick and my elder. I won't allow you to say such things about my father."

"It's God's truth. I swear it is." Gayla stubbed out the cigarette. "Your father admitted to me his involvement in the robbery years ago. He told me that he killed the bank teller, too. Frank Murdock was an unexpected scapegoat."

Rosellen shook with fury, clenching her hands so tight her short nails dug into her palms. "You're lying. I don't know why, but I know you are."

"No." Gayla shook her head firmly. "I've lied in my time and been justified in doing it, but this time I'm telling the truth."

"If you've known this for years, why haven't you told anyone before now?" Cason demanded.

"How could I? I don't know if I would have had the courage to expose Henry while he was alive. He was the sheriff. No telling what he would have done to me. And I didn't know where you were. You'd vanished a long time before Henry admitted to me what he'd done. But when I heard yesterday that you were back in town it was like heaven giving me a second chance to do something good, to right a terrible wrong before I enter Glory."

"Glory, hell!" Rosellen exclaimed. "I don't give a damn where you go, but you're not going to get to heaven by telling these outrageous lies."

Gayla ignored Rosellen and said to Cason, "I knew I had to see you and tell you the truth."

"What truth?" Rosellen demanded, on the edge of being hysterical for the first time in her life. She wanted to clobber the woman. "You call what you said truth?"

Her brothers had taught her to wrestle and fight with her fists. She could shoot, ride, and tie knots better than most men, but she didn't know how to make this woman stop lying. "Saying these horrible things about my father doesn't make them true."

"What proof do you have?" Cason asked, brushing Rosellen aside again.

She shoved his arm away, refusing to be left out. "There is no proof," Rosellen shot quickly at him, her head pounding with denial. "There can't be, because what she's saying is a pack of lies. Can't you see this woman is crazy?"

Cason towered over Rosellen. She sensed the power, the raw emotion, he held in check. He stood so close she could feel the heat of his anger.

His gaze drilled into hers. "If you haven't got the

guts to hear this, get out. I intend to find out what Gayla has to say."

Rosellen struggled to stay calm. Some force she couldn't control seemed to be closing in on her. She was tall, strong, and smart. She took great pride in being able to take care of herself. She couldn't match Cason Murdock's strength, but she wouldn't be intimidated by the ruthlessness she saw burning in his eyes.

"I'm not surprised you're lapping up everything she has to say. She's absolving a cold-blooded killer—your father—and accusing an innocent man." Rosellen shook with anger and frustration.

His hard, cold gaze stayed on her face. "You're in my way."

Cason's tone was threatening, but she didn't care. "My father was sheriff of this town for twenty years, and no one ever breathed a bad word about him. Now this whore is trying to ruin his good name. He's not here to defend himself, but I am, and I won't stand for this."

"You don't have to," Cason said, glaring down at her. "You can hightail it. It's time somebody told the truth about what happened fifteen years ago, and I intend to get the real story."

Inwardly Rosellen trembled, but she couldn't back down. "By all means, you stay and listen to her horse dung, because that's exactly what her story is."

"I don't have any proof to offer either of you," Gayla said in a voice husky from years of smoking. Her eyes watered generously with more tears. "I'm only trying to do what I should have done years ago. I swear I'm not lying."

"The hell you're not."

"Your father pretended to go out of town for the day, but instead he rode to an abandoned mine and met his partner. He left his horse and his badge there, and he dressed up in pelts and fur like an old trapper, thinking no one would recognize him. Then he and his partner rode quietly into town so they wouldn't draw anyone's attention. They only meant to rob the bank. Henry didn't mean to kill the teller, but the young man recognized him, and Henry pulled the trigger before he realized what he was doing."

"You're lying," Rosellen insisted, but Gayla kept talking.

"Your father was foolish to think he could rob the bank in the town where he was sheriff and not be recognized, no matter the disguise.

"Stop this," Rosellen whispered.

"It was the gold and silver fever that ruined Henry Lattimer. He wasn't the only man who went bad because of greed. It happened all the time. Every time there was a big strike hundreds of men went crazy."

A faraway look shone in Gayla's glistening eyes, and her expression softened once again. "Everybody around here was getting rich. Poor Henry couldn't be content with what little the town paid him to keep the peace. It was a hard job. Dangerous, too. There were times when my girls were weighing in more gold dust in a single day than Henry was making in wages the whole month. It was hard for him to see such prosperity and not have a pinch of it for his own, so he decided to take what he thought he rightly deserved from the town."

"That's a ridiculous story. I never heard my father complain about the amount of money he earned."

A derisive smile lifted the corners of Gayla's painted lips. "Honey, that's what men have whores for. We hear a lot of complaints the wives and children never hear."

"You're a bitch!" Rosellen exclaimed at the unexpected slight.

"Sometimes." Gayla smiled. "But I'm not lying."

"How does my father fit into this story? And why was he killed?" Cason asked.

Gayla turned her attention to Cason. "Henry felt terrible about killing your father."

"Then why did he?" Cason's voice was cold. His eyes had hardened.

"Your father was panning near the mine where Henry had left his clothes and horse. Back then a man could find a nugget or two of gold or silver from an abandoned placer if he had the patience. When Frank saw the two trappers come riding up he walked over to let them know he'd already staked a claim on the mine. Henry knew he couldn't get his horse and change his clothes without Frank wondering why he'd been in disguise."

"Henry knew he was caught," Cason muttered.

Gayla nodded. "He couldn't leave a witness. He had no choice but to shoot Frank and take him in as one of the robbers."

"How did the sheriff convince the townspeople that my father was involved?" Cason asked.

"It didn't take much. Your family hadn't lived in Poppy long. No one knew Frank that well. Henry said that as he was returning to town he rode up on two men changing their clothes. He claimed that they started shooting at him when they saw who he was and that he killed one and the other got away with the money. I don't think anyone asked too many questions about details."

"He made himself a goddamn hero. That bastard," Cason swore.

"No!" Rosellen shouted and grabbed hold of Cason's arm. "Can't you see that this woman's words are as worthless as fool's gold? You didn't know my father. He would never have done anything like that."

Cason's fingers closed around her wrist and tightened. She gasped with shock as his touch sent a shiver of intense warmth sparking through her.

He jerked her hand away from his arm and flung it aside. "Save your praises for the church. I don't want to hear you sing anymore. What your father did killed my mother, too. I won't forgive your old man, and I can't forget what he did."

Rosellen felt as if she'd been slapped. Now he was trying to blame her father for his mother's death, too? This man had incredible gall.

"You are a damned fool if you believe anything that whore says." Rosellen was at the breaking point. She couldn't listen to any more. "Her lies have gone too far. My father never killed a woman, and he never killed a man who didn't deserve it."

His eyes flashed with a new challenge. "I'm going to make you eat those words."

"We'll see about that," she countered.

Cason swung back to Gayla. With a dangerous edge to his voice, he said, "Who was the other man with Lattimer, and where is he now?"

"I don't know where he is. He was Henry's cousin," Gayla said, continuing her story as if she'd never been interrupted. "Henry said they were as close as brothers when they were boys. I know his name was Dodge, and he had a wide, jagged scar on the back of his left hand. Henry said that Dodge kept his promise for years, sending him money each month as his part of the take. He didn't want it all showing up at one time. He thought someone might get suspicious."

"Stop this." Rosellen tried again to cut off the woman's words.

"Henry said he told his wife it was an inheritance from a distant relative that a lawyer was sending. She didn't have any reason to doubt him. When the money stopped coming, Henry went to Denver to check on Dodge but couldn't find a trace of him anywhere.

Henry came back depressed and spent a whole night drinking some of my best whiskey. That's when he told me the whole story."

"What else can you tell me about this man?" Cason asked.

Gayla looked down at her trembling hands. "He lived in Denver. That's about all I know."

Livid with anger, which she could no longer control, Rosellen turned on Cason Murdock. "I've had enough of this. If I hear one word of these outrageous lies on anyone's lips in this town, I'm coming after you. I don't care if you're old and sick or wearing a six-shooter strapped to your hip. I'm coming after you, and when I find you my gun will be loaded."

Chapter

❖ 2 ❖

Cason watched Rosellen Lattimer storm out of the room. She was so rigid with pride that her slim hips barely swayed, but the trousers and gun belt she wore did a good job of outlining her shapely figure.

Loyalty was important to him, and Cason had never seen a woman so full of it. He understood why she defended her father so strongly. He knew how furious she was right now, how helpless she felt.

Cason had been there.

He knew the debilitating taste of despair and frustration that wouldn't go away no matter how loud you shouted. He knew what it was like to have no one listen to you. He had been through the very same thing fifteen years ago, and he'd walked away just as devastated as she looked.

Cason would have liked to think he'd shown just as much pride in his walk when he led the horse that carried his father's body out of town.

He'd always known his father was innocent, but until now he'd had no hope of ever proving it. He believed every word the saloon owner said.

It was too damn bad that cold-blooded murdering sheriff was already dead. Cason would have loved to see Henry Lattimer squirm before Cason put a bullet right between his eyes, just the way the man had killed his father.

Cason had never forgotten.

Suddenly his heartbeat raced with the memory. He gazed beyond the pink flocked paper on the whore's bedroom walls and allowed his mind to drift back in time to that hot summer day when Rosellen's father had ridden up to the house to tell Cason that his father was dead.

Sometimes at night Cason could hear the sound of his mother's pitiful wailing. He remembered the way his heart had pumped furiously in his chest as he ran all the way to town. He couldn't believe what the sheriff said was true. He had to see for himself.

At times he could feel the helplessness and denial, and he could hear the gut-wrenching cry of pain that tore from his throat when he saw his father propped up outside the jailhouse with a bullet hole in his forehead, his half-closed eyes motionless, unseeing. The heat and stench of his blood-soaked clothes and flesh had drawn the flies that were swarming around his lifeless face.

The townspeople stood around his father's stiff body joking, laughing, drinking. They clapped the beaming sheriff on the back, congratulating him for having killed the bank robber and murderer.

Cason had tried to push the men away, yelling that they'd killed the wrong man. A strong arm shoved him down into the dirt. A clump of spittle landed in his hair.

No one listened to him.

No one helped him as he lowered his father's body to the ground. Cason took off his own sweat-soaked shirt and covered his father's face.

And he remembered something else. Standing beside the sheriff, looking up at him with adoring eyes, was a little girl with golden blond hair streaming down her back.

Rosellen Lattimer. She was all grown up now and just as pretty as she'd been fifteen years ago.

"Too damn pretty," he muttered aloud and shook his head to clear his thoughts of the past.

So Rosellen Lattimer wanted to be a sheriff like her murdering bastard of a father. Cason grunted softly. She would never be sheriff in Poppy, Colorado.

Not if he could help it.

"Is she Henry Lattimer's only daughter?" he asked.

Gayla chuckled low as she lit another cigarette, then settled back against the pillows again. "Oh, God's heaven, yes. The town couldn't have survived two like her." Gayla inhaled, then blew the smoke out through her nose.

"She was always known as the sheriff's little hellion when she was growing up. He let her get away with anything—starting fights at school, shooting glass panes out of abandoned buildings, and spying in bedroom windows to see who was sleeping with whom.

"Rose got into more trouble than most of the boys in town. Yet she walked through the streets like she owned them. To hear Henry tell it, he whipped his boys a time or two—they were as mean as snakes— but he turned a blind eye and a deaf ear to everything Rose did. From what I saw today, she hasn't changed a pinch worth of gold. She's still the town hellion."

Hellion? It sure fit. Cason remembered her asking him what he was doing in *her* town. But for some reason her high-and-mighty attitude hadn't really bothered him. It had intrigued him.

"Talk has it that her brothers were responsible for Rosellen being so hard to handle."

"How many brothers?"

"Three." The cigarette slowly burned in her hand and Gayla continued without pausing, seeming to relish the story she was telling. "Those boys helped ruin her, true enough. Wouldn't a one of them tell her no. Many was the day I saw Henry grab one of those boys by the ear and give him a dressing down, but he never said a word to that tart-mouthed little hellion, even when she drank a whole bottle of whiskey and smoked a handful of cigarettes."

Cason remained silent and watched Gayla stub out the half-smoked cigarette. He wondered why she bothered to light them.

"That girl was sick for three days. No, sir, it wasn't just her brothers' fault. It was her parents' fault, too. They're the reason she's been wearing trousers since she was sixteen and toting that gun since she was old enough to be married."

Gayla paused. "Not that any man has been foolish enough to try to court her."

She'd never been courted? Cason could believe that.

He remembered how she'd strode so comfortably into the saloon packing her six-shooter. Most men would have been intimidated by her, but not Cason. Truth was, he would have found her challenging, stimulating, if not for who her father was.

He didn't want anything to do with Henry Lattimer's daughter.

Gayla chuckled softly, and Cason's attention was drawn back to the woman. "I could've made a lot of money with a lively girl like her. Men pay good money for a woman who has a lot of fire and knows how to move in bed. I'd bet a night's take she'd be a wild one."

Cason would also have laid bets that she'd be one hell of a woman in bed, but he didn't want to think about Rosellen and beds, or about the passion he sensed smoldering deep inside her shapely body.

When he looked at Rosellen, he didn't want to see anything except the faint resemblance to the man who had killed his father in cold blood and driven his mother to madness.

"Rose thinks I'm lying, but I'm not," Gayla continued. "I wouldn't lie about a thing like this. There's no reason to upset anyone's life. I'm dying, and I'm trying to mend a terrible wrong."

She paused as if she expected Cason to say something, but he didn't feel a flicker of sympathy for the woman. She had never tried to find him when she'd learned the truth from Henry Lattimer. She had also admitted that she probably wouldn't have had the courage to tell the truth even if she'd known where Cason was.

"I was going to take Henry's confession to my grave, until Delta told me a handsome, wealthy stranger named Cason Murdock was in town and my girls were taking dollar bets on which one he'd finally take upstairs."

Any other time that bit of news might have amused him, but right now Cason wasn't interested in any of Gayla's girls. He wanted to know more about the man named Dodge.

"Think back to the night Lattimer confessed he was the murderer. What else did he say?"

"Well, as I remember, I had a sip or two with Henry, and it's been a long time."

Cason would have offered her money, pressing her to remember, but a dying woman had little use for money. "I need more information about his cousin. Was he a big and tall man, or was he short and slight?"

"He was a strapping man, like Henry. He came to visit Henry once. I guess that's when they hatched their plan to rob the bank."

"Had he always lived in Denver, or did he go there after the robbery?"

"He must have lived there, but I don't know for how long." She paused. "Are you going to look for him?"

"Of course."

"It's been too long. You won't learn anything. It must have been eight or nine years ago that Henry made that trip to Denver. He said it was as if his cousin had vanished. He found some people who remembered a man named Dodge with a scar on his left hand, but nobody knew what had happened to him."

"Did Lattimer say how the man lived in the city? Did he spend wisely, or did he squander the money on drinking and gambling?"

"Henry didn't really talk about his cousin, just about what he did. You know, not sending the money anymore."

A movement caught Cason's eye, and he saw that Delta was lounging in the doorway.

"I really would like to help you, Cason," Gayla said. "You and your family were done wrong. If I think of anything else, I'll send for you, but I need to rest now."

Cason looked up at the whore in the pink satin robe. She had propped herself against the doorjamb again. Her robe was tightly belted at the waist but hung open revealingly everywhere else. The expression on her face invited him to give her a closer look.

But Cason's mind drifted back to Rosellen. He remembered the anger in her piercing blue eyes, the fierce denial in her tone, the strength of character that kept her from cowering before Gayla's story.

He took his first deep breath since entering the room. Rosellen's qualities were the things that attracted him, not Delta's brazen display of her body.

"I'll show you out," Delta said with a sugary smile.

"That is, if you're ready to go." She winked at him. "If you're not, my room is upstairs."

"I'll find my own way out." Cason strode past Delta without bothering to spare her a glance.

He was wound as tight as baling wire, unable even to consider taking the whore up on her offer. When he crawled into a woman's bed he didn't want anything on his mind but her, and she was the last thing he was thinking about right now.

He had come back to Poppy with only one goal in mind—to destroy the town that had shown his parents no mercy. Now he had another aim—to clear his father's name.

Never had he allowed himself to think that might be possible. He couldn't let the opportunity pass without seizing it.

During the past two days he'd seen that Poppy had grown from a wild, lawless boom town to a peaceful mining community safe enough for the local families to consider electing a woman as their peace officer.

He wondered why Rosellen wanted to be the sheriff. Why did she feel the need to tote a gun? Her attitude showed she was strong and brave enough to be the sheriff for the people of Poppy—but she wasn't going to get the chance.

Cason intended to destroy Poppy, Colorado, and make it a ghost town.

Chapter

✦3✦

Rosellen fumed as she stomped up the porch steps of the modest home where she'd lived all her life. Her head was pounding, and her feet ached where her brand-new boots had rubbed blisters on her heels. She stopped outside the door and took a deep breath. She didn't want her mother to suspect the anger, frustration, and helplessness churning inside her.

The white clapboard house with its picket fence looked deserted, but Rosellen knew her mother was inside putting supper on the table. The overgrown buffalo shrubs and saltbush and the closed shutters helped keep out the bright summer sun, making the house cooler during the hottest days of the year.

The nerve of that saloon woman, Rosellen thought, trying to pin a multiple murder—such a heinous crime!—on the man who'd been sheriff of Poppy for twenty years. Had the charge not been so serious, Rosellen would have laughed in the woman's face.

As soon as Rosellen was made sheriff, she was going to find a way to close down the Silver Nugget. She didn't care how popular the saloon was with the men in town. She'd teach that lying whore to besmirch her father's good name.

Rosellen took another deep breath. She'd hoped the brisk walk from the saloon to the edge of town where she lived would cool her temper, but it hadn't. It had only made her hotter and given her time to realize she was unprepared to deal with what she'd just heard.

And then there was Cason Murdock to consider. Her pulse hammered. No, she couldn't dwell on him and the way he made her feel. She must forget about him, even though he was the first man who had ever held her interest. She would think about the many things she would have to do when she became the sheriff.

She opened the door and stepped inside the small house. "Mama, I'm home." She took off her dark brown hat and plopped it on the cast-iron hall stand. Then she unfastened her gun belt and holster and hung it beside the hat.

After leaving the Silver Nugget she'd thought about going straight to the livery and saddling her horse. She'd wanted to ride her mare fast and hard until they both worked up a lather, but knew she couldn't. If she was going to be the sheriff she had to stay calm. She couldn't go tearing out of town hell-bent for leather whenever something didn't go her way. Those days were in the past. The hellion no longer existed.

Many times she had heard her father say, "No town wants a sheriff who can't hold his temper."

She'd been trying hard to control hers and act responsibly for almost a year now. Ever since she realized she could do a better job taking care of Poppy than the two blowhards the mayor's committee had hired as her father's temporary replacements.

Rosellen stepped into the living room, looking for any object that seemed expensive. There were two silver candlesticks and a gilded bronze-and-marble clock on the mantel. A rosewood side table with brass mounts stood by her mother's rocker, and a set of delicate English china that was used only on special occasions was displayed in a fine mahogany china cabinet. In the dining room a silver tea and coffee service graced a satinwood side table.

They had some things in their home that could be considered extravagant for a small town sheriff's salary, but they had them because her parents had always been penny-wise, *not* because her father had helped rob the bank.

Rosellen battled the urge to scream from the pain of not being able to force Gayla to admit she was lying. And Cason had soaked up every word the woman said like a sponge.

"Oh, good, you're home."

Rosellen turned at the sound of her mother's voice. "I called out to you. I guess you didn't hear me."

"I was on the back porch throwing out the dishwater," Evelyn Lattimer said as she walked into the front room wiping her hands on a calico apron. "You know I like to wash the pots before we eat."

Rosellen nodded. Her mother was tall and thin like Rosellen. For years they could have passed for sisters, but recently streaks of gray had begun to show in Evelyn's neatly pinned chignon, and lines of age had appeared around her eyes and mouth.

Looking at her mother's sweet face, Rosellen couldn't imagine asking her if her father had ever received a monthly inheritance, if he'd gone to Denver a few years ago, or if he had a cousin named Dodge.

No, Rosellen told herself emphatically. She wouldn't allow the lies of a woman of low character to make her doubt her father and disturb her mother with questions.

"I have the table set and supper ready. We can sit down as soon as you wash up."

Rosellen wasn't hungry, but she knew her mother liked to dine early on Tuesdays. It was the only night of the week her mother left the house. She walked to their neighbors' house next door and met with other ladies to quilt or sew but mostly to gossip.

Rosellen always looked forward to her time alone in the house. She would usually fill the washtub in the kitchen with hot water, then sprinkle a little of her mother's vanilla and coconut oil into the water and soak until the water turned cold.

Tonight she desperately needed that time so she could pull herself together. She was reeling from Gayla's accusations and the chained power she sensed smoldering inside Cason Murdock.

"Your face is flushed, Rose. You're not getting the grippe, are you?"

"No, Mama. I'm just hot because I walked fast," she fibbed. She brushed past her mother, not wanting her to look too closely at the frustrated wrinkle in her brow. "I know you don't like for me to be late on Tuesdays."

"That's so considerate of you, dear. Men appreciate a woman who's thoughtful."

Cringing with frustration, Rosellen stepped inside the privacy of her bedroom, closed the door, and leaned against it for a moment to catch her breath. Her mother never missed an opportunity to remind her of the qualities that would make a man happy.

Rosellen certainly wasn't interested in pleasing a man. Years ago she'd proved she could outshoot, outsmoke, and outthink most of them, and that was the way she liked it.

Cason Murdock drifted across her mind again. There was something about him that appealed to her, something she didn't understand. She only wanted it to go away. He was the son of an outlaw. What was wrong with her?

She pushed away from the door. Right now she wanted nothing more than to keep her mind blank while she took off her boots, rested her feet, and washed from the basin.

Three short raps on the front door brought her head up. She knew it had to be one of her brothers. They had the same knock. It wasn't unusual for any one of them to stop by on his way home from the mine, but never on Tuesdays. Curiosity skittered up her back.

Rosellen headed back to the front room. A tingling of suspicion crawled up her neck. From the hallway she saw all three of her brothers walk into the parlor.

"I don't understand why you're all here," Evelyn said as she made herself comfortable in the low-backed rocker.

Rosellen didn't, either. Christmas and the Fourth of July were the only times all three of her brothers made it to the house at the same time.

Something was wrong. Rosellen stood as if rooted to the floor. Fear that they had heard the same vile story from Gayla clutched at her heart. Did they intend to tell their mother?

Jarred, the oldest and shortest of the tall, blond, blue-eyed brothers, took one of the wing chairs. Simon, the middle son and heaviest of the three, fitted himself into a corner of the brocade settee. Walter, who was seven years older than Rosellen, and was also the tallest of the Lattimer brothers, sank into the other corner of the settee.

Rosellen gathered her courage and walked into the room. "What's wrong?" she asked.

"We're glad you're home, Rose," Jarred said. "It's really you we've come to see."

"You wanted to see me?" She looked at all three

of her brothers. Concern showed on their faces. Her knees suddenly weakened.

Jarred turned to Evelyn. "Mama, we don't want to keep you from your sewing group."

"Oh, don't worry about that. We haven't even had dinner yet, and I have plenty of time. I want to know what's happened to bring you all here."

Rosellen sat down in the green upholstered armchair. She looked at her brothers and, in as normal a voice as she could muster, asked, "What's this about?"

"We're worried about you, Rose," Simon said.

Rosellen wondered if they'd heard Gayla's lies and were worried about their mother, too. "So?" she managed to say more confidently than she felt at the moment. "That's nothing new. You worried about me when I took my first drink, made my first high dive into the pond, and shot my first jackrabbit."

"Can't you be a lady? Why do you always have to act so damn tough?" Walter asked.

"Watch your language," Jarred reprimanded his youngest brother with a stern expression.

"Sorry, Mama."

Jarred turned to Rosellen. "The stunts you're talking about made us worry because we would have gotten in trouble if you'd been hurt."

"He's right," Simon said. "This time it's you we're concerned about. When I stopped by yesterday afternoon Mama told me you're serious about this sheriff job."

Rosellen relaxed a little now that she knew what they wanted. Maybe Gayla had taken her threat seriously and decided not to breathe a word of her lies to anyone else.

"That's right," she said. "I scheduled a meeting with the mayor and his committee tomorrow morning to talk them into hiring me as the new sheriff until a new election can be held. I thought I'd made it clear to all of you that I wanted to do this."

Simon leaned forward. The buttons on his shirt strained against his ample stomach, which hung out over his belt buckle. "We're here because we don't want you to pursue this any further."

"Being sheriff is dangerous," Jarred added.

"Cut the concern," she snapped. "Since when have I been afraid of getting hurt?"

"That's always been your problem, Rose," Walter said impatiently. "You never have been. You'd take any dare anybody threw at you."

"We're afraid for you," Jarred said in his best older-brother tone, as he gave Walter a look that told him to stay quiet. "We want you to settle down to finding a husband and forget this silly notion that you can be the sheriff."

"I don't want a husband, thank you very much. And what do you mean by silly?" she asked, her anger rising. "I'm serious about being sheriff."

"It's a man's job. You aren't capable of doing it," Walter said flatly.

"Thanks for the vote of confidence, brothers," she remarked, unable to keep the pain of disappointment out of her voice.

Always the peacemaker, Simon explained, "Walter didn't say that exactly right, Rose. Being sheriff is too dangerous a job for any woman to handle."

Jarred leaned toward her. "Mama was right when she said it was time for you to take off your trousers and wear a dress every day, not just on Sundays. You're not a kid following us around town anymore. You're a pretty young woman, and you should dress and act like one."

"Find a nice man to marry," Evelyn added.

"And stop wearing that damn gun."

"Walter." Jarred warned him again.

Rosellen bristled. "I haven't followed any of you around since you married, but I guess you haven't noticed how I've changed."

The truth was that she was trying hard to show everyone in town she'd grown up since her father died. She looked at her brothers. Acute disappointment filled her. She had assumed they would support her in this decision. They had always stood up for her in the past. What happened? She couldn't believe they weren't going to support her now when she really needed them. She thought they knew how much this meant to her, how much she wanted to be the next sheriff.

"All of you should know better than anyone that I'm not afraid of any man. And even if I was, Poppy's not the wild town it was years ago when Papa had to break up a fights every night and when drunks would fire their guns in the streets. Poppy has settled down into a quiet, churchgoing town."

"It would only take one fight for you to get hurt," Simon said.

"Or one stray bullet from a gunfight and you'd end up with six feet of dirt in your face," Walter blurted out.

Evelyn gasped.

"Sorry, Mama."

"All right, let's be realistic, Rose. How would you break up a fight in a saloon filled with drunken men throwing chairs, tables, and whiskey bottles across the room?" Simon asked.

"How do you think?" she snapped. After her horrible meeting with Gayla and Cason Murdock, Rosellen wasn't up to this fight with her brothers, but she wouldn't back down. "The same way Papa did. I'd fire my gun into the air until I had their attention, and then I'd haul their butts down to the jail and let them sleep it off."

"It's not that easy, Rose."

Her voice grew louder, reflecting her frustration. "Of course it is. I can't count the times I've stood outside the saloon and watched Papa end a fight. Thanks to all of you, I know how to wrestle a man to the ground and cuff him if I have to."

"We just let you win," Walter injected.

"Like hell you did, and I'll prove I can best you any time you're ready."

"Rose," Jarred cautioned, "stay away from the mayor's committee and let them find someone else or—"

"Or what? You'll tie me to a chair in my room like you used to do when you didn't want me following you? Don't you understand that if I leave it up to the mayor and his committee to hire a temporary sheriff, they'll end up with someone who'll leave, like the first one did, when another town offers him five dollars more a month. Or they'll get an old codger like the last temporary sheriff they hired, a sot who spends his nights drinking and his days sleeping it off. How can anyone like that take care of Poppy?"

"That's why they're taking their time to make sure they find the right person."

"That's me."

"No, it's not," Jarred said firmly, flatly, honestly.

"I can't believe this." She rose, frustration, disappointment, and determination fighting inside her for control. "If I can't get my own family to support me, how am I going to convince anyone else? I was counting on all of you for help."

"We hear talk at the mine, Rose," Walter said. "Only a handful of men think you can handle the job, and that's only because they remember you riding your horse so fast down main street that you scared all the other horses in town and made them bolt."

"And the dust the horses kicked up ruined three women's lace parasols."

"What I did when I was growing up has nothing to do with the person I am today. We all had our fun when we were younger. I've changed. I'm responsible. For two years I walked the streets with Papa checking to make sure oil lamps were out and doors were locked. I know how to write out the paperwork on bounties, and I've met most of the U.S. marshals, judges, and even some of the outlaws that work this area. When men talk about me at the mine, tell them I'm the best person for the job."

"No man is going to take a woman sheriff seriously," Walter said.

"How do you know that?"

"Because women are supposed to cook and sew and take care of children."

"It's our fault. We never should have taught you how to shoot and ride and drink."

"The problem is, you don't know that you're a woman, not a man," Walter added.

A flicker of recognition struck Rosellen. The way that Cason Murdock had stared at her when she first walked into the saloon floated across her mind. No, Walter was wrong. She knew she was a woman, and she knew what it felt like to be looked at like a woman.

"All right," she conceded. "Maybe I was a hellion a few years ago, but I've changed. And in time I can earn the town's respect. I know it."

"It won't work."

"I'm only asking for a chance to prove I can do this."

Walter said, "We've been thinking that maybe I should quit my job at the mine and be the sheriff."

Rosellen sucked in her breath as if she'd been sucker-punched in the stomach. "What? You, Walter?" Her eyes darted from brother to brother, and in their guilty faces she saw that they had discussed this possibility at length. "You've talked about this?" Betrayal cut her like a sharp knife to the heart.

"Rose . . ."

"Don't do this to me, Walter." Her voice trembled. Moisture stung her eyes, but she blinked it away. Double damn, her mind whispered. She didn't want to fight the tears, too.

"We've only talked about it. Nothing's been decided," Simon admitted quickly.

She could never win the support of the mayor and his committee if one of her brothers wanted the job. They were all well liked in town—and they were men. "You know how much I want this job, Walter, and you don't want it at all. You just don't want me to have it. That's selfish and unfair—of all of you."

"It's not that, dear," Evelyn said. Her eyes told Rosellen that her mother didn't like seeing her unbearable pain. "They don't want you to get hurt. They're afraid for you, and so am I."

"Well, don't be," she said, sniffling to keep back the tears. "Mama, Karen Forehand died last week trying to have her baby. Remember, I went to school with her. She was my age, and she's dead. If I were married right now that could have been me dying."

"Don't say that, Rose."

"It's true."

"No, dear," Evelyn said. "Some women just aren't made for having babies. You're tall and well shaped. No reason to think you won't be just like me. I never had more than a few pains with any of my children."

"The point is, Mama, that everyone is going to die sometime. It's like the preacher says every Sunday morning. God's in charge of our lives. Whenever it's my time to meet my Maker, I'll be ready, and it won't matter to me if it's at the end of a smoking gun barrel or trying to give birth."

She looked at her three handsome brothers. She loved them, but they had broken her heart. "I'm going to meet with the mayor tomorrow." She looked directly at Walter. "I'd like to have your blessing, not your competition, but either way, I'm going."

Rosellen strode over to the hall stand, picked up her gun belt, and buckled it around her hips. Her father had never left the house without his gun, and neither did she.

"Rose, where are you going?" her mother asked.

"For a walk," she said, tying her holster to her thigh.

"Rose, come back here. We didn't mean to make you angry," Jarred said, following her to the door.

"You didn't. You made me sad. I thought all of you had more confidence in me than you do."

"Don't go, Rose. You haven't eaten," Evelyn said in an exasperated voice.

"I'm not hungry."

"We're only thinking about you and what's best for you," Walter added.

"I don't need your kind of help."

"You're not being reasonable, Rose," Jarred said.

She stood by the door and looked her oldest brother in the eye. "If you don't want to help me get that job, then stay out of my way."

She left the house, closing the door quietly when what she wanted to do was slam it and rattle the windows in their frames. But she'd changed. She didn't do things that way anymore.

Her first few steps reminded her that the new boots had rubbed her heels raw, but there was no way she was going back into the house to put on her comfortable old boots. She would just suffer. She turned left and started walking toward Front Street. There was nowhere else to go.

Dusk had settled, leaving dark purple clouds to color the edges of the sky. The heat of the day had passed and a vagrant breeze stirred past her, feathering loose strands of her hair and cooling the damp skin at the nape of her neck.

Poppy sat low in a fertile valley that stretched like a lavish never-ending meadow spotted with trees, gardens, and houses. It was surrounded by mountains and canyons, isolated buttes, and rocky crags that hid some of the richest resources in the world—gold and silver. In the distance the towering Rockies majestically rose up on either side of the town and trapped hot air that could hover over the area like a wool blanket for days.

Rosellen felt a sudden longing to return to the time when she had been free to ride out to the foothills and watch herds of deer, elk, or antelope graze in the tall grass and nip leaves from low hanging branches. Sometimes she had taken off her boots and waded in a stream so clear and cold her feet had gone numb.

Often, as a child, she had risked missing supper and facing the anger of her parents by staying out after dark so she could watch the wide expanse of sky melt from brilliant shades of blue to fiery orange and purple.

But now as she strolled into town, her boots kicking up dust, she knew those carefree days of her wild youth were over. She had grown up, and she was changing.

The town was quiet. Most of the men who came into Poppy for a shot of whiskey or a game of cards were home eating their supper. A little later in the evening, Front Street would come alive. Piano music would be heard from one end of the main street to the other. There would be laughing, talking, gambling, and loving.

Loving? Rosellen shook her head. What had make her think about that?

Cason Murdock. He was the first man to make her stomach flutter and her heart kick up a notch. Almost every eligible man in town had wanted to court her, but she'd never shown interest in any of them. Why did the first man to catch her eye have to be Murdock?

"No way in hell," she muttered, dismissing that thought as quickly as it had come to her.

Murdock was probably a fast gun, a murdering outlaw like his father, and she wouldn't waste one more second thinking about him or about Gayla's ugly lies.

She ignored the blisters on her heels and kept walking.

How could she persuade the town leaders to accept her as sheriff if she couldn't even get her own family to support her? It was as if her brothers didn't know her and what she was capable of. How could they even think of considering Walter for the job when they knew how badly she wanted it?

Dammit, they'd taught her to be as strong and tough as they were, and now they expected her to start acting like the women they'd married. Well, she wasn't going to do it. She'd stopped smoking and drinking, and she was trying real hard to stop cussing, but she wasn't going to stop being tough. Poppy needed a sheriff who cared about the town, and she wanted to be that person.

"Damn, damn, double damn," she whispered.

Just because she liked to race her horse through town and because she had swiped an apple pie once or twice from Miss Leddy's coolin' window didn't mean she was an irredeemable hellion.

It wasn't like she had ever hurt anybody, and her father always paid Miss Leddy for the pies. Poppy was filled with abandoned buildings, like any other boom town. Every youngster—well, every boy in town—had knocked out a few windowpanes. It wasn't her fault that girls didn't know how to have as much fun as boys.

The loud crack of a gunshot shattered the stillness of the twilight, startling her. Rosellen jerked her hand to the handle of her Colt, then froze for a moment.

Her heart pounded like the hooves of a thousand stampeding horses. The shot had seemed to come from in front of her.

She quickly glanced around but saw no one. She pulled her gun and ran toward the sound. A stranger stood in the middle of the street, holding his gun on someone lying on the ground.

Heartbeat hammering, she slowed and quietly moved toward the two men. She recognized the man on the ground as Shoestring Palmer. He had been hit in the shoulder. He held his hand over the wound. Blood seeped through his trembling fingers and gushed down his arm.

When she was about twelve feet from them she stopped, steadied her aim on the stranger's chest with both hands, and said, "Drop the gun."

The stranger snapped his head up and looked at her but kept his revolver pointed at Shoestring. His clothes and long scraggly hair and beard were splattered with the ash-colored mud that caked the belongings of every sourdough who wandered into town. Even though most claims were owned by large companies like the Comstock, there were still plenty of prospectors scratching, digging, and panning, hoping to strike the next mother lode.

"You'd best put that gun down, little lady, before you hurt yourself."

His gaze was fierce. What had she gotten herself into? What would she do if the man didn't listen to her? Did she have the courage to pull the trigger and shoot him? She didn't know. She only knew she had stepped over the line and she couldn't back down.

Rosellen didn't let her eyes or her hand waver, but her knees were doing a two-step. She had to stay in control and not allow this man to intimidate her. Out of the corner of her eye she saw two townspeople walk out of the general store, but they remained on the boardwalk.

"Mr. Carmichael and Mr. Wilkins are coming out of the general store. They'll tell you I'm the best shot in this town and that I'm not afraid to pull this trigger."

"Go ahead and fill him full of lead, Rose," Shoestring encouraged her. "He shot my shoulder up bad and it's killing me. I need the doctor."

The stranger glared at her. "This ain't your fight or anyone else's in town."

"You made it mine when you put a bullet hole in Mr. Palmer's shoulder."

The man's lip curled upward. "Who are you?"

"I'm the person who's going to shoot you if you don't drop that gun right now."

"He cheated me. He deserves to die."

Rosellen tried to think what her father would do in this situation. "Maybe you're right and maybe you're not. What do you have to say for yourself, Mr. Palmer?" she asked, knowing that other people had accused Shoestring of pinching more than his share of gold dust from their pokes.

"Ain't a word of it true."

"It is too. The nails on his thumb and forefinger are long and curled and can hold a lot of gold dust. You check 'em. I'm telling you he pinched more'n what a bottle of whiskey is worth."

Rosellen had heard most of the tricks of the trade for miners and prospectors who dealt in gold dust rather than coins or paper money. A pinch of dust was said to be worth a dollar. Most men thought that big pinches and small ones equaled out over time, but someone was always trying to find a way to hold more gold.

She'd heard tales of men who tried to pinch more than their share by constantly squeezing small rocks to create dents in their thumbs and forefingers so the pinch would pack the indentions with extra dust and flakes. Some rubbed their hand through their greased hair before pinching so more of the gold dust would cling to their fingers.

Rosellen was pretty sure Shoestring was guilty as charged.

She realized she wasn't afraid of this man or his gun. She was afraid of not being able to show the town that she could end the danger this man presented.

She cleared her throat. "What you're saying might be so, but I'm not going to let you kill him over it. Drop your gun and step away."

The prospector glanced around. Rosellen noted that several people had gathered and stood watching. But no one stepped up to help her. The back of her neck had grown damp. Her arms felt weak from holding them in the same position so long, but she forced herself to keep her aim on the stranger.

"What kind of town is this that allows its womenfolk to handle a firearm?" he asked of no one in particular.

Someone eased up beside her. Rosellen sensed his power immediately.

"The kind who knows she can take a man like you. If I was you, I'd do what she says."

Cason Murdock.

Rosellen was relieved and furious at the same time. She didn't want his help. She could certainly handle this without him, but just knowing he was beside her gave her the extra courage she needed to see this through.

"I don't need any help from you, Murdock," she said in a low voice.

"Doesn't look like you're going to get it from anyone else around here."

"That's because they know I can take care of myself."

"I wasn't brought up to let a woman handle a fight if there was a man around to do it."

"And I wasn't brought up to let any man do my fighting for me." Then in a voice loud enough for everyone to hear she said, "Get out of my way and stay out of this, Murdock."

The sourdough looked at Cason with piercing eyes. "You going to let that woman talk to you like that and get away with it?"

"She's in charge. I'm just watching her back in case you have a partner."

Rosellen's knees almost buckled at Cason's words. She'd forgotten one of her father's hard-and-fast rules. Never forget to watch your back.

She could have been dead by now. She stole a quick glance at Cason. His gun wasn't drawn. He simply stood beside her, letting the stranger know he was there if she needed him. A flicker of admiration pricked her.

"Was I supposed to let him cheat me and not do anything about it?" the stranger said.

"You didn't have to shoot him," Rosellen said. "Next time take your complaint to the sheriff."

"Well, where is he? I would rather talk to him than you, anyway."

"We don't have a sheriff right now. You've had your justice by shooting him. Now, I'm going to suggest you stick that gun back in your holster, get on your horse, and ride out of here before there's more trouble than you want."

"He shot me!" Shoestring yelled. "You can't let him just ride away like that. He should be hanged from the nearest tree or at least thrown in jail."

"This man's not the first to complain about your nails being too long. Keep them cut short or one of these days you're going to find someone who has better aim than this man."

The prospector lowered his gun and let his arm hang limp at his side. "I ain't never been run out of town by a woman before." He shoved his gun in his holster, shook his head, and walked away.

Rosellen seemed to be frozen in position. She couldn't take her eyes off the man's retreating back. Had she actually convinced him to leave without more shooting?

"He busted up my shoulder. You can't let him get away with that," Palmer yelled again. "Somebody do something! Stop her. Stop him!"

No one moved to help Shoestring.

"You can put your gun down now," Cason said.

She continued to watch the prospector until he mounted and headed his horse out of town. Rosellen turned toward Cason as she slowly lowered her Colt. Her arms were stiff, her head was pounding, and her knees were trembling.

She knew she should be grateful. Cason's presence had given her the edge she needed to stay in control, but instead of thanking him for bolstering her courage, she said, "If you butt into my business again, Murdock, you'll be the next person I run out of town."

Cason's eyes narrowed just enough to challenge her. "You think I'm afraid of you?"

"That would be the wise thing to think."

"Like it or not, that prospector would never have

backed down if someone hadn't stepped up beside you."

"I see you're still believing things that aren't true."

"No, that's your job."

"I don't know why you came back to Poppy, Murdock, but I don't like it. I'll be watching you. And I intend to be on you the first time you step out of line."

"On me?" A derisive smile lifted one corner of his mouth. "I'll count on it, Rosellen."

He said her name with such masculine passion that her skin tingled as if it had discovered something for the very first time. The feeling frightened her, thrilled her, seduced her.

Rosellen wanted to smack that cocky, handsome expression off his face, but she controlled herself and said, "Somebody come help Shoestring walk over to Doc Harmon's place."

Cason thumbed back his hat and gave her a sardonic grin, then turned and walked off.

"Rose!" Jarred yelled.

She looked up to see her brothers racing toward her. She hadn't seen them run like that since they were kids. They were worried about her. In an instant she forgave them. She understood their fears. Being sheriff *would* be a dangerous job, but she hoped she'd just proved to all of them that she could handle it—and next time she would do it without any help from Cason Murdock.

"Rose, are you all right?" her mother asked, joining them.

"Of course. I'm fine, Mama."

"I knew damn well you didn't need to be sheriff," Walter blurted out.

"Why do you do this to us?" Jarred exclaimed. "You could have been killed."

Rosellen's heart fell to her feet. She had been ready to forgive her brothers for not supporting her because she thought that now they would realize she *could* handle the job as sheriff.

"He had his gun pointed at Shoestring, not me," she answered defensively as the rest of her family, Mr. Wilkins, Mr. Carmichael, and other townspeople gathered around her, all of them talking at once. Their words blurred into babble. Rosellen stood quietly and let them talk.

Through a break in the crowd she saw Cason, standing back, watching. Unexpectedly, a rare sense of longing filled her, and she remembered how her senses had reacted when she first saw him. Suddenly she wanted to ignore all the people surrounding her and rush over to Cason. She wanted to thank him for his help. She wanted him to take her in his strong arms.

Rosellen's mouth went dry. What was wrong with her? She was the daughter of a well-respected sheriff. How could she be attracted to the son of a cold-blooded murderer?

Chapter

→ 4 ←

The next morning Rosellen worried as she paced back and forth in front of the living room window that opened on a dense patch of pines, birch, and cottonwoods at the back of the house. She'd put on extra-thick winter socks not wanting to make the blisters on her heels any worse until her new leather boots softened and shaped themselves to her feet.

Her stomach was empty, but she hadn't been able to eat a bite all morning. She hadn't thought about food yesterday, either. When she'd returned home last night she'd insisted her mother go on to her sewing group. Rosellen had filled the washtub and soaked in the cold water until her skin wrinkled.

She'd easily gotten over her encounter with the mud-caked prospector, but this morning she had to cope with the disappointing fact that her brothers didn't have enough faith in her abilities to support her for sheriff. It made her angry to know that they were more than willing to encourage Walter, if he wanted the job. She also had to deal with the very real fear that Gayla might tell her crazy story to someone else in town.

And then there was the burning truth she could no longer deny.

Cason Murdock.

She had seen him only twice, but he had affected her as no other man ever had. In the past it had been so easy to think of other men as one of her brothers or like a father, but not this one. He created a brand-new feeling inside her. And as much as she hated to admit it, she was glad he'd stepped up to help her last night.

Rosellen felt as if something were crawling around in her stomach every time she looked at Cason and whenever she caught him looking at her. For a wild moment last night when her family and the towns-people were surrounding her, all she wanted was to escape into Cason's arms.

How could that be? She was sure she hated the man and all that he stood for, yet every time she'd closed her eyes last night she had seen him standing by the bank watching her accept praise and reprimands from those gathered around her.

Why wasn't she able to keep him from invading her thoughts? Why did she remember his long, powerful legs and slim hips as he'd eased up beside her? She had sensed his strength and confidence. Why did it bother her that he'd dismissed her so easily when he first saw her?

He meant nothing to her. She'd never cared whether a man gave her a first glance, let alone a second. Until a year ago Rosellen had had her father, and she had her brothers. She had never needed any other man in her life.

She had no choice but to put all those thoughts aside for now. In less than an hour she would meet with Mr. Vestly and some other town leaders. This was her chance to make her formal announcement that she intended to be Poppy's new sheriff and she needed their support now and later when an election would be held.

She rubbed the back of her neck and rolled her shoulders from front to back a few times. Her stomach rolled and rumbled disagreeably. Her knees were weak and her hands shaky. Damn Gayla, Cason, and all her brothers, too. She wasn't going to spend another moment thinking about any of them.

"Sit down, Rose, you're going to wear the heels off your new boots," Evelyn said as she walked into the room tying her apron around her waist.

"If I wear these off, I'll have new ones put on," she answered. She folded her arms across her chest in defiance and kept walking back and forth in front of the window.

Rosellen loved her mother, but Evelyn had never understood her wanting to be just like her father. Her brothers had never loved Poppy and its people as much as Rosellen had. They had never followed her father around and watched him walk from one end of town to the other, talking to the people, settling their disputes. Henry Lattimer would listen to their complaints, offer suggestions, and keep his eye on strangers. He'd taken care of Poppy. And now Rosellen wanted to do that.

"Are you going to buy a new rug, because you're wearing that one out, too?"

"If I need to," Rosellen said, sensing no reprimand in her mother's voice and giving none in her answer.

"Your father paid a lot of money for that rug. I'd like to know where you think you're going to get that kind of money."

Rosellen cringed, then immediately reprimanded herself. She didn't like being suspicious of every little

"I remember now," Jarred said, his eyes narrowing as he struggled to recall the past. "No one knew what happened to Murdock's boy."

"That's right," Evelyn agreed. "A while after the shootings, Henry rode out to the Murdock place to check on the bank robber's widow and son. When he came back, he said there was another grave beside Mr. Murdock's with his wife's name on it, but there was no sign of the boy. Everyone knew his mother had been in a sickbed since they moved to town. Henry assumed the woman died and the son buried her, then left without a word to anyone."

Rosellen started putting the pieces together. Yesterday Cason had said something about his mother being killed too. Could it be that when she heard her husband had been killed she lost the will to live?

No wonder Cason was so bitter toward her father. Rosellen shivered at the thought of losing both her parents in so short a time. She remembered how difficult it had been adjusting to her father's death. Losing both would be devastating. She braced herself. She had to stop that kind of thinking right now. She didn't want to feel sorry for Cason Murdock.

"Where do you suppose he got his hands on the kind of money it takes to buy a mine?" Evelyn asked.

"And shut it down," Jarred added.

"His father was an outlaw," Rosellen spoke up. "Where do you think he got the money?"

"From robbing banks?" Evelyn asked.

Jarred nodded.

Rosellen rose from the arm of her mother's chair. "I won't have the likes of Cason Murdock in my town. I won't have him shutting down the mine and putting my brothers and neighbors out of work."

"He bought the mine, Rose. He can do whatever he wants to with it."

"Not in my town, he can't." Rosellen walked over to the hall stand and plucked her gun belt from it.

"Don't go off half cocked and do something crazy," Jarred said.

"Rose, the town can survive without the mine," Evelyn insisted, coming up behind her.

"No, Mama, it can't, and there's plenty of ghost towns in Colorado to prove it." She fitted the wide leather band around her hips and buckled it.

"What about your meeting with Mr. Vestly and the other men?"

"Oh, damn," Rosellen whispered, then cringed, softly hoping her mother hadn't heard her swear. Evelyn Lattimer hated for any of her children to cuss, but right now Rosellen wanted to cuss a blue streak.

She pushed the strap through the loop with a flourish, then quickly tied the leather string that held the holster around her thigh. "I'll stop by and tell them I'll have to meet with them later."

"Rose, listen to me. This man is dangerous."

She glared at Jared.

"All right," he went on, "you proved last night you're not afraid of danger, but this man is no old prospector with a shaky hand. Murdock's already showing his muscle by posting guards around the mine in case there's trouble. I don't know where he got his money and I don't know why he wants to close the mine, but I do know he's not the kind of man you need to go messing around with."

"Listen to your brother, Rose, and stop talking this nonsense," her mother pleaded. "You have no business taking on a man like Murdock. Let Mr. Vestly and the town committee handle this."

"Mr. Vestly and his committee couldn't even find us a decent sheriff. What makes you think they can handle Murdock?"

"Then the men who work at the mine can band together and protest or strike. Let them take care of this," Evelyn pleaded.

"Mama, if I can keep Murdock from closing down the mine that should be all I need to get those men to support me for the job as sheriff.

"Rose, stop and listen to yourself. For once in your life take the time to think and act level-headed."

"No, I won't have him putting the welfare of my family or my town in jeopardy," she said, ignoring her brother's plea. "Was he still at the mine when you left?"

Jarred opened his mouth to speak, then hesitated for a moment before saying, "I'm not going to tell you anything that would get you into trouble. You can't handle everything, Rose."

"No, but I can handle this."

Jarred sighed heavily and shook his head. "He was still at the mine when I left, but there's no use in going there. I doubt his guards will let you see him."

"Dear, dear," Evelyn said, twisting the hem of her apron. "You can't do anything, Rose. He's posted guards. You'll be shot."

"He's just protecting his own, Mama," Rosellen said. "And that's exactly what I plan to do. If there's no mine, the men will have to go where they can find work to feed their families. Jarred, Simon, and Walter will have to move. Do you want that?"

"No, of course not, but what can you do?"

"I don't know yet. I'm going to find him and have a talk with him. He obviously doesn't know he's come to the wrong town, and I aim to set him straight once and for all."

"Look, Rose, wanting to be the sheriff is one thing, but you can't go taking on men like Murdock," Jarred said.

"He's not a Saturday night drunk you can lead to the jail and throw behind bars," her mother added.

Rosellen looked from her brother to her mother. "I'm not afraid of this man, and neither his money nor his gun impresses me."

She grabbed her hat off the hall stand and walked out the door.

Chapter

→ 5 ←

The middle-aged woman smiled at Cason and picked up his empty plate. "You want a cup of coffee with that bread pudding?"

"Yes, for both of us," Cason answered, glancing at Buster to dissuade the woman from trying to start a conversation with him again. No one in the town would want to talk to him once word got out that he was shutting down the mine. And that was the way he wanted it. Not even the courageous Rosellen Lattimer could tempt him to seek her out and talk with her again.

Especially not her. He didn't even know why she'd crossed his mind. He had more important things to think about than the daughter of a man he hated with a burning passion.

Cason forced his attention away from Rosellen and thought about Buster. His longtime friend and partner wasn't happy with him, but Buster hadn't said anything. Before they came to Poppy, Cason had made it clear to the old man that he didn't have to be involved in this, but Buster said they'd been together too many years to go their separate ways.

Long hours in the sun and the hard work of prospecting had aged Buster's face. He was small in stature but years of a pick-and-shovel life on rocky mountainsides had kept his body muscular and well toned.

Shortly after Cason met up with Buster he had discovered that the easterner was an educated man, and Cason had always thought he was way too smart to be panning for gold and silver. That proved to be true. After years of hard work, however, their vagabond life high in the Rockies had paid off when they struck a mother lode of gold in a mountain canyon at the mouth of a free-flowing creek.

Cason didn't like disappointing Buster. He'd always treated Cason like a son, and they had great respect for each other. Cason would have frozen to death the winter they met if Buster hadn't taken him into his camp.

Before Cason met Buster he took unnecessary chances with his life and didn't worry about dying. For a long time after he lost his parents, he wanted to die.

Cason had lived dangerously and played dangerously until he met Buster. During their first couple of years together he'd saved Cason's life on more than one occasion and taught him everything he knew about panning, mining, and using dynamite to open the side of a mountain.

It had been easy to slip under Buster's wing and let the older man teach him what he hadn't learned during the few years he'd been in school. Cason's mother had always been too sick to teach him much of anything and his father had seldom been home. Buster taught Cason to be a gentleman—when the occasion called for it—and how to use a gun.

"You were quiet all through your meal," Cason said as the waitress walked away. "What's the problem?"

Buster looked up at him with small, knowing eyes. He twitched his nose so tight his long sideburns and handlebar mustache moved slightly. "Can't a man eat his dinner without talking?"

"I guess so, but you don't usually."

"Well, I was thinking."

So was I.

Buster sat back in his chair and stuck his forefinger inside his tight collar, and pulled on it. Even though Buster was the well-bred son of a wealthy family he prided himself on being just a common man.

"What were you thinking about? Closing the mine or my trip to Denver?" Cason asked.

"Both, but mostly I don't want to see you go off searching for gold and coming back with pyrite."

"We've chased more than one dry mine filled with fool's gold. And I know the difference at a glance. I'm used to coming up empty-handed."

"But we don't have to chose dreams anymore. You're not a careless man, Cason."

Using caution was the first lesson Buster had taught him and it had paid off every day of his life since. "I know what I'm doing."

"It's *why* you're doing it that has me worried. What makes you think you can take stock in anything that madam told you?"

"What she says makes sense."

"And you want to believe her."

"I do believe her."

"Maybe she's just a clever woman spinning a yarn in order to get a little attention. There's plenty of them around, and they all like to embellish a tale."

"What would be the purpose? She didn't ask for anything in return for telling this story, and she says she's dying. What would be her gain?"

"Hell, I can't figure out what's in their damn minds.

But you know what I always told you about gold-digging females."

Cason smiled. He knew: "Never trust a woman who's living and walk softly around the dead ones." He had heard more than one tale from Buster about loose women and churchgoing women, too. Cason had always figured most of them were right out of Buster's imagination.

"Maybe she's looking for a way to make herself more acceptable when she gets to the pearly gates," Buster offered in explanation.

"She's telling the truth. I've always known my father didn't have anything to do with robbing that bank or killing that teller. After that bastard killed my father I couldn't even get the doctor in this town to sell me my mother's medicine."

Buster nodded. "I know what you went through."

Cason leaned over the table, his voice rising a notch. "No, you don't. You weren't there. You only know what I told you."

The dining room of the hotel was suddenly quiet. Cason's gaze darted around the room. Other diners had stopped eating and talking and were looking at him. Slowly he sat back in his chair and relaxed again. He'd hoped that one day he wouldn't be so passionate about his past, but that day hadn't come yet, and he knew it wouldn't come until he cleared his father's name and destroyed the town of Poppy.

"This is the first clue, the first chance I've ever had to clear his name. I won't pass it up. If you have any problems with staying here and closing down the mine, just say so. I'll do it when I get back."

"It's not that and you know it. Got nothing else I want to do anyway."

"What about all those places you told me you were going to visit when we struck it rich? You haven't made any plans to go to any of them."

"All that was just talk. What's in San Francisco and Mexico City that I haven't already seen some other place?"

"Well, you used to say you were going to go back east and pay your kinfolk a visit."

Buster's eyes took on a thoughtful quality. "I might do that someday, but not right now. You have me worried."

"No reason for you to worry. You made sure I knew how to take care of myself."

"I know, but I see something in your eyes I've never seen before, and it disturbs me."

He'd never been able to keep anything from Buster. The man was too damned astute. "What do you see?"

"Hope."

Cason's stomach knotted as tight as a cold-water cramp. He shifted in his seat. He didn't know if it showed, and he damn sure wasn't about to admit that his partner was right. Buster was too intuitive. Always had been. Cason was good at hiding his true feelings from everyone but Buster.

The townspeople had cheered and celebrated when Henry Lattimer killed Cason's father. Now it was Cason's turn to seek vengeance. He couldn't say he remembered the faces of any of the townspeople that day. But he remembered the sheriff and the little girl who had stood beside him.

He'd never forgotten her. That had to be the reason the grown-up Rosellen was on his mind today. He couldn't stop thinking about the blond, blue-eyed beauty.

"Not even when we first started finding flakes and small nuggets did I see hope in your eyes that we'd hit a mother lode."

"Getting rich was never important to me. It's only what money can do for me that I'm interested in. When I came to Poppy, all I wanted was to buy the mine and shut down the town. Now a woman has given me the opportunity to clear my father's name and prove to everyone that Frank Murdock wasn't a murderer. I can't walk away from that."

"I know that what happened to your folks has burned like a fire in your belly since you were a boy."

Cason couldn't deny the truth of Buster's words, but he couldn't heed the warning in them, either. "I plan to search every street and saloon in Denver. Someone should remember a man with a jagged scar on his left hand."

"And he could be he dead or living in Mexico, too."

"I won't know until I try. I'll let you know where I'm staying when I get settled."

Buster sighed and straightened in his chair. "Do what you have to do. I'll take care of things for you here."

"If it looks like there's going to be trouble at the mine, hire more guards."

Buster cocked his head to the left and then the right, stretching his neck as far as he could to either side.

"If those damn collars bother you so bad why do you wear them?" Cason asked.

"It's the mark of a true gentleman to be able to dress like this when he's not on his way to church or going to a funeral."

Cason smiled as a faded memory crossed his mind. "Do you remember that when I started digging with you my clothes had so many holes in them I was embarrassed to go into town with you for supplies?"

An expression of fondness settled into Buster's sun-hardened features. "I remember."

"You told me that clothes didn't make the man. It was what's inside a person that counted at the end of a day. Have you changed your mind?"

Buster rubbed his chin and looked around the room

before smiling and saying, "Yeah. I feel like a gentleman when I'm all strapped up in a suit like a dandy."

"You look like one, too."

"We were out on the hills prospecting too long, Cason. I've noticed that most men in town don't wear six-shooters on their hips anymore."

"You're wasting your breath, Buster. I'm not giving up my revolver for that derringer you insisted I buy."

"We aren't worried about claim jumpers and timber wolves anymore. I should have never encouraged you to practice shooting each day."

"My aim has saved our lives many times, as you well know."

The waitress placed a bowl of bread pudding and a steaming cup of coffee in front of each man. She smiled sweetly at Cason. "You two gentlemen seemed to be having a good time. I saw you smiling just before I walked over."

"We are," Buster told her. "We've been friends for years."

"Can I get you anything else?"

Cason didn't bother to acknowledge her friendly greeting as he said, "We're fine." After a moment's hesitation she walked away.

Buster blew into his cup before taking a sip, then said, "You had planned to ride out to where your parents are buried. You still planning on doing that?"

"No time. The short line is heading out at five o'clock this afternoon. I'm going to be on it."

The distinct sound of boots tramping on plank floors caught Cason's attention. His senses sharpened: *Rosellen.*

He remembered the light tap of her step, the clink of the fancy spurs on her new boots. He set down his cup and waited for her to stand before him. He knew what she wanted. What he didn't understand was the tightening in the pit of his stomach. Why did the thought of matching wits with her again excite him?

When he first saw her, he'd thought, How better to get back at Henry Lattimer than to challenge the daughter who had stared at him with such adoring eyes? But Rosellen was no shy young woman who could be easily seduced.

Rosellen stopped at the table and glared down at Cason. "Murdock, I want to talk to you."

Buster immediately stood up and backed away. Cason remained seated. "This sounds *official*," he said, deliberately mocking her. "Does that mean you had good news from the Mayor's Committee today?"

She hesitated long enough to let him know his question had caught her off guard. He could tell she hadn't expected him to know about that meeting, but he'd learned a lot in the two days he'd been in Poppy.

"After that courageous display with the old man you ran out of town yesterday, I was sure they'd make you the new sheriff first thing this morning."

Cason deliberately let his gaze fall to the front of her brown shirt and stared at her breasts. He watched as her breath became faster, making her chest rise and fall with each breath. He affected her. Damn, it felt good to know she wasn't as tough as she wanted everyone to think she was. It felt good to know she was looking at him as a man and not as the son of a murderer.

He lifted his gaze back to her face. Her cheeks were flushed. He'd bet half his fortune that she was as angry as a mama bear who'd lost her cubs. He knew the last thing she'd want would be to feel curls of desire for him.

"But, no, maybe not," he said. "I don't see a tin star pinned on your chest."

"Thanks to your poor judgment, I had to cancel my

meeting, not that it's your concern. I've been looking for you most of the morning."

Cason enjoyed watching Rosellen squirm like a worm dangling on the end of a fishing line. He shouldn't even be talking to her. She thought his father was a murderer and here he was bantering with her—and enjoying it.

He purposely kept his voice low and seductive as he said, "Now that you've found me, what do you plan to do with me, Rosellen? Are you ready to be *on* me?"

From behind her, Buster cleared his throat, and Cason rose from his chair. His old friend never failed to let Cason know when he'd forgotten his manners.

"This is my partner, Buster O'Malley. Buster, this is Rosellen Lattimer."

Buster glanced from Rosellen to Cason and back again. "Is this the—er—one of the ladies you were telling me you met yesterday?"

Cason nodded and watched Rosellen while she spoke to Buster. Damn, she was pretty. Sparkling blue eyes, honey-blond hair. Her cheeks and nose looked as if they'd been sprinkled with gold dust. He looked at her breasts again, but for a different reason this time. Full, firm, nice. Her small waist and softly rounded hips fit neatly into the men's trousers she wore.

"Pleased to meet you, ma'am—er, miss."

It was unusual for Buster to stumble over his words, especially in front of a woman. Cason couldn't imagine what had his friend tongue-tied.

"Call me Rose," she told Buster.

At least her name was one feminine thing she didn't shy away from.

This was the third time Cason had seen her, and each time she'd been wearing the old army Colt. It was no wonder she'd never been courted. A man would have to get past her gun to get under her clothes, and most men weren't up to that kind of challenge.

Most men.

Not Cason.

His gaze drifted back to her face. Her lips were puckered in anger at him. Again. He bet she was a heart-stopping beauty when she smiled, and he bet she could challenge any man's endurance in bed and win hands down.

All of a sudden Cason yearned to plunder those well-shaped lips with his own, and that thought aroused him as quickly as a youngster looking for the first time at a naked woman.

His thoughts went back to what Gayla had said yesterday afternoon. He agreed with her. A woman like Rosellen should be in the sporting business so that any man who wanted to could have a taste of her fire.

And if she wasn't the daughter of Henry Lattimer he'd have been the first one in line to show her just how hot she could get.

Chapter

→6←

$\mathcal{I}$t bothered Rosellen that just looking at Cason could cause an urgent heat to crawl up her neck and flare across her cheeks. She didn't want to be affected by him in any way, but she couldn't deny any longer that she felt different—softer when she was around him.

Rosellen had given Cason's partner a quick glance and a short nod, but she couldn't have missed the fact that he had only one arm. The sleeve of his twill jacket had been neatly folded and was pinned up on his shoulder.

Unlike Cason, who was casually dressed in a white collarless shirt and dark brown trousers, Buster was fashionably outfitted in a brocade waistcoat, starched collar and elaborately tied striped cravat. The wax and curl of his mustache was as immaculate as the rest of him.

"I think I'll excuse myself and let the two of you have a private conversation," Buster said.

"There's no need for you to leave," Cason told his friend. "This shouldn't take long."

"Are you afraid to be alone with me, Murdock?" Rosellen asked, knowing the question would raise his ire.

He looked up, and instead of giving her an angry look, he offered her a knowing smile. "I'll meet you any place any time, Rosellen."

She tried to hide her surprise at his suggestive attitude by keeping a firm expression on her face.

"I'm not afraid to be alone with you," he continued. "I only meant that you couldn't have much to say to me, because we don't know each other, and I think we both want to keep it that way, don't we?"

His lack of anger bothered her more than she expected. She was furious, and she wanted him to be angry too. She remained rigid, forcing herself to talk hard, short, and tough. "We're straight on that, I guess, but how long I stay here and talk to you will depend on whether or not I get the answers I'm looking for."

Buster poked his finger down the collar of his shirt again and twisted his head to the side. "This conversation sounds too serious for me to get involved in. I think I'll go find that waitress and see if she can get Rose a cup of coffee while you talk to her," he said and turned away before Cason could stop him.

Cason pulled out a chair, picked up his Stetson from the seat, and placed it on the table. His gaze swept languidly over her face.

She looked him over, too. There was a tightness around his mouth and a slight squint to his dark eyes. She realized that something bothered him deeply and he was trying desperately to hide it. He wouldn't be happy to know that his concern showed. She could have sympathized with that, but she was trying hard not to.

"Sit down and start talking."

Rosellen sank onto the chair. Her empty stomach

rumbled as she caught sight of the two bowls of warm pudding, which hadn't been touched.

Everybody in town knew that no one made better bread-and-raisin pudding than Miss Leddy at the hotel. She caught a whiff of the pungent cinnamon and cloves and the sweet vanilla that had been cooked into the bread. Rosellen's mouth watered in anticipation of the rich taste, and she moistened her lips.

"Would you like some pudding?"

Oh, yes, she thought and wondered if he could read her mind.

"To sweeten you?" he added confidently.

"No," she answered. "I'm not hungry."

"Then tell me what I can do for you."

She forced her gaze off the dessert and looked directly into Cason's eyes. "Keep the mine open."

"What else?"

"I want you out of town."

"By when?"

"Sundown."

"Is there more?"

This was going better than she'd hoped. "Yes. Why don't you tell me what bank you robbed to get enough money to buy that mine, so I can haul you down the street and throw your butt in jail?"

His eyes narrowed slightly. "I've never seen a woman try as hard to be a man as you do, Rosellen."

He deliberately said her name every chance he got. Damn, that bothered her. And why did it resonate so smoothly whenever he said it? Everyone else made "Rosellen" sound like two names. Only Cason rolled them together and made them sound the way it was meant to sound—like one word.

At an early age she had insisted that everyone shorten her name to Roe, but to no avail. Rose seemed to be the name that stuck with her. She'd always hated the fact that her brothers were given strong masculine names and she'd been given the most feminine name she could imagine: Rosellen. Her mother was the only person who ever slipped up and called her that until Cason.

She squared her shoulders. "I'm not trying to be a man, only a strong woman."

Cason leaned back in his chair, lifting the front legs off the floor. "Why not be what you are, Rosellen? A beautiful woman."

She deliberately looked around the dining room to avoid Cason's eyes. If she could see that he was hiding his true feelings he might be able to see that she hid the fact that she wasn't as tough as she pretended to be.

Rosellen nodded to Mr. and Mrs. Coleman when she realized they were watching her from across the room. A quick glance told her that other townspeople were eyeing her, too.

Cason Murdock was just too damned attractive. She didn't understand how she could find anything about this man appealing, but she did. Every time she saw him, she discovered she was drawn to him like a prospector to a gold strike.

She hated him for thinking her father killed the bank teller. She hated him because he was the first man who had ever made her want to be held in a man's arms. And even now she wondered what his lips would feel like pressed against hers.

She had to stop that kind of nonsense thinking. It was a violation of her father's memory even to consider this man attractive let alone think about kissing him.

Mr. Atkins the assayer stared as he walked past her table. She gave him a nod of greeting, which he returned with curiosity written all over his face.

"Why not get back to the original subject?" she snapped, but her voice no longer had an edge. And

Cason was too damned calm. How could any man be so relaxed, knowing he was going to put more than one hundred men out of work?

"I didn't rob any bank. Buster and I hit a main vein in the southeastern part of the state."

"I'm not buying that."

"It's as probable as you being the next sheriff of this town."

She quietly sucked in her breath. He knew exactly where to hit her. She couldn't let him get to her. Her gaze dropped to the pudding again. Plump, juicy raisins lay nestled in a puffy dumpling that floated in a fragrant sauce. Her mouth watered again.

Rosellen squeezed her hands into fists. She had to stop thinking about food and Cason Murdock and keep her mind on the business at hand. It was because of him that she was hungry in the first place. If he hadn't shown up in town she wouldn't have missed her supper last night, breakfast this morning, and the noon meal today.

Maybe she was too tired to match wits with him. She had always prided herself on holding her own with any man, but he was winning the verbal battle, and that was making her all the more irritable.

"I won't keep the mine open, but I plan to be on the five-o'clock train that connects with the Denver and Rio Grande, so I will be out of town by sundown. That gives you one of the three things you wanted. Happy?"

"No."

It bothered her the way he kept looking at her with those dark brown eyes. She'd never met a more confident man. She wished she knew what was making her think these crazy thoughts about a man she couldn't possibly like.

"Look, I don't know where you've been or what you've been for doing the past fifteen years, but you obviously don't know what shutting down the mine will do to this town. It employs over one hundred men. If they don't work the mine, they'll have to leave town and find jobs elsewhere so they can feed their families. Poppy will become a ghost town."

Cason remained silent, watching her. She had a feeling he was deliberately not saying too much to avoid telling her anything he didn't want her to know.

"What about the fact you won't make any money if you don't work the mine?" she asked. "The vein's not dry. I'm told there's plenty of gold left in the mountain."

"I don't need any more money."

"The people of Poppy do. They need their jobs. You can't be that coldhearted."

He said nothing.

She trembled with frustration. What was this man's weakness? If he wasn't hungry for money and he already had power, what *did* he want?

"Closing the mine is a heartless thing to do."

So suddenly it stunned her, Cason jerked toward her, an angry scowl on his face. "Don't talk to me about heartlessness. You don't even know what it means. I was a young boy in this town. Not one damn person helped me when—" He stopped abruptly and leaned back in his chair.

He didn't move a muscle, and he didn't blink as he regained control of his temper. "I won't change my mind."

An inexplicable feeling of compassion washed over Rosellen. For a moment he'd let his mask slip, and she'd seen his rage and hurt.

There was a sadness in Cason Murdock's eyes that she didn't understand, but his sudden outburst had given her a glimpse of a different man from the one who seemed so hardened. Something more than her

"Good. Make the damn trip. You won't find anyone in Denver, because there's no one to find. Gayla made up the whole story to make a man she remembered as a little boy feel better."

"You must be trying so hard because you want to convince yourself. You're not going to convince me."

"I can't believe you're doing this. These people haven't done anything to you. It was my father who killed yours. These people are innocent. Dammit, Murdock, just tell me what I can do to keep you from closing down the mine."

"Nothing."

"Everyone has a price."

"I have more money than I can spend, but if you're politely trying to offer me your body I'll have to consider that."

A shocked gasp escaped Rosellen's lips. Not from what he said but from the way her body responded to his suggestion. Why had a thrill of excitement raced through her at his insulting comment?

"You bastard."

"You're the one who wanted to know my price."

"And you know I was talking money."

"How could I have known? And I agreed only to consider the idea. I'll let you know when I make up my mind if I'm interested."

She took a deep breath, but refused to let her chin fall or her shoulders sag. "Go to hell."

He lowered his lashes over his dark eyes. "Go fight a battle you can win, Rosellen. This one has already been settled."

"Not as far as I'm concerned. I'll keep after you until you board up the doors of the mine. As long as there is one family left in this town to fight for, I'll be knocking on that door, trying to get it open."

She rose and left the dining room.

* * *

"She's a hot-tempered one," Buster said, taking the seat Rosellen had vacated. "I bet she's just the kind of woman Shakespeare had in mind when he wrote *The Taming of the Shrew.* No man will ever tame her."

"A pretty face and a viper's tongue," Cason mused.

"I bet she'd be a handful under the blanket. No need to throw extra wood on the fire with her around."

Cason didn't respond. For some reason Buster's comment bothered him. He didn't want to talk about sex and Rosellen to Buster.

"We could make a wager as to how long it'd take you to get her in the sack. . . . Hey, you listening to me?"

Buster was too perceptive. Somehow he'd picked up on the smoldering embers that had been ignited between him and Rosellen. She'd picked up on those feelings, too, although Cason knew she would never admit to it. He saw her response to him in her eyes, heard it in her gasp. Just like him, she was fighting it hard.

"Yeah, I'm listening. While I'm gone I want you to see about having stone markers made for my parents' graves."

"Be glad to. You want them big with fancy writing?"

"Just make sure the headstones are bigger than Henry Lattimer's," he said, thinking it was a small thing to do for his parents, but it was the only thing he could do.

"All right. Consider it done." Buster tugged on his cravat and said, "You think anybody in this town knows the whole story about how your mama died and everything?"

"You're the only person I've ever told, and that's the way I want it. Remember that."

"I never had a loose tongue, even when I was a drinking man. You know that."

Cason nodded. He knew Buster was loyal to a fault, but Rosellen had Cason's thinking screwed up. "I think I'll spend a few minutes upstairs at the Silver Nugget before I have to go to the depot. It'll be a long train ride to Denver."

"Have you seen a woman over there that's caught your eye?"

He'd seen one that caught his eye, but she didn't work at the saloon. "Not yet, but I thought I'd have a look."

"I knew that quick-tempered Rose had your blood simmering. The air between you two was so hot it was smoking like a two-ton smelter."

"I think you're the one who's excited about her," Cason said, hoping to take the heat off himself. "You can't stop talking about her."

"Me?" Buster's eyes widened in surprise. He strained his neck against the tight collar.

"Maybe you should go to the saloon with me."

"I'll go later when I have more time. You'll be pushing it to pay for an hour and still make that train."

"I'll make it." Cason pushed back his chair, picked up his hat, and walked off.

Buster was right. Rosellen was the woman he wanted. He might as well admit it to himself and be done with it. He sure as hell wasn't going to do anything about it even though something about her was driving him crazy with need.

Maybe this was happening because she challenged him on a level that no other woman ever had. Maybe he knew that, because of what her father did to his family, she was forbidden. Maybe he wanted to punish her for what her father did.

He didn't know what it was. He only knew he

wanted to see Rosellen again. He wanted to talk to her again, and he wanted to know what she was like in bed.

But that wasn't going to happen, so he headed for the saloon. Maybe a whore would help him forget about the golden-haired Rosellen Lattimer—until he returned to Poppy.

Chapter

→ 7 ←

*R*evenge.

That was what he wanted. No wonder Cason Murdock wouldn't give an inch.

During the walk home Rosellen had finally figured out what Cason was up to. He was hell-bent on revenge, and he knew that she wanted to stop him. He wasn't going to give her anything that might help her.

Since her father was already dead, Cason planned to get back at Henry Lattimer for killing his father by destroying the town. Somehow he must have known how much her father loved the people of Poppy and how he dedicated his life to taking care of them.

She burst through the front door of her home. Through the arched doorway that led into the parlor she could see her mother sitting in her rocker by the unlit fireplace.

"That man Murdock has a heart that's as black and hard as solid iron ore, Mama," Rosellen complained. "I don't know what I'll do yet to stop him from closing the mine, but I'm not going to stand idly by and watch him make Poppy another Colorado ghost town."

Cason appeared to have plenty of money. She squeezed her eyes shut for a moment. Having grown up in a mining town, she knew that very few people had enough money to buy a mine that was producing. And now that she knew revenge was his motive there was no point in appealing to his sense of right and wrong. Vindictive people were interested only in getting even.

Cason's handsome face flashed before her again. It wasn't vengefulness she saw when she looked into his eyes. It was sorrow. He'd tried to hide it behind his coldhearted attitude, and she sensed a lot of anger in him, but there was something deeper behind the man than he wanted to show.

Rosellen plucked her hat off and sailed it onto the hall stand. What in the hell was she doing trying to analyze a man who wanted to destroy her family, her town? She must be going soft.

"That's the way of it with outlaws, gunfighters, and rich men like Murdock, Mama," Rosellen continued. "They think they can ride into a peaceful community like Poppy and take over. Well, I won't have it. Not in my town. A man like Murdock thinks everyone will be afraid of him, but I'm not. I've rescheduled my meeting with Mr. Vestly and his committee for tomorrow."

She untied her holster, then unbuckled her gun belt and hung it up.

"I don't know why they don't just give me the badge. They know I'm the best person for the job."

Her mother hadn't said a word, so Rosellen glanced her way again. It was an odd time of day for her mother to be resting. Evelyn's face was as grave as the preacher's when he used to caution Rosellen about throwing spitballs across the aisle in church on Sunday mornings.

Rosellen walked into the living room and gave her

mother a closer look. Her face was drawn, and her lips and cheeks were pale. She didn't look as if she'd heard a word Rosellen had said. For the first time, Rosellen noticed that her eyes were red and swollen as if she'd been crying. Evelyn hadn't looked so bad since the day her husband died.

"Mama, what's wrong?" she asked, kneeling in front of her.

"I'm not feeling too well right now, Rosellen." She dabbed at her eyes with her apron.

Rosellen's heart rose up in her throat as she remembered those were the last words her father had spoken before suffering heart failure.

A wave of fear sliced through her. "Don't move. I'll go get the doctor."

"No, no, dear. Don't go. I'm not sick." Evelyn stopped Rosellen with a cold hand. "But I don't think I can talk about it with you just yet. It's too dreadful."

Rosellen heard the pain in her mother's voice, and it frightened her. "You must tell me what's wrong."

"Here you go, Mama, I have some water for you," Simon said walking in from the kitchen. "Rose, I'm glad you're finally home."

"Simon, what are you doing here? What's going on?" Rosellen stood up. She didn't know what was happening to her family. Her mother was sick. Her brothers were leaving work in the middle of the day. Cason Murdock had returned to town and upset everyone's life.

"Jarred and Walter are at the mine. I told them I'd come home and stay with Mama."

"Why? Did she send for you? She was fine when I left. What happened?"

A grim expression twisted his lips. "We didn't want either of you to be alone. Obviously you haven't heard. I was afraid you might have."

"Heard what?" she asked as a niggling dread

washed over her. All of a sudden Rosellen felt as cold as her mother's hands.

Simon shook his head. "I didn't want to be the one to tell either of you, but I was afraid to wait until later, for fear someone else might let the news slip. There's some gossip going around the town about Papa."

Rosellen's chest tightened, cutting off her breath. A buzzing started in her ears.

"No, Simon," Evelyn said jumping to her feet and grabbing hold of his arm. "There's no need for her to know." She turned to Rosellen. "I don't want you to know what ugly things have been said about your father. I know how much you loved him."

"She has to know," Simon said. "The story is spreading through town like a cold wind, Mama. Here, drink your water. Rose needs to hear this from family, not from someone on the street."

Tears spilled out of her mother's eyes, and Rosellen's heart almost stopped. She knew the answer but she couldn't stop herself from turning to Simon and demanding, "What gossip?"

"I didn't want you to hear it, Rosellen." Her mother's voice was soft, whimpering. Tears rolled from her swollen, frightened eyes.

"Mama, why don't you go lie down. I'll tell Rose everything."

"Yes. I think I do need to lie down for a little while." She sobbed out loud as she left the room.

Rosellen's heart broke for her mother as anger burst to life and burned like a searing blue flame inside her chest. She could handle her own pain, but she wouldn't let anyone do this to her mother and get away with it.

As soon as Evelyn was out of sight, Rosellen pivoted toward her brother and said, "Tell me what you heard."

Simon ran his hand through his close-cropped blond hair. "I don't know how such a ridiculous thing could have gotten started, but apparently someone overheard the woman who owns the Silver Nugget Saloon telling someone else that Papa was involved in the bank robbery that happened years ago and that he killed two men. Have you ever heard such an outrageous lie?"

"Someone, hell. Double dammit," Rosellen whispered softly even though the anger inside her was as fierce as a January blizzard.

She remembered how Delta had looked at her when she entered the saloon. Rosellen should have known the woman was eavesdropping on them. The whore probably couldn't wait to start spreading the pack of lies Gayla had told. Rosellen should throw that little hussy Delta in jail for daring to breathe her father's name.

"Who could have thought up such a preposterous lie? And why? Papa's been dead over a year."

"I know who started this," Rosellen muttered. And she could only imagine why, and money would be her first guess. Delta probably had somebody pay her for the dirt she heard.

"Who? And how do you know?"

"I just do," she answered, trying to brush Simon off.

"No, Rose, you think you do," her brother said. "As usual, you're jumping to conclusions that are going to land you in trouble. Tell me what you think you know, and I'll check it out."

"I'll take care of this, Simon."

Rosellen had told Gayla and Cason she'd come after them if she heard one word about this, but she hadn't thought about Delta.

"Rose, why don't you let Jarred and Walter and me handle something for a change? We're not kids anymore. You don't have to prove anything to us by being so tough."

Tough? She wasn't tough; she was scared. She felt light-headed and sick to her stomach. She should have done more yesterday to prevent this from happening. "I won't have anyone hurting Mama."

"We don't want anyone to hurt her or you," Simon said, "but we're not going to accuse anyone until we have some facts. The first thing we have to find out is what this person is trying to accomplish by spreading this rumor."

Rosellen knew. The story was too juicy for Delta to keep to herself, and she had probably made a tidy sum of money off the information, too.

Simon pursed his lips for a moment, then said, "We have to consider the possibility that's it's someone who doesn't want you to be sheriff and who hopes this will make you back off."

"Simon, are you saying this is my fault?"

"Of course not." He hitched his brown trousers up and over his rounded middle. "But right now you're the one who wants to be sheriff."

"I don't believe this." Rosellen shook her head and started pacing. "Simon, if it was anything like that, the person would just persuade Mr. Vestly not to recommend me as the temporary sheriff."

"Well, whoever is behind this rumor has a reason for spreading it, and it's not going to hurt Papa, so the person must have someone else in mind."

"The only one I'm worried about is Mama, and I'm fighting mad."

"Rose, don't get your back up. This gossip will blow over in a few days. Papa was a good man. Everyone in town knows that, and no one will believe this ludicrous story."

Rosellen walked over to the window and stared at the white picket fence that surrounded the front lawn.

How could so many things go wrong in so short a time? Yesterday morning she'd awoken thinking she'd be the next sheriff of Poppy, but now she wondered if there would even be a town if she couldn't stop Murdock from closing the mine.

What was she going to do now that the horrid lie would be on everyone's lips? Damn Cason Murdock for coming back to Poppy.

She thought back to how he had pushed her aside so he could cling to every word Gayla said. She'd seen how desperate he was to believe the woman.

Suddenly a thought struck her. He wanted to be justified in destroying the town so he'd needed for others to believe Gayla's lies too. What if Cason went to Denver and paid someone to pretend he was this so-called cousin named Dodge? What if that man came back and told the whole town everything the woman said was true? What if everyone in town believed him?

Double damn.

She had to do something. Cason had the money, the means, and the motive to do something like that. Rosellen knew how powerful the desire for revenge could be.

Rosellen looked around the parlor. Her eyes were drawn again to those things that others might have thought were too expensive for someone on a sheriff's salary to afford. She took a steadying breath and knew what she had to do. And she didn't want her mother or any of her brothers around to tell her not to do it.

"Simon, I want you to take Mama home with you. Powder her nose and around her eyes to hide the redness. Make sure you walk down Main Street with her and stop and talk to everyone you see. Act as if nothing's wrong."

"Have you lost your mind? You can see Mama isn't

up to doing that, and she doesn't want to talk to anyone right now."

"She has to."

"Why? What good can something like that do?"

"I want everyone in this town to know that the Lattimers don't believe a word of this bare-faced lie that has been spread around. We aren't hanging our heads in shame for anyone. Henry Lattimer didn't do anything wrong, and we have no intention of trying to explain something that never happened. Now, go get Mama and head out. I've got some thinking to do."

The heavy satchel in Rosellen's hand made the taut muscles in her arm burn, but she kept up a brisk pace as she stepped up on the boardwalk that ran along Front Street. Fury raged inside her, and she took each stride with determination.

Everything that had gone wrong in her life during the last two days was Cason Murdock's fault. If he hadn't come back to town, Gayla wouldn't have thought up such outlandish lies, Delta wouldn't have spread the gossip around, and Rosellen wouldn't be doing all this fast walking and making her feet sore again.

She noticed a few stares and a lot of long glances as she marched into the heart of town. She kept her head up, but didn't break her determined stride.

With her free hand she waved to Mr. Carmichael. He was loading supplies into a wagon but took time to say hello to her. She nodded to Mrs. Patterson as they passed each other in front of the dry goods store, and she stopped long enough to hear Mr. Wilkins tell her what a fine job she did running that troublemaking prospector out of town. He also told her that Shoestring's shoulder was going to be all right.

Rosellen didn't stay long. She had two more stops

to make before the train pulled out of the station, and she was running out of time.

She stepped off the wide planked walkway and into a dark alley that led to the back of the saloon. This way would save her about five minutes walking time, and she needed every minute she could get.

It was hot and humid in the narrow passageway that few people dared to venture into. When she made it to the bottom of the steps she dropped her brocade satchel to the ground and climbed the steep stairs two at a time.

Her legs were weak and trembly by the time she made it to the top. She took a deep breath and rested against the railing. She should have taken time to eat something before she left home, but by the time she'd packed her clothes and written her mother a note there was no time.

She'd been starving since she saw Cason ignoring Miss Leddy's bread pudding. As far as she was concerned, that was just another mark against him. Not having the good sense to eat that delicious dessert when it was hot was just another thing to add to her long list.

Rosellen climbed onto the narrow balcony that ran alongside the upper floor windows of the Silver Nugget Saloon.

Years ago Rosellen had heard that when Gayla bought the building she'd had the stairs and balcony built and opened two exits that led out of the back alley. She wanted her customers to have an easy way to come and go discreetly or hurriedly if the need arose. Just another one of the many reasons she was well liked by most of the men in town.

Rosellen's father had never let her come with him to the back of the saloon, but she'd hidden behind water troughs and rain barrels more than once and watched men go and come from the alley.

She'd seen her father climbing up the steps, too, but until now she had never allowed herself to think that he might have been doing anything other than official business when he entered the saloon that way.

Standing in front of one of the four windows, Rosellen clenched her fists, and for a moment she felt light-headed again. She didn't like doubting her father's character. He was a good man who loved his wife, his children, and his town. He went to church every Sunday and said a blessing at the supper table every evening. Murdock didn't know her father and had no business judging him.

She wouldn't, couldn't, allow herself to think anything else. He'd had a reputation as a man who had turned a small, lawless mining camp into a community with a church and a school. She shouldn't have to defend him. The way he lived his life spoke for him.

One of the windows opened into a hallway, but Rosellen didn't know which one. She'd never been on the second floor of the saloon, so she had no idea which window she needed to go through. The best thing to do was climb in the first window and see where that took her—and hope it wasn't an occupied room. She'd find her way around once she got inside.

Rosellen hadn't felt so mischievous since the time all three of her brothers had dared her to climb up a lattice trellis and look into a bedroom window to see who was sleeping with the widow Martin. The woman had seen Rosellen looking in and screamed. Mr. Finway had stumbled over his feet trying to put his trousers back on and ended up with a broken leg.

Rosellen cringed as she remembered. That was just one of the many stupid things she'd been dared to do in her younger years and that she now wished she hadn't done.

When she got her wind back, Rosellen grabbed hold of the frame and, after a couple of tugs to get it started, slowly raised the window all the way up. Surprisingly it only made a slight scraping sound. A lacy curtain panel was sucked out the window, and she pushed it aside. She bent at the waist and swung one booted foot inside the room, straddling the windowsill. She then lowered her head and swung her body into the room.

She heard the click of a gun cocking. Her hand went to her weapon. She jerked her head up and hit the bottom of the window as she swung her other leg into the room.

Rosellen grunted and looked up.

She blinked rapidly, not believing her eyes. Standing on the other side of the bed was Cason Murdock, buck naked, pointing his six-shooter at her heart.

Chapter

➤ 8 ◆

Rosellen felt her heart slamming against her chest, beating in double time. It almost hurt to breathe. Cason was a magnificent man. Powerful and dangerous.

He kept the gun pointed at her as she rose from the window and turned fully toward him. She forced herself to keep her gaze on his face.

Rosellen's hands dropped to her sides. She hardly dared to breathe. A quick glance around told her he was alone. Surprising. She wondered if he'd just arrived or if one of Gayla's girls had already been in and left.

Cason didn't move to pull on his trousers, or to cover his body with the sheet, his shirt, or his hat. He could have grabbed the red satin robe that lay on the foot of the bed, but he didn't reach for any of those things.

He wanted her to look at him.

But why? Did he want to intimidate her, frighten her, or seduce her? She wasn't sure which, but she couldn't let him do any of them. Rosellen knew if she ever showed this man a weakness he'd find a way to use it against her.

With deliberate slowness she let her gaze travel down his strong neck, over his broad, muscular shoulders and chest, then lower. His stomach was flat, firm. His hips were lean, narrow. She noted that he must have worked outside with his shirt off, because the skin below his waist was much lighter than his face, neck, and chest.

She couldn't help looking at his entire body. Her gaze inched lower. She saw curly dark golden blond hair and—*Big*.

A thrill shimmied up her spine. She didn't want to blink and miss one second of inspecting Cason's splendid, handsome body.

"Are you through looking me over?"

Her gaze flew back to his face. The tautness of her body increased. *Damn, don't let me blush.*

His expression was reckless. His words and how he said them could have been considered teasing had it not been for the intense fire of arousal she saw in his eyes. The sensual set to his full lips was suggestive of the way she'd been staring at him.

Cason lowered his gun to his side. Without conscious effort her gaze followed the movement of his hand.

"I can stand here longer if you need more time."

Damn him. He was having fun at her expense.

Hoping he wouldn't notice, she lightly cleared her throat before attempting to speak. "I have three older brothers. I've seen the male body."

"But you haven't seen me before."

"That sounds like a challenge."

"Then it must be."

Her breathing was so shallow she wasn't sure she was getting any air. A raw tension dominated the air between them, but Rosellen couldn't let him know just how his brashness stirred her blood.

She deliberately looked at his entire body again before meeting his eyes. "You all look alike," she lied.

"Really?"

"Disappointed?"

"Not convinced," he challenged in a low, seductive voice. "I can't say I've ever had a woman look me over so thoroughly before."

She deliberately, wantonly looked at his forbidden parts again. She could have sworn *it* was growing. She waited a long time before she moistened her lips and managed to lie with a straight face, "I'm not impressed."

"Liar."

"Go to hell," she muttered and meant it.

Rosellen didn't want to respond to this man on any level and certainly not a sexual one, but right now she was overflowing with desire. She wanted to walk over to him, flatten her hands against his broad chest, and slide her palms all the way down to— She tightened the reins on her wayward thoughts.

With little effort he was getting to her. Real bad. She had to stay calm and think clearly.

She had seen her brothers naked when they went swimming in the frigid water of a swollen stream, but that had been years ago when they were much younger. And she didn't remember any one of them looking anything like the irresistible man standing so proudly before her now.

Cason released the hammer on his pistol and laid it on the night table beside him. "You were half a second from being a dead man."

"That would be something, considering I'm a woman."

"Prove it."

Her eyes narrowed. She jutted one leg out to the

side and rested both hands on her hips. "What are you talking about, Murdock?"

He stretched out his arms. "If you're applying for a job, you're overdressed."

"No, you're underdressed. I thought you had a train to catch," she snapped, thinking she might have been racing around for nothing. "Change your mind?"

"No. But it's going to be a long ride to Denver. I thought I'd stop by for a quick—"

"Save it," she blurted, interrupting him. She didn't want to be a source of amusement for him any longer. "I can guess the rest."

The door opened, and a dark-haired young woman waltzed in. "I have the liquor you wanted, handsome. I hope you're ready for me." She stopped short. "Oh." She drew her brows together. "Hey, what's going on here?"

"Nothing," Rosellen said quickly.

"What are you doing in my room with my customer?"

Rosellen heard jealousy in the woman's voice. "I was looking for Delta, and I see I have the wrong room."

"Last door on the right," the prostitute said, folding her arms across her chest and looking annoyed as she caught sight of the open window.

"I'll just hurry out so you two can . . . get down to business." She threw a glance at Cason. He wasn't at all disconcerted by what had happened.

"Next time walk in the front door and ask before you come upstairs," the girl snapped.

"You can be sure I will." Rosellen kept her chin up as she stalked to the door and stopped. Her gaze swept over Cason again. "Carry on."

Rosellen was trembling as she closed the door behind her. She hadn't expected to see Cason and certainly not so—so nude. Now that she had, she would never forget the smallest or the largest detail of his body.

She *had* looked him over thoroughly.

With a steadying hand she leaned against the wall and took a deep breath. She wasn't sure her wobbly knees were ready to walk down the hall to Delta's room until she composed herself. She rubbed the tender spot on her head that she just now realized was paining her.

Why had it affected her to see him nude? Why should she be impressed with his magnificent build? She didn't want to think of him in any way except as a man she had to watch. But she didn't have time right now to think about those funny feelings squirming around inside her. She would have to deal with those things later. She had to see Delta and Mr. Vestly before five o'clock. If Cason was going to be on that train, so was she.

Rosellen pushed away from the wall and walked down to Delta's door. She knocked, then opened it without waiting for an answer. Delta sat at her dressing table combing her hair. She gasped and spun around when she saw Rosellen.

The woman jumped off her stool. "Get out of here."

"Not until you and I have a talk."

Delta ran to her nightstand and jerked open the drawer. Rosellen rushed over to her and grabbed her wrist as she pulled out a revolver. With her shoulder, Rosellen dived into Delta and they fell onto the bed, wrestling, kicking, and grabbing hair.

Putting all her strength into squeezing Delta's wrist, Rosellen forced her to drop the gun. With the toe of her boot she kicked the firearm to the floor and out of Delta's reach.

The prostitute was strong, but Rosellen had learned long ago how to wrestle and subdue an opponent. She grabbed Delta's arm and flipped her onto her stomach. With quick movements she forced Delta's arm behind her back, then pushed her knee into the whore's backbone.

"You're hurting me, you bitch! Let me up, damn you!" Rosellen pressed Delta's face into the bedcovers to muffle her shouts.

"Why did you pull a gun on me?" Rosellen demanded, trying to catch her breath. "Someone could have gotten hurt."

"Everybody knows how wild you are. I was afraid you were going to shoot me."

"Damn," Rosellen swore. "Have you ever known me to shoot anyone?"

"I knew you were angrier than a mad dog."

"That's because you spread that lie about my father. Now you're going to tell everyone it's not true."

"No. No, I didn't do it," she mumbled into the coverlet, struggling against Rosellen's firm hold.

"Yes, you did, and I don't like people talking about my family, making my mother cry."

"I didn't tell. Get off me."

"You told somebody."

"No, damn you. I'll swear it on the preacher's Bible."

"Did Gayla do it?"

"No."

"Murdock?" she asked, but for some reason she was sure he hadn't said a word.

"No, it was the man who delivers our whiskey each month. He was in the back room stacking crates. He heard everything Gayla said. He made George, the bartender, pay him fifteen dollars before he'd tell all he heard."

Anger crawled up Rosellen's back. *Fifteen dollars?* That bastard *sold* the gossip? "Who did he tell other than the bartender?"

"I don't know who else he told. I don't know who George might have told. Now let me up. You're hurting me."

Rosellen released some of the pressure on her back. "What's the whiskey salesman's name?"

"Alford Clark. I'm sure you've seen him around town."

Rosellen remembered seeing the wagon marked Clark Whiskey Sales, but she'd never spoken to the man. "You better not be lying to me," she said and slowly started turning Delta loose.

"I swear I'm not. I hear things all the time around here, but I stay quiet. I've heard what Gayla does to her girls when they gossip."

A memory flashed through Rosellen's brain. Yes, she remembered, too. One of Gayla's girls had been accused of telling people that Wilbur Clandon's wife was pregnant and it turned out it wasn't so. He'd just used that to justify coming to the Silver Nugget for what he wasn't getting at home.

Gayla had dragged the young whore out of bed and thrown her out into the street with nothing on but her robe—no shoes or coat, even though it was the middle of February.

Satisfied for the moment that Delta hadn't spread the rumor, Rosellen let her go and jumped off the bed. She picked up Delta's gun, put it back in the nightstand, and shut the drawer.

Delta swung her feet off the other side of the bed and cringed against to the far wall, whimpering. Her eyes were wild. "You're crazy. You almost broke my arm. I'm going to tell Gayla what you did. I'm going to tell the whole damn town what you did to me."

"From the way you were wailing like a banshee I think they already know. Now, when will the whiskey salesman be back in town?"

"He comes at the same time each month, I guess."

"You better hope he shows up and tells the same story you do, or I'll be back."

"No one breaks Gayla's rules," Delta said rubbing her back. "I didn't spread that story."

"For now I'm going to believe you, but if I find out you're lying about this, I'm going to come back and mess you up so bad no man will ever take another look at you." That was as close to an apology as Rosellen was willing to give.

"I wouldn't lie to you," Delta said, rolling her shoulders. "Truth is, I liked your father. Henry was a good man. He always treated me real nice. Sometimes he made me feel like a lady."

Rosellen swallowed hard. Delta was sending her a message and she read it loud and clear. Now all doubt was erased. Her father's visits to the saloon weren't just to haul drunken cowboys and miners to jail.

She straightened her shoulders and summoned her pride. He might have visited the whores like a lot of other men in town, but he hadn't killed anyone. She still had that to prove.

Not afraid to show Delta her back, Rosellen turned to leave and stopped short. Her breath thickened in her throat. Cason stood in the doorway, watching her. The bartender and two other saloon girls were there, too.

Double damn.

Looking at Cason, fully dressed, hat in hand, she knew all her troubles could be traced back to him. She hated being so acutely aware of him, but she didn't know what she was going to do about it.

"I guess this is why they call you the sheriff's little hellion," he taunted her.

Cason's remark stung. Maybe she used to deserve that name, but she was going to change that. She had to, if the citizens of Poppy were going to respect her.

Rosellen was trying hard not to get so angry that her emotions took control of her actions, but the minute she'd heard about the gossip she'd reverted to her old way of wanting to fight whomever she didn't see eye to eye with.

Sometimes she thought there was no use in trying to handle things like a grown-up or in a ladylike manner. She'd acted without thinking things through for too long.

No self-respecting sheriff would rough up one of the townspeople, even if she was a whore, especially over a rumor that no one would believe anyway. But Rosellen had been forced to jump Delta when she grabbed her pistol. Delta was as nervous as a cat in the middle of a pack of dogs. She could have pulled the trigger and accidentally shot her.

Rosellen hated being called a hellion—especially by Cason, though she would never let him know that. And she couldn't let anything Cason Murdock said get to her. He meant nothing to her, and she surely didn't owe him an explanation about her life. What he thought about her wasn't worth a nickel to her.

She didn't want to be the hellion she used to be. She'd grown up. She was almost twenty-one years old. When her brothers had gotten older they'd all married and settled down, stopped roughhousing. And she could do it, too.

Just as soon as she'd finished her business with Murdock.

Cason was staring at her. She had two choices, leave by the window or the door. Her bag was down by the stairs and she was running out of time to make it to the train station by five o'clock. She couldn't possibly look any worse in Cason's eyes than she already did.

Straightening her shoulders, Rosellen strode over to Delta's window and opened it. "You should keep this locked. Anyone could come in here. You wouldn't want that, would you?"

Rosellen crawled out, leaving the window open behind her.

As she started down the steps two at time, she wondered if Cason had found time to enjoy the whore before he dressed and walked to Delta's room.

"Rosellen, you can't barge into my office like this." The portly man stood up so fast that one side of his braces popped off the waistband of his trousers and hit him under his double chin.

She set her canvas satchel by her feet. She'd already been to the bank and taken out the smallest amount of money she thought she could get by with, knowing that she and her mother had limited funds to live on until she got the job as sheriff.

"I'm sorry, Mr. Vestly, but I had no choice. I've waited outside your office as long as I can. The first whistle has blown. The train's going to be pulling out of the station any minute now, and I have to be on it."

"What are you talking about?" he said, fumbling with short, stubby fingers to fasten his suspenders.

"I don't have time to explain everything, but I will tell you that where I'm going has to do with that man named Murdock who bought the mine and now wants to close it down."

Suddenly his face reddened, and Rosellen knew he was remembering the gossip that by now would be all over town. She could see it in his eyes.

"Oh, yes, I—I heard about that, too. I mean, the, ah, committee plans to meet with Mr. Murdock about that and persuade him not to close it."

"I've already tried."

He lifted his bushy eyebrows in surprise. "You've talked to him?"

"Yes. He won't budge. He's leaving on the train for Denver. I'm going to follow him."

"What? Why?" The sagging skin around his face shook. "If he's going, good riddance."

"He's leaving his partner and his hired guns here to do his dirty work."

"Well, we'll talk to them. You can't go chasing after that man. What do your mother and brothers have to say about this?"

They didn't know yet. "There's no time to explain all that right now. The man left in charge of closing the mine is Buster O'Malley. You can try talking to him, but I don't think it will do any good; he seems devoted to Murdock. I don't know how long I'll be gone, but I'm hoping you'll hold the job of sheriff open for me."

"Rose, you're not making any sense. You're talking too fast and saying too much."

"I know." She took a calming breath. "I also know that Walter may talk to you about the job, and I want you to know I'll run against him just as I would any other man. I just need some time before you make your final decision."

"Rose, I don't know." He shook his head again. "I've never promised you the job."

"I can take care of Poppy, Mr. Vestly. All I'm asking for is a chance. I can do it, but I have to deal with this man Murdock first." The second whistle blew. "I have to go. Just give me your promise you'll wait until I get back to appoint a temporary sheriff and give me a fair chance."

He rubbed a palm over the crown of his head, barely ruffling the long, thinning hair that had been slicked away from his face with an oily hair tonic. "I'll try."

Rosellen wrinkled her nose in frustration. "I'm going after Murdock to try to stop him from destroying this town. If I succeed, I deserve that job. You remember that." She picked up her satchel and rushed out the door.

It had never bothered her before that the train station was so far out of town. It must be close to half a mile, she thought as she started running, knowing she had cut it too close. Her boots rubbed against the already sore skin on her heels. But she couldn't slow down. She wasn't sure she was going to make the train as it was.

Her mother and brothers would be furious when they read her note and discovered that she'd followed Cason to Denver, but she didn't have time to think about that now.

Murdock had left her no choice in this matter. She didn't want him closing the mine, but right now her immediate problem was keeping him from doing something dishonest to discredit her father in the eyes of the townspeople.

The running and the heavy burden made her breathless and hot. Her hat fell to the back of her shoulders and the late afternoon sunshine beat down on her head. She hadn't had time to eat anything since the noon meal yesterday, and hunger was beginning to sap her strength. She felt weak and trembly, but she kept her legs pumping.

She had to make that train. If she missed it, she would never find Cason in a city as big as Denver. The survival of the whole town depended on her.

Just as Rosellen jumped onto the boardwalk at the depot, the train whistle blew for the third and final time, signaling that the big steel-and-iron machine was leaving the station. Puffy black smoke billowed into the clean mountain air. The engine was already chugging away from the small plank building. Rosellen held tightly to her satchel and ran as fast as she could.

Gasping for breath, she caught up with the last car

and ran to stay even with it, waiting for a chance to hop onto the open platform at the back of the train. The high-pitched screeching and rattling of the wheels speeding on the tracks was frightening, deafening, but she was too close to give up.

She stretched her arm wide as she ran alongside the massive locomotive and grabbed hold of the handrail on the platform as the train picked up speed. The force wrenched her shoulder painfully and jerked her wrist, but she held tight. With all the strength she could muster, she tried to pull herself up on the iron platform, but the heavy bag in her hand dragged her backward.

Struggling to control her balance, Rosellen managed to swing one leg up on the first step. Just as she thought she was going to make it, her sweaty hand slipped from the iron handrail.

Rosellen tried to scream but fear swooshed all the air out of her lungs.

Chapter

→ 9 ←

Cason was hot and bothered. Tormented. His trousers were too tight as he bent and took a seat at the front of the train. He hadn't been expecting anything explosive. Just a quick, gratifying poke to let off a little of the steam rising between him and Rosellen.

Now he had time to sit back and think.

When he'd heard the window slide up, he'd rolled off the bed ready to put a hole in somebody's gut. But then he'd seen the shiny mule-ear boot cross over the windowsill.

That woman had him hotter than a boiling smelter. She'd looked him over from head to toe—several times. She'd never batted a nervous eye as he stood there naked as the day he was born.

He should have been embarrassed, but he hadn't been. He should have been ashamed of himself for standing there encouraging her to look at him, but he hadn't. He should have taken a shot at her and scared the hell out of her so she'd think twice before she crawled in anybody else's bedroom window.

But he hadn't. He'd played with her, and she'd matched him challenge for challenge.

The hellion. Damn if that name didn't fit her. She was trouble with a capital T.

Most of the men he'd known didn't have the courage, the spunk, or the determination of Rosellen Lattimer. Hell, most of the men he knew didn't have her kind of loyalty, either. She must have gotten it from her mother. Cason couldn't imagine the bastard coward Henry Lattimer having any.

And, dammit, he liked the fact that Rosellen had accepted his challenge and looked him over again. Now he wanted to look at her the same way, but he couldn't. He had to remember she was the daughter of the man who had destroyed his parents. And he had to be unforgiving, no matter how deliciously she disturbed him.

Cason stirred in his seat and pulled down on the legs of his trousers. He had to stop thinking about her or it was going to be a long, frustrating trip to Denver.

The whistle blew, and the train lurched and slowly started moving. Cason turned and looked around the car. There were only eight or nine people on board the short line that would connect to the main line in Pueblo. Good. He was glad the train wasn't crowded. Less chattering. He could put his hat over his face and sleep off his frustration.

Cason glanced out the window as he slumped down in the seat. "Damn!" he muttered, rising to take a closer look. There was Rosellen, running as fast as she could, trying catch the train.

A hand caught her wrist. Strong fingers dug deep into her flesh. A shadow loomed over her. Rosellen was yanked upward, wrenching her shoulder. The toes of her new boots scraped across the iron platform. She slammed against the rock-hard chest of Cason Murdock, flattening him against the back of the railway car.

She tried to steady herself, but the train lurched and swayed as they rounded a curve, throwing her against him once again and slamming him into the rickety iron railing. Rosellen wanted to jerk away from him, but she was too breathless and weak with relief to move. She dropped her satchel and rested her forehead against Cason's shoulder.

"You brave little fool. That was a crazy stunt for you to pull. You must be demented," Cason shouted to be heard above the shrill whistle that suddenly blared above the fierce clanking of iron on steel.

"I think I am," she managed to say even though she was sure there was no air left in her lungs.

"You would have been killed just now if I hadn't spotted you," he admonished, setting her away from him.

Rosellen's legs were so trembly and the train was rocking so hard that she could hardly hold herself up straight. A burning pain in her shoulder made it feel as if the bone had been ripped from its socket.

"You were the one who almost got me killed," she said breathlessly. "What did you mean by grabbing hold of me like that? You made me scuff the polish off my new boots, and you hurt my arm."

His brows drew together in a frown of disbelief. "I saved your little ass and you know it."

"I don't know any such thing," she fibbed without regret and rubbed her sore wrist where his fingers had latched on to her skin like steel bands. "I didn't need your help. I had hold of the railing and was pulling myself up when you grabbed me and almost made me lose my balance and my satchel."

"That's a lie." He spoke calmly, confidently.

Rosellen had to lean against the railing to hold herself upright. She wasn't certain she'd recovered enough to take a step yet.

The hazy late afternoon sky, patches of dark green trees, and a narrow blue stream rushed by her in a blur of motion. Wind caught strands of her hair, slipping it free from its ribbon.

"I wasn't going to fall until you yanked on me," she said, not knowing why she was unwilling to let go of the argument when she knew she was being less than truthful.

Cason stared at her with dark brooding eyes. The tepid wind whipped at his hair, blowing it away from his face as the locomotive chugged along at a rapid pace. The whistle blew again, signaling the train's departure from the outskirts of town.

"Like hell you weren't. But that aside, what are you going to do now? You're on the wrong train."

"What do you mean?" she asked, then moistened her dry lips. Now that she was breathing again, her heart was fluttering because he was so close. "This train is going to Denver, isn't it?"

He nodded. "But you can't be going there. You said you thought it was a waste of time, remember?"

"Still do." She took a deep breath, feeling calmer, safer.

"So I guess you're going because you have nothing else to do but waste your time," he said meeting her gaze with his relentless stare.

"No, as a matter of fact, there couldn't be a worse time for me to go. Thanks to you, my family needs me more than ever, and the town needs me, too. But I'm obviously on my way to Denver." She swung her arm—the one that wasn't aching—out to the side as if to show him the rolling, tree-dotted landscape rushing past them.

"I don't need your help to find the man called Dodge," he said. "You can get off at the next stop and go back and help your family and your precious town."

She wanted to laugh, but she was too tired. All she managed was a soft grunt and a half smile. "You don't know, do you?"

His eyes narrowed with a sudden unease, and that gave her a small feeling of satisfaction. After all he'd put her through, if she worried him even a tiny bit she was glad.

"What?"

"I'm not going because I want to help you find this figment of Gayla's imagination. I'm going to keep an eye on you. From now on, Murdock, I'm your shadow. I don't plan to let you out of my sight until you are back in Poppy, empty-handed."

His gleaming brown eyes slowly looked her up and down. "Even with you dressed in men's trousers, your hair a mess of tangles, and a smudge of dirt on your face, the offer is—very tempting. But I travel alone."

His suggestive comment sent her pulse racing, and that angered Rosellen even more. She bit back the curse hovering on her lips and simply said, "Not anymore." With the back of her hand she rubbed first one cheek and then the other, hoping to erase the dirt from her face.

"I guess you've already proven you'll follow me anywhere by joining me in the upstairs room at the saloon."

Indignation reared its head, and her eyes widened in shock. He was itching for a good cussing-out, and if she hadn't been trying to change her ways, she would have obliged him.

She brushed her hair away from her face and settled her hat on her head again. He could get deeper under her skin than a burr in a wool saddle blanket.

"You know I wasn't following you there. I was looking for Delta."

"So you said."

"So I proved."

"You missed the spot. It's here." He rubbed his thumb across the small area between her upper lip and her nose.

A jolt of desire shuddered through Rosellen at his gentle touch, and she swatted his hand away. She felt like stomping her foot in frustration as her body betrayed her again. "You won't be so cocky after I've tailed your butt a few days."

"You think so?"

"Yeah."

He quirked an eyebrow. "Why would I mind a woman chasing after me?"

White hot needles of fury punctured her. She was amusing him. "You son of a backwater—" Rosellen bit back the curse and clamped her mouth shut. She couldn't allow him to continue to rile her into saying things she didn't want to say.

A rueful smile lifted one corner of his shapely lips. "Are you too chicken to finish your sentence?"

Rosellen felt as if steam was lifting out of her cheeks at his accusation. She would have bet every coin she had in her pocket that someone in town had told him she'd fought all her brothers and every boy in school at one time or another for calling her a chicken or a yellow-bellied coward.

She gritted her teeth, refusing to let him goad her into saying any more inappropriate things. She'd been fighting too hard to change, and, dammit, she was going to succeed.

"Look, I'm following you because I don't trust you. Who knows what you'll do when you finally admit to yourself that Gayla was lying?"

His brow puckered into a frown. "Nobody follows me if I don't want them to."

"Really, Murdock? Did you learn how to elude trackers when you were robbing banks?"

His mouth tightened. "Go ahead and think that if it makes you feel better about the crimes your father committed."

"The only thing Henry Lattimer did was rid the world of a bank robber and murderer."

"I'm going to enjoy proving you wrong."

His eyes narrowed, and she knew she'd hit a nerve. "Just remember, you're going to have to go through me," she said.

"My pleasure."

"It won't be as easy as you seem to think to ruin my father's good name."

"He did that to himself years ago, and the woman who knew about it didn't have the guts to tell on him. You just don't want to believe it."

The conviction in his voice startled her. "No one messes with my family and gets away with it."

"Could I possibly consider that another challenge?" he shot back.

"It's a promise."

"Let's get something straight, Rosellen. I can't keep you from going to Denver. I'm not going to try, but *I* travel alone."

"Stop flattering yourself, Murdock. I'm not planning on traveling with you. I'm following you."

"Do you really think you could keep up with me if I wanted to lose you?"

She met his smoldering dark eyes with an intense stare. "Try me."

"Are challenges the only thing you know how to issue?"

She rotated her aching shoulder a time or two, then said, "They've served me well in the past."

"Why don't you try issuing an invitation once in a while?"

"For what?" she taunted.

"This."

In one fast, easy motion he stepped in front of her and flattened her against the back of the passenger car, pinning her body to his. He lowered his head and covered her lips with his.

Her surprised gasp dissolved into a soft moan as his lips moved over hers with haste, power, and searing hot passion. In a futile attempt to dislodge him, she twisted and pushed against his chest.

In answer to her pitiful effort, Cason pressed his lower body against the soft womanly part of her that no man had touched and stroked her with suggestive movements. As quick as a lightning strike a hunger awakened inside Rosellen.

Deep. Dark. Thunderous.

She opened her mouth and accepted his tongue as it thrust deep inside her mouth. His kiss was vicious, savage, and left her dizzy with inexplicable sensations she'd never felt before.

She heard his uneven breathing. And a breathless fluttering started in her chest and flew down to her stomach. His hand came up and cupped her chin, lifting her face, tilting her head to give him greater access to her mouth.

Rosellen tingled with discovery.

Somewhere deep inside herself she knew she should be fighting him, stopping him, but all she could do was match his wild, passionate movements. Thoughts of her hatred vanished and were replaced with need. Rosellen had no control over the raging desire shooting through her.

Cason's wide hand slid down her neck, across her chest, over her breasts, around her waist, past her revolver, and settled on her backside. His fingers spread across her bottom and pulled her up tight against his fullness, and then he slid his hand back up to her breast. He flattened his palm against her softness.

The rhythmic motion of the train jarred her body and her senses. A low moan escaped her lips. She squirmed and found herself moving, rocking against his hardness as her mind recalled the image of Cason standing boldly, handsomely naked in front of her.

"I knew there was a fire inside you, Rosellen," he whispered into her mouth before capturing her lips again in a long drugging kiss.

Her heart danced with excitement. She slid her arms up and over his shoulders to his strong back, pulling him tighter against her. His body was firm and warm. He tasted of spicy cinnamon.

"You're as hot and beautiful and rare as molten gold."

His words enveloped her, heated her, thrilled her more than she would have thought possible, but she didn't want to talk. She only wanted to feel.

Rosellen tried to get closer to that unexplainable urgency that was driving her to match Cason kiss for kiss, touch for touch, and movement for movement. The sensations spiraling inside her were as fast and unstoppable as the train they were on.

Cason captured her lips with his again, sucking them into his mouth and releasing them quickly, expertly, over and over again. His lips were possessive, demanding, thorough. He thrust his tongue powerfully into the depths of her mouth. Rosellen gasped with a pleasure so exquisite that she felt limp and weightless. She didn't want to stop the sensations that were hurtling through—

Suddenly she realized that Cason's lips were no longer on hers, though his body remained rock-hard against hers. She opened her eyes and saw his face was mere inches from hers. He was smiling at her, but he was not laughing.

"There is a woman underneath those trousers you wear. A woman who is very hot."

"You bastard!"

She pulled away from him and pinned herself in the corner between the railing and the car. She drew in a ragged breath and rested her palm on the handle of her Colt. The land rushed by her, making her dizzy. Maybe if she'd had something to eat she would have been stronger and not so susceptible to Cason's kisses.

A spark of worry leaped into Cason's eyes. He motioned for her to come toward him. "Watch out. You're too close to the edge of the platform. Come back this way before you fall off."

She wasn't sure she'd care if she did. All Rosellen wanted to do was crawl into a corner where she couldn't be seen. Shame filled her. She couldn't believe this had happened to her. She hated this man, hated what he wanted to do to her family and her town. Yet his kisses thrilled her, excited her beyond reason. She didn't know why she responded to him with such mindless abandon.

"Are you all right?"

Concern etched his face, but she didn't care. "Of course not," she answered with a hissing breath, hating him for making her feel such wonderful things. "I kissed you, didn't I?"

"So?"

"I'm trying to decide if I should draw my gun and shoot you—or myself."

Cason steadied himself by holding on to the railing. "I don't want you to shoot either of us."

"Given the way I'm feeling right now, one of us has to go."

Chapter

❖ 10 ❖

"Take your hand away from that gun," Cason said as quietly as he could and be heard over the clanking of the train. "The kiss wasn't that bad."

"That's the problem. It wasn't bad at all," she complained. "Oh, God, you touched me, too. I can't believe I let you do that."

"I guess we got a little carried away, considering we're standing out here on the platform in the open."

"A little? You had me ready to take off my clothes for you," she admitted honestly.

His eyes zeroed in on hers. "You're not angry because I kissed you. You're mad at me because you enjoyed it."

"Hell, yes," Rosellen said feeling disappointed and disgusted with herself.

She calmed down once the wind hit her face and cooled her off. She didn't think she'd ever been so heated, so frantic. She'd been kissed before—several times, in fact, by one of Walter's friends when she was seventeen. She didn't remember it as being anything like what just happened between her and Cason.

"I'm missing something here," he said. "Why do you want to shoot one of us?"

She lifted her hand away from her gun, brushed a flying strand of hair away from her face, and secured it behind her ear. "Because you don't like me and I don't like you, but we both liked the kiss."

"I haven't admitted to liking anything."

Confounded by his blunt statement, she stumbled over her words. "B-but you did, didn't you? I—I mean you acted as if you enjoyed it."

"Yeah," he finally admitted as the train chugged along the tracks, rocking them. "I liked it. A lot."

"Well," she said, angry at him from bruising her ego and at herself for being so vulnerable to him. "I'm not going to change my mind about you, and it's doubtful you'll change yours about me."

She had been powerless to push away from him. Something exciting and wonderful had happened between them, and the only thing she knew to do about it was to forget it. If she pondered it, she'd go crazy. One thing she was sure of was that she couldn't let her emotions run rampant and make her susceptible to him again.

"You're a very tempting woman, Rosellen. Maybe you should think twice about following me."

Rosellen looked into Cason's eyes. His tone had grown serious. He was warning her. Trouble was, she never heeded a warning.

"No. Once I'm committed, I don't back down."

She raked the back of her hand across her mouth several times, but knew that nothing would ever scrub away the taste of Cason from her lips.

"Didn't you get enough kissing when you were with that woman at the Silver Nugget? Did you have to go and kiss me, too?"

"You started it."

"What? How? You lying pile of—"

"All right," he cut her off. "The kiss shouldn't have happened. Leave it at that."

He had the decency not to smile at her, and she grudgingly admitted to herself that she appreciated that.

"I never touched the woman at the saloon. I was waiting for her when you came in, and after you left . . . I decided I really didn't have time for her, so I dressed and walked down the hallway to see who was screaming bloody murder."

A sudden thrill of satisfaction tumbled through her. Why should she care one bit whether he'd bedded the whore? Rosellen put her hand to her forehead. The rocking motion of the narrow ledge was making her ill. She needed to sit down and rest. She needed water and food.

"Next time do your lip smacking there in the saloon and stay away from me."

Rosellen remembered thinking the moment she saw Cason that he was dangerous. She just hadn't known how dangerous he was until now.

He was the son of an outlaw. Why had she submitted so passionately to him? She hated everything he stood for. He wanted to destroy her family, her town, and now he wanted to destroy her with his powerful kisses. She couldn't let that happen again.

There was no longer any doubt in her mind. She was a woman and he was a man, and the attraction between them was so powerful it erased all barriers.

Cason Murdock had ridden into town and turned her life upside down.

"You don't look so good. Let's get inside where you can sit down."

A faint flicker of compassion showed in his expression and Rosellen moaned silently. The last thing she wanted was for him to feel sorry for her. She wanted to go inside and sit down, but she felt too light-headed to walk. And her stomach hurt from lack of food and water. Her heels were burning from the constant rubbing of her new boots, and her shoulder was killing her.

"I feel as if I've been trampled by all three of my brothers when they were wearing their boots and spurs."

"You don't look that bad," Cason answered dryly. "I don't see any blood."

"I'm surprised you think I have any blood."

"I know for a fact you have *very hot* blood pumping through your veins, Rosellen."

There it was again. That indescribable *thing* that made her want to forget who he was and just enjoy him. She repressed the urge.

"Well, you're wrong. I'm as cold as the highest summit in the Rockies. Remember that the next time *you* think *you* want to kiss *me*."

"Very hot," he repeated.

A shiver of anticipation of something she couldn't explain made her tremble. Rosellen shook it off and reached down to pick up her satchel at the same moment Cason went for it. Their hands met on the handle. Goose bumps of desire peppered her again, and she snatched her hand away.

"I'll carry this for you," Cason said, reaching behind her and opening the door. "You can hardly walk right now."

Double damn. It was going to be a long train ride to Denver.

Rosellen followed Cason into the passenger car. The scent of cheap pipe tobacco hung in the air. Most of the velvet-covered seats were unoccupied, but she heard whispered chatter as they walked down the aisle.

They were on the east-west spur of the Denver & Rio Grande Railroad, which connected with the southern tip of the north-south main line that ran from Pueblo all the way to the city of Denver. The short line was brand new and not yet well traveled.

The train had only five cars hooked to the engine. The last one carried passengers; the other four were for livestock, cargo, or prisoners.

Rosellen walked slowly down the aisle, glancing at every passenger. Most of them looked back at her. A kindly-looking older woman smiled at her, an old man nodded to her, and a balding middle-aged man stared at the revolver strapped to her hip. Rosellen also noticed a young couple holding hands.

"Right here," Cason said when she made it to the front of the railcar. Rosellen took a seat by the window and Cason shoved her satchel onto the brass storage rack above their heads, then sat down opposite her.

Rosellen rested her elbows on her knees and dropped her head into the palms of her hands.

"Are you all right?" he asked, when she didn't move for a long time.

"No, and you've asked me that three times already," she answered in a gravelly voice. Her throat felt parched and sandy. "I still don't have my breath back."

"You're breathless from our kiss?"

Oh, God, she thought. What they did was so much more than just kissing. And the hell of it was that he knew it too.

She took her hat off and laid it on the seat beside her, then caught him watching her and said, "Drop dead, Murdock."

He grunted. "If you're going to get that upset about it, just go right on believing that I was the one who kissed you."

"That's the way it happened, but it doesn't change the fact your lips met mine."

"Tongues, too."

Rosellen bent over and pulled her boots off her sore feet and wiggled her toes. "I can't believe I didn't shoot one of us."

"It's over, Rosellen. Forget it." He sighed heavily. "I only brought it up to try to make you feel better."

She met his gaze and knew she wanted something more from him. "Why did you kiss me, Cason?"

His eyes searched hers. "I could lie and say I had a lapse in my sanity, but the truth is that I did it because I wanted to."

Rosellen shook her head. "All I can think is that I must have lost my mind," she mumbled and turned away from him.

She looked out the window at land sweeping past and untied the black ribbon that held her hair in place. With trembling fingers she combed through the length of it and gathered up all the loose strands before retying the bow.

"You're not looking much better." He picked up his canteen and handed it to her. "Here, drink this. It doesn't look as if you had the good sense to bring water with you."

"I thought about it, but because of *you* I didn't have time to get any."

She looked at the container. Her stomach lurched. No use in being foolish. She took the water and drank slowly at first, then threw her head back and closed her eyes as the wetness coated her dry throat. She wanted to let the cooling liquid run out of her mouth, then down her chin and neck to the valley between her breasts, refreshing herself the way she used to when she was younger and drank from summer springs. But she didn't dare waste a drop.

When she lowered the canteen, she noticed that

Cason was watching her. Rosellen saw in Cason's eyes what she'd heard in his voice: he didn't want to be attracted to her any more than she wanted to be drawn to him.

Her stomach growled. She swallowed hard and handed the canteen back to him without a thank-you.

The sun sank lower in the sky, and the train chugged along, gently rocking. Cason was worried. He couldn't believe he'd allowed the little hellcat to tempt him into kissing her, but her lips had been so inviting. And damn if he wasn't itching to kiss her again.

He wouldn't have touched her if she hadn't come crawling in the saloon window. If he'd had his fun with the whore he would not be sitting here frustrated, aching to draw Rosellen close to him again.

She was off limits, he reminded himself. He couldn't do what he had to do if he started feeling soft for anyone in the town of Poppy. And he especially didn't want to feel anything for the fiery-tongued daughter of Henry Lattimer.

Cason took a folded napkin out of his carpetbag and unwrapped a large sandwich. If he ate something, maybe he could get his mind off Rosellen and sex.

The bread looked fresh and soft. Chunks of well-cooked beef poked out from all four sides. His stomach rumbled with hunger. He lifted the sandwich to his mouth to take his first bite and caught Rosellen staring at him.

He lowered the sandwich without taking a bite. "You didn't bring any food with you either?"

She eyed him warily. "What's it to you?"

"You look hungry."

"What do you mean? How can anyone *look* hungry?"

"Your eyes are as big as digging pans, and you're almost drooling."

"You can stretch the truth farther than anybody else I know, Murdock."

"You're trying to be as tough as leather, Rosellen, but you can't sound hard when your stomach is growling like a black bear. And I can't enjoy my food with you staring at me as if I'm eating your dinner."

"Go ahead and eat your sandwich. I won't look at you."

Rosellen folded her arms across her chest and gazed out the window. She breathed in deeply and remembered the scent of Miss Leddy's bread pudding.

"Did you bring anything to eat in your satchel?"

"I didn't have time. If I'd stopped for food I would have missed the train."

He started to bite into the sandwich again but stopped and said, "Oh, hell. Here, eat this." He extended the sandwich to her.

"I'd rather starve than eat your dinner."

"Fine with me." He took a bite. The sandwich was delicious.

Rosellen's stomach immediately rumbled at her rejection of his offer. Cason looked at her more closely than he really wanted to. She was pale. The delicate hand she now held under her chin was shaky. He didn't want to care that she was hungry, but, dammit all the way to hell, he did.

"When's the last time you ate?" he asked.

"None of your business."

His tone didn't change. If he had to feel sorry for her he would, but he didn't have to like it. "Did you eat at all today?"

"No, thanks to you," she grumbled again, throwing him a frustrated glance. "I missed breakfast this morning and my meeting with Mr. Vestly. I missed the noon meal, too, and because of you I'll probably miss my chance to be the next sheriff of Poppy."

"So I'm the cause of all your problems."

"Every last one of them."

"Good." That was some consolation. "You're hungry, so take this and eat it before you faint and I'm forced to pick you up off the floor."

"All right. I'm too hungry to argue any more." She accepted the sandwich and took a big bite, then chewed daintily. "Mmm. This is so good." She took another bite. "The bread is soft, and the beef deliciously tender." A moan of satisfaction escaped her lips.

Cason had never heard anyone carry on so about food. She was driving him crazy with her noises. Didn't she know it was in a man's makeup to want to please a woman? Every little contented sound she made sent chills of excitement washing over him, making him wish all the more that he'd bedded the whore.

"I'll pay you back," she said after she'd eaten enough to quiet her stomach rumblings.

"With what?" He held up his hand. "Before you say anything, I don't need food, and I don't need money."

She wiped the corners of her mouth with her fingertips. "Then I'll consider this a debt that doesn't need to be repaid."

Cason stretched his long legs out into the aisle and made himself more comfortable as he watched Rosellen. She didn't know it, but she'd already repaid him by enjoying the sandwich so much. It didn't matter what Rosellen tackled—a sandwich, an enemy, or a kiss—she went after it with all she had.

She took another bite and, after swallowing, said, "Why are you staring me?"

"I'm wondering what kind of woman crawls through a whore's bedroom window."

"The kind who has a job to do and is looking for a shortcut. I had to see Delta, stop by the bank, go to Mr. Vestly's office, and catch the train."

And she had made it. He tried not to be impressed by her, but he was.

"Why did you jump the woman at the saloon?"

"You were standing there when I looked up. I thought you must have heard everything," she said, then popped the last bite of the sandwich into her mouth.

"I had to dress, remember?"

"Delta went for her gun."

"Why?"

"She knew why I had come for her. I thought Delta was the one who had spread Gayla's lies about Papa."

Cason uncapped his canteen again and handed it to her. She took it and drank thirstily from it, vowing to find a way to pay him back—and not with kisses.

"Did she?"

"Not that she's admitting." Rosellen dabbed the corners of her mouth with the end of the napkin and sipped the water again before handing it back to Cason. "She swears it was one of the liquor distributors who overheard Gayla's confession while he was stacking crates in the back room."

"You think she's telling the truth? She looked to me like she was too afraid of you to lie about anything."

"I guess I believe her. I didn't have time to find the whiskey salesman, but when I get back I'm going to look for him."

A sadness crept into her eyes. "I intend to disprove Gayla's lies. My father didn't commit those crimes. He couldn't have. He loved the people of Poppy. It was *his* town. He wouldn't have robbed or killed any of them."

Cason slowly nodded. Thank God she was reminding him why he had to keep his distance from her. "I know how you feel, Rosellen. You don't have to convince me of anything. I felt the same way fifteen years ago when your father told me my father was a murderer. Poppy was *my* father's town, too. He worked there, and I went to school there. Why would Frank Murdock steal from his neighbors and kill one of them?"

Rosellen looked stunned, then indignant. "My father was the *sheriff*. He was sworn to uphold the law, not break it."

Incredulity struck him with force and angered him. "Do you think that badge made your father better than any ordinary man trying to earn a living for his family?"

"Yes. Yes, he was better, because he had to be better," she insisted. "He had to set a good example for the whole town."

She wasn't going to bend an inch.

Good. As long as she kept reminding him what a fine fellow her father was he'd have no trouble keeping his hands off her.

Chapter

→ 11 ←

The screeching and clanking of wheels on tracks and cars jerking and bumping together stirred Rosellen from her deep thoughts. It was dark when the train started slowing down to pull into its first stop. The bright round moon lit the night with a silvery glow that belied the lateness of the hour.

Everyone else in the car had been sleeping for some time, including Cason. Rosellen had spent her time thinking about him, their kiss, and her desire to be the sheriff of Poppy. She'd worried about what her mother and brothers would say after they read her hastily written note. She didn't expect them to understand why she had to follow Cason to Denver.

Rosellen stretched her arms over her head and rolled her shoulders a few times to loosen stiff muscles. Scattered lights from the town twinkled at her from a distance, offering a welcome she was too tired to enjoy.

She rubbed her ankles, her toes, and her sore heels

a couple of times before stuffing her feet back into her boots.

Her stomach was full, and her head felt much better. Her legs no longer felt weak and trembly. She had Cason to thank for that. Although he hadn't actually spoken to her since shortly after she finished the delicious sandwich that was supposed to have been his dinner.

When it became clear that they couldn't talk about their fathers without anger rising between them, Cason had burrowed into his seat, stretched his long legs farther out into the aisle, put his hat over his face, and slept.

She didn't mind. She didn't want to talk to him anyway, she assured herself. But for reasons she didn't understand it had bothered her that she couldn't see his face.

While he was sleeping, she had a perfect opportunity to study him. She wanted to discover what it was about him that had made her respond so passionately to his kisses and his embrace.

Her behavior shocked her. If she'd never been kissed before, she would have assumed that any man would make her feel that way, but she had been kissed, more than once, and the earlier kisses had been nothing like Cason's kisses. She'd had no idea she was capable of such earth-shattering sensations.

The locomotive continued to chug into the night, but the hissing and clanking of steel and iron subsided as the cars came to a grinding, bumping stop. Along with the other passengers, Cason stirred and came to life. He pushed his hat away from his face.

Moonlight fell across his features. He looked up at her with sleepy, dreamy eyes that held her motionless. His expression was relaxed and clear of the anger and frustration that had been etched there. She liked the way he looked now. Rested, approachable.

Staring at him, she saw a man she wanted to know more about. She knew bits and pieces about his father and mother, but she found herself wanting to know the entire story. Why had his father's death also ended his mother's life?

She didn't know what was wrong with her. She should have been upset, but instead she was seeing everything about Cason in a new light, and she knew it must be because of that kiss. This had to stop. She had to resist feeling sorry for Cason. She had to keep her distance from him.

"You're staring at me. Haven't you ever seen a man wake up before?"

"Have you forgotten that I grew up with three older brothers?"

He sat up straight. "How could I? You keep reminding me."

"Well, it's hard for me not to stare at you when you're sitting right in front of me with your legs sprawled out in the aisle."

"Did you enjoy watching me?" he asked with a hint of a smile on his lips.

"I especially enjoyed looking at you when you had your hat over your face," she fibbed.

"I bet you enjoyed it more when I was undressed."

"To tell you the truth, I didn't see much difference between your face and your skinny butt."

Cason laughed for the first time. It was a natural hearty sound and, to her surprise, not at all unpleasant.

"You didn't see my butt. I never turned around."

"Thank God. Now, if you'll move, I'll go outside and see if I can find some food to replace your dinner."

"Don't worry about it. Remember, it's a debt that doesn't need to be repaid."

She didn't like him using the word "debt." "I feel

bad that I ate the whole sandwich and didn't leave any for you."

"I wouldn't have given it to you if I'd been hungry. Does that make you feel better? Does it renew your faith in the kind of man you think I am?"

"Yes," she answered testily. "I should have known you weren't just trying to be nice. Now I can't get out until you do, and I need to pay mother nature a visit," she said. "I have a feeling we won't be in this town long."

"In that case." He uncrossed his ankles and drew in his legs. Then he rose and allowed her to go ahead of him to the door.

Rosellen mentally shook herself, then turned into the aisle and fell in behind the other passengers disembarking the train.

A funny feeling had attacked her insides the first time she saw him, and it hadn't stopped. She'd never felt this way about a man before. She'd always hated the thought of thinking about men and kissing and touching.

The first time Walter's friend had kissed her, she had hauled off and socked him. He'd forgiven her and talked her into trying it again, but she hadn't liked anything about his lips on hers. When he poked his tongue into her mouth, she'd felt as if she was kissing a snake.

But she'd had no such feelings when Cason kissed her and his tongue probed the inside of her mouth. She'd eagerly accepted and encouraged his every touch as if their kiss was supposed to happen.

Rosellen groaned with contempt for herself. How could she have wanted his touch? How could she want to feel all those desires again? What madness had fallen upon her?

Why couldn't she shake those feelings?

Rosellen and Cason were the last to disembark.

Some of the passengers greeted friends and family members who'd come to meet them, and new people made their way onto the platform to board the train. It would be that way throughout their journey. Once the train reached the main line at Pueblo, they would head north. But they'd stop at most of the towns between Poppy and the state capital.

The men let the ladies line up first for the outhouse. Rosellen took her turn, then waited not far away for Cason. She really didn't expect him to try to shake her until they arrived in Denver, but there was no harm in being careful.

Rosellen looked over at the dark depot and farther away to where a few lights twinkled in the distance. It looked like quite a hike into the town. She was truly indebted to Cason for giving her his food, and she should have thanked him.

Instead of shoving him away she'd welcomed his kiss. Instead of washing the taste of him from her mouth she'd savored it. What was there about Cason Murdock that made her want to forget the past that hung between them?

A warm breeze blew across her face and fluttered her hair. The big round silver moon lit the platform better than any gaslight could have. Her gaze drifted back over to Cason. He stood taller, straighter than most of the men in the line. She liked the way his broad chest tapered into slim hips. Like her, he wore his gun belt low and the holster strapped to his thigh.

Rosellen knew that wearing a firearm was less common now than it had been just a few years ago. The boom-and-bust era of Colorado tent-city mining camps and towns was fading into the past like the stagecoach, oil lamps, and the revolver on the hip. But knowing she wanted to be sheriff, Rosellen was reluctant to give up hers.

Suddenly Cason left the line and walked over to

her. He peered down at her and said, "Why do you keep staring at me?"

"I wasn't staring. I'm watching. I told you I don't plan to let you out of my sight."

"Are you going to follow me in there?" He pointed toward the outhouse.

"Of course not. But I will watch to make sure that if you go in, you come out."

"As if I'd want to stay in there."

It was such a ludicrous thought that Rosellen nearly smiled, but she simply said, "I only meant I don't want you sneaking out and vanishing into the night."

His eyes flashed. "You know, Rosellen, we haven't been at this more than a few hours, but I don't like being shadowed, even by a very hot woman."

"Hot?" she questioned indignantly. "I'm tired of you saying that about me. The only thing hot about me is my temper whenever I look at you."

"You're lying, and I'll be happy to prove it to you again. Anytime you say."

She pressed her lips together for a moment, then said, "I'm not afraid of you, your threats, or your kisses. I'm sticking to you like gold dust to grease."

One corner of his lip lifted in an unpleasant smile. "Only for as long as I want you to. I'll lose you whenever I get ready, and you won't be able to do a damn thing about it."

"I'll match my skills against yours anytime."

"That time will come."

"You wouldn't want to ditch me unless you had something to hide or unless you plan to do exactly what I've suspected from the start."

"Which is?"

"Hire some old codger to play the part of this fictitious man named Dodge, then bring him back to Poppy to tell the story you're so desperate for everyone to believe."

"Do you really think it would be that easy to get a man to admit to having committed murder and robbery? Even if I offered him a large sum of money, what good would it do him if he was sitting in jail or swinging from a tree?"

"There could be dozens of reasons someone would agree to such a scheme."

"Name one."

"Maybe he'd do it so that his family would have enough money to live on, or maybe he'd save it until he got out of prison and then spend it all on whiskey."

"And maybe I'm beginning to believe you just want to follow me because you like being around me as much as you like being in my arms."

She glared at him. "You must be dreaming, Murdock. I'm following you because I don't trust you."

"You admitted you enjoyed our kiss every bit as much as I did. And I have a feeling that you're hankering for me to kiss you again."

Denial leaped to her expression. "You're not dreaming; you're crazy. However, I'm sure you've had a lot of practice in seducing innocent young women."

"Not enough."

He pulled her to his chest and claimed her lips in a demanding, passionate kiss that stole her breath away as easily as it had the first time he kissed her.

His embrace was powerful. The taste of him had a drugging effect on her. She warmed to his touch immediately and slid her arms around his neck.

To her chagrin, the kiss lasted only long enough to send Rosellen's senses reeling before he let her go and stepped away.

"And if you continue to follow me," he said with a rueful expression lingering on his lips, "there's no telling what else I might do, Rosellen. It's your choice."

She searched her fuzzy brain for a comeback, but the effort was useless. Cason turned and walked off, leaving Rosellen infuriated that he'd had the nerve to kiss her in front of other people.

But even as she thought that, she was tempted to run her tongue across her lips and savor the taste of him. She had to find a way to fight his sensual effect on her. She folded her arms across her chest and gave his back the evil eye until it was his turn to go inside the outhouse.

He was playing with her and enjoying every minute of it.

Huffing with annoyance, Rosellen stomped her foot and turned away but bumped into someone who was hurrying up behind her.

The young man shoved Rosellen, and she stumbled backward but caught herself before she fell.

"If you're not in line, move out of the way. I have to get to the outhouse."

His slurred words and gruff voice made Rosellen turn and look into the face of a young man with glassy blue eyes and a ruddy complexion. The smell of liquor struck her full force.

He drew back and stared at her, blinking slowly. "You're not a man." The words seemed to have been dragged from his throat.

It was clear to her that he was well into the bottom of the whiskey bottle that poked out of his jacket pocket. She didn't remember seeing him on the train, so she assumed he was either one of the new passengers or a person from the town. It would be just her luck to have to deal with a drunkard all the way to Denver.

"And I'm not in line," she said dryly and pivoted away from him.

"Wait a minute." He grabbed her arm and swung her around to face him. "You talk like a man too, but I can tell by your face that you aren't. Never seen a man as pretty you are, but I've never seen a woman wear men's clothes, and you're packing a gun, too." He chuckled, slurring his laugh as well as his words. "You trying to scare somebody with that six-shooter, little girl?"

Rosellen jerked free. Her eyebrows drew together, and she gave him another menacing glare. "If you touch me again, I'll flatten your nose."

He laughed, and fumes of stale whiskey sailed past her. If they'd been in Poppy she'd have swung his arms behind his back, cuffed him, marched his rotgut-swilling ass down to the jail, and made him sleep it off.

"That's mighty big talk for a little girl like you. Why would a woman as pretty as you want to talk and dress like a man?" he asked, leaning in close to her.

"So I don't have to put up with the likes of you." She turned to walk away again, but he grabbed her arm a second time and brought her up short.

Rosellen started to swing her fist around and sock him under the chin but remembered to think before she reacted. She was working hard not to settle everything with a fight or with cussing. As sheriff of Poppy, she would run into many men like this, and she might as well learn right now how to handle them.

Rosellen flinched. "Get your hands off me and step away. You're drunk, and you need to sober up."

The man wiped his nose with the sleeve of his jacket. "What are you going to do if I don't let go of you?"

She'd seen her father handle men who'd had too much to drink. Talk calmly but firmly to him, she reminded herself. Don't get him mad; no one fights dirtier than an angry drunk. If talking doesn't work, grab his wrist, then twist and yank his arm behind his back and jerk it up as hard and fast as you can. That'll bring him to his knees so you can cuff him.

Rosellen didn't have any cuffs, but she was ready to bring this bastard to his knees.

"Is something going on here that I can help with?" Cason asked, stepping up beside Rosellen but keeping his gaze on the young man.

"This is between me and the little girl here. Go on about your own business, stranger."

"I don't think I can do that."

Fury raced through Rosellen. Cason had stepped up to help her *again*. It was bad enough that he'd helped her with the prospector in Poppy, but at least that man had a gun. Did he think she couldn't handle herself with a man who could barely stand up by himself? Did he think she was a damsel who needed rescuing?

Suddenly an idea struck her. If he wanted to help her, fine. She'd let him, but he would do it on her terms.

She smiled sweetly. "Cason dear, I'm so glad you're here. I was just about to tell this gentleman I was waiting for my husband. You came along just in time."

The drunkard dropped her arm like a hot poker. "You didn't tell me you were married."

"You didn't ask."

"I was wondering if you two were married when I saw him kiss you," said a gray-haired older woman with a knitting basket hanging from one arm. "I figured you must be husband and wife, showing that much affection in front of everybody. I thought it was so romantic the way he just swept you up in his arms in front of me, God, and everybody else."

"Oh, yes, we are happily married," Rosellen fibbed again, batting her eyelashes rapidly at Cason, daring him to speak up and make a liar out of her.

The woman looked Rosellen up and down. "It was hard to tell because it looked like you two were having a little spat when you first boarded the train."

"Oh, we're too much in love to have unkind words between us." Rosellen smiled and pressed her breasts against Cason's arm. The move sent a thrill of desire

131

streaking across her midsection. Being coy was unlike her, but she refused to back down from the role she was playing.

"That's just the kind of thing I like to hear," the woman said. "I was just coming over to see if I could help. I saw this man was bothering you. I'm glad your husband was able to take care of him for you."

The man held up both hands and started backing away. "I ain't bothering nobody. I was just walking past on my way to the outhouse and stopped to say hello. I'll be going now." He turned and stumbled off at a fast pace, but Rosellen heard him mutter something about it not being natural for a husband to let his wife dress like a man.

Rosellen glanced at Cason. He was furious. Rosellen smiled with satisfaction. That would teach him to butt into her business and expect her to sit back and take it.

"Are you two going all the way to Denver?" said the petite gray-haired lady.

"Yes, ma'am," Rosellen confirmed.

"I'm Nadine Oliver. Let me go find my husband Walt, and we'll introduce ourselves properly. We're going to Denver too. It will be so nice to have someone to talk to." She hurried away.

Cason snarled at Rosellen. "What the hell do you think you're doing, telling people we're married?"

"You always seem so set on coming to my aid. You butted in with the old prospector and again just now with that drunkard. I decided if you really wanted to help me I'd let you but on my terms for a change."

"How the hell is telling these people we're married going to help you?"

"I remembered my father saying that men didn't usually bother married women."

"I should have known your father told you that."

"It worked, didn't it? Did you see how fast that

drunk backed off when I told him you were my husband?"

"Well, next time you think about doing it, don't. Let's get one thing straight, Rosellen. I'm not here to look after you. You are on your own."

"I don't need your help."

"You would have starved if I hadn't had food and water with me."

"That was only because you kept me so busy in town today that I didn't have time to get anything to eat. And for a man who doesn't want to help me, you always seem to be showing up at my side."

"That hardscrabble prospector could have shot you. I didn't see any of the townspeople stepping up to help you. And that drunk was ready to haul you off into the woods."

"As if he could have."

"And I sure came in handy when you needed a husband just now."

"If I were pretty and had on a velvet dress with my hair piled high with curls, you wouldn't have minded that I'd said we were married."

"You are pretty. And right now I'm more interested in what's under your trousers than any velvet or silk skirt. I don't want to be your husband or any other woman's husband. And I damn sure don't want to be bothered all the way to Denver by a little old woman who can't shut up."

"It's only until we get to Denver. Don't worry. I'm not going to make you marry me just because you kissed me."

His eyes narrowed. "What are you talking about?"

"Well, you kissed me, didn't you? People who kiss usually get married."

Rosellen couldn't believe those words had come out of her mouth. Why was she teasing this man? It was so unlike her. She was supposed to be keeping her distance from him. She had only meant to chastise him for trying to butt into her business, but instead she found herself playing with him. Maybe hell had frozen over.

"I've kissed plenty of women and never thought about marrying any of them. If you think a kiss means we're going to get married, you've been smoking locoweed."

"It would if my mother or any of my brothers had seen the way you kissed me. They've been trying to marry me off for three years now."

"Are you trying to scare me off, because if you are it won't work. I'm going to kiss you again and again, Rosellen." He took a step toward her. "And who says I'll stop there. I might get carried away and take those trousers off you, because, like you, I can't seem to get enough."

She backed away. Clouds sailed across the moon, making it difficult for her to see his face clearly. She was actually enjoying this heated conversation. She didn't understand any of these dizzying tingles that went off inside her whenever Cason talked about kissing her.

"Your brain is crazy and full of cow chips if you think I want you to kiss me again."

"Crazy, am I? Let's see." He reached for her arm, but she easily sild away from him.

"No." She swallowed hard and stepped back again.

Cason's gaze met hers. "You can't have it both ways, Rosellen."

She moistened her dry lips. "What do you mean?"

"You can't follow me and run away from me at the same time. Make up your mind which one you're going to do."

That was exactly what she was trying to do. It surprised Rosellen that she didn't find the truth threatening or distasteful. For a wild second she wanted to goad him into making good on his promise to kiss her again. She wanted to know if those toe-curling sensations running deep inside her were the kinds of feelings that happened only once in a lifetime or if were they could be duplicated time and time again.

"Why are you nice to me sometimes and so mean to me at other times?"

He looked deep into her eyes, and she shuddered from the soul-searching gaze. "When I kiss you, I forget who you are and see only a beautiful, desirable woman. At other times I remember the truth—that your father murdered mine."

She gasped in outrage at the bold lie he spoke so easily. "You're chasing the pot of gold at the end of the rainbow, Murdock. Didn't anyone ever tell you, it's not there? You might as well believe in fairy dust and elves."

"Prospecting for close to fifteen years taught me a lot of things—patience, how to deal with loneliness and disappointment—but the main thing it taught me was that you can't tell if a vein of gold runs through a mountain by looking on the outside. You have to blast a hole in the ground and dig away the rubble before you can find the precious metals that run through the land."

"Meaning?" she asked, too confused by her feelings for this man to sort out what he was trying to say.

"You're looking at Gayla's surface and not realizing the wealth of information she has stored in her memory about the past—about your father."

Rosellen tensed. "That woman doesn't know anything about my father. The only thing you're digging up is pyrite."

The train whistle blew, and the conductor yelled, "All aboard."

"Sometimes it's fool's gold," Cason agreed. "I've dug pyrite out of the earth before. But one day Buster and I hit a lode that made all the digging every day for fifteen years worth every shovel and wash pan, every Long Tom and every sluice we worked. It's a chance I'm willing to take."

"Then watch your back, Cason, because I'll be right behind you."

Chapter

→ 12 ←

Bright early morning light awakened Cason, piercing his eyes. His lashes fluttered, chasing away sleep. His head hung at an uncomfortable angle. His feet were cold and numb from being cramped into one position for so long.

Cason stirred, trying to clear the fuzziness from his brain. The sky was such a light shade of blue it almost looked white. For a moment he thought he was back at the mining camp with Buster, sleeping on the hard ground, but he couldn't figure out why he was so damn dizzy.

He shook his head and cleared his thoughts. He remembered he was on the train heading for Denver. No wonder the sky seemed to be rushing past him. He rolled his neck and shoulders a few times, stretching stiff muscles. His eyes focused as he caught sight of the innocent-looking woman lying curled up on the burgundy velvet–covered seat in front of him.

Rosellen.

Had she really told those people last night that they

were married? He'd never met so bold a woman. She reminded him of gold. Most of the time gold was hard, but as soon as it was heated it became soft and malleable, and in any form it was precious.

Cason ran his hand through his hair. Why was he thinking about Rosellen like that? But his gaze drifted back over to her and he knew why. She awakened desires inside him that no other woman ever had.

She lay propped up against the window, using her fringed buckskin jacket as a pillow. Shards of sunlight fell across her cheeks and nose. Cason was reminded again that her complexion looked as if it had been brushed with fine flakes of the purest gold found in the Rockies.

Morning light glimmered off her golden hair. Her dark wheat-colored eyebrows arched upward. Her lashes were long and curled ever so slightly. Her soft hand lay beside her face. Her fingers were long and slim, her nails short and clean.

She'd removed her boots and tucked her sock-clad feet underneath her. Her long legs were bent at the knees and tucked close to her chest. The way those trousers fit told him that her limbs were shapely.

Some men were intimidated by tall, slender women who carried themselves well. Not Cason. He found her very attractive. And as he studied Rosellen, from her beautiful face down to her toes, he decided she was perfect. He couldn't find a flaw in her looks anywhere.

And he liked her sharp wit, appreciated her courageous attitude, admired her unwavering loyalty. Cason's gut twisted. But she was Henry Lattimer's daughter. She thought his father was a murderer. She thought her precious town deserved to thrive.

But knowing all those things didn't keep the stirrings of sexual hunger from growing as he watched her.

Her chest rose and fell evenly. She was in a deep sleep. For all her big talk and tough behavior, right now she was merely a soft, supple woman whom he wanted to take to bed.

To hell with the fact that her last name was Lattimer. When his body felt the way it did now, the man who sired her didn't matter. It was only when he was able to think rationally with his head and not with what was between his legs that it mattered who Rosellen was.

Cason closed his eyes and remembered the way her lips felt against his when he kissed her—soft, passionate, eager. But what he'd liked best was that she was untutored. Whoever she had been with in the past hadn't taken the time to teach her how to kiss, but she'd made up for that with her enthusiasm.

He liked the way she fit in his arms and up against his chest. He hadn't expected to be so instantly aroused by her yesterday when he kissed her. He'd thought that quickness had left with his youth.

He wanted to reach over and nuzzle the warmth of her neck. He remembered the sweet womanly scent of her skin, and he ached to kiss that soft skin behind her ear. He wanted to gently awaken her with seductive whispering.

A crashing jolt threw Cason forward, unseating him. His knees crashed to the floor, and he grunted in pain as he lunged in Rosellen's direction. He caught her in his arms before the train threw her, too. Steel and iron hissed and screeched against each other in a deafening sound that hurt his ears. He expected the train to jump the track at any moment. He braced himself against the back of Rosellen's seat and held on tight.

Cason was yanked back, then forward again. His knees knocked against the metal casing holding the seat. Rosellen's forehead smashed his upper lip against his teeth when she tumbled forward in his arms as the train continued to lurch. Her fingers dug into the fabric of his shirt as she made a startled sound.

"Hold on," he managed to say.

The force of the train slowing down kept him from righting himself immediately. Screams of shock and fear echoed across the railcar as the eight or ten passengers on the train scrambled to regain their seats.

"What on God's earth happened?" Rosellen asked, trying to squirm out of Cason's arms.

Cason grunted again as he struggled to stand up on his aching legs. "I don't know." He looked out the windows on both sides of the car to see if he could spot anything amiss. "It's my guess there's something on the tracks—debris of some kind, and they're stopping fast to avoid a collision."

The screeching and whining of the wheels grew louder until the train shuddered to a grinding stop, throwing Rosellen and Cason into each other again. His arms tightened around her.

Rosellen looked up at him. "You'd think they'd be able to stop this thing without throwing us out of our seats."

Their eyes met. His lower body started thinking for him again. He remembered the taste of her on his lips. He was going to kiss her. She was going to let him.

Shouts and loud talking from the front of the train drew his attention but not enough to make him back away from Rosellen.

"Are you sure you're all right?" she asked, slipping out of his arms. "You look as if you're in pain."

He was, but not the kind she was referring to. "I feel as if I busted both knees when I fell to the floor, but otherwise I'm fine," he said. "How about you?"

She smiled at him. "I guess you're a pretty good cushion. I don't think I have any bruises."

Cason couldn't remember the last time he'd felt his heart rise up in his throat so quickly. Rosellen had actually smiled at him. It wasn't a big beaming smile, and it had been slow to form on her lips, but, damn, it was worth the wait.

"I'd better see what's going on outside."

"Wait." She touched his arm, and Cason stopped. "Look, Murdock, I've been thinking. Since we're going to be on the train together and then later in Denver, maybe we should declare a truce."

"Tired of arguing?"

She hesitated for only a second. "Something like that, and I guess I've realized it's not getting us anywhere."

Cason nodded. She was not only beautiful, intelligent, and courageous but she also knew when to quit. He wondered how many more things he was going to find to like about her. And how long could he resist her when she was so affable?

"I was just thinking the same thing," he said. "You were wrong last night when you said we didn't like each other. The fact is, we do. It's our fathers who are the problem. I don't like the way you feel about mine, and you don't like the way I feel about your—"

The front door of the passenger car slammed open with crushing force, revealing two strangers. One held a pistol in either hand, and the other man held one gun and a burlap sack.

"This is a holdup! Don't anyone move," the taller man barked.

Cason tensed and moved to stand in front of Rosellen to shield her from harm.

The back door burst open, banging against the wall so hard one of the hinges gave way. Two more men rushed in with six-shooters aimed to fire.

"We've got you covered!" one of them yelled. "Stay where you are and don't make any sudden moves."

Kerchiefs covered the lower halves of their faces, and black dusters hid their shirts and most of their trousers. They looked from passenger to passenger, pointing their guns at first one then another.

One traveler reached for his weapon, and a robber shot him without warning. The man dropped his gun, grasped his chest, slumped to his knees, then fell to the floor. A woman standing near him screamed.

"Does anybody else want to be a hero?" the tall robber yelled.

Cason remained silent, wondering why he'd thought train robbing was a thing of the past. From the corner of his eye he saw Rosellen's hand inch toward the handle of her old gun, but Cason was quicker and grabbed her wrist. He shoved it down by her side and held it tightly, then moved to stand closer to her so the robbers couldn't see her trying to get to her gun.

"Don't move a muscle," he whispered in a low, growling voice that wouldn't tolerate an argument. "You're going to get yourself killed and probably some of the other passengers, too."

Rosellen glared up at him. "They just shot a man," she muttered through clenched teeth and tight lips.

"They'll shoot you, too, just as quick."

"I can get the drop on them. They won't expect a woman to have a weapon."

"If they see a gun they won't care if you're a woman."

The robber chuckled. "Doesn't look like we're going to have any more dead heroes today. Too bad. Raise your hands over your heads. All of you. If I see any of you without your arms stretched high, I won't ask any questions. I'll just shoot."

Cason squeezed Rosellen's wrist tighter and whispered, "When I let go *don't* go for your pistol if you want to live long enough to tail me."

"I want to see those hands now!"

Cason released her, half fearing she'd do something

foolish. In an uncompromising tone he said, "You can't be a hero every time. Get them up."

He stared at Rosellen and breathed a shallow sigh of relief when, like him, she raised her hands above her head.

A volley of shots sounded in the distance. Passengers gasped and mumbled; some of the women cried. Cason knew what was happening. The conductor and the engineer must have put up a fight.

He glanced at the four robbers inside the car and noted that the man holding the burlap sack was the youngest, while the man doing all the talking to the passengers was the oldest and clearly the leader.

"Looks like the boss picked the wrong train to hold up," the robber closest to Cason said to his partner. "There's not enough people on board to pay for a good bottle of whiskey and a cheap whore."

"Shut up," his partner said. "The boss knows what he's doing. You heard him last night, same as I did. What we really want is that rich bitch who boarded the train last night. Besides, fewer people mean less chance for trouble. Don't none of us aim to have our necks stretched from no sheriff's braided hemp."

Cason and Rosellen looked at each other, then at the young couple who'd boarded last night. The woman was whimpering softly behind the man. If they were wealthy, as the robbers claimed, Cason had a feeling the man who went for his gun must have been traveling with them as a bodyguard.

"That's better," the leader said. "Now, before you go thinking either one of the men driving the train is going to come save you, don't bother. Those shots you heard were my man taking care of them, so they won't be helping you or giving us any trouble."

"What do you want from us?" a man in a bowler hat called out to them.

"This is just a passenger and livestock train," someone else added. "There's no gold or silver on board"

The leader's laughter had a hard edge. His breath sucked his kerchief in and out. "The only gold we're looking for is what's in your pockets. One of my boys heard that a rich young lady was boarding this train last night. I aim to take her and hold her for ransom."

The young woman whimpered loudly and everyone looked her way.

The leader laughed, a hollow, forced sound that set Cason's mouth in a grim line.

"Thank you for pointing yourself out to me."

"I won't let you take Mellie," said the man who stood next to the distraught woman.

"If you give us any trouble I'll kill you. Now, my boy here is going to walk down the aisle. Keep your hands up. If he tells you to do something, do it. If we see a hand go down, we'll shoot."

"Most of us are poor miners. We don't have money or valuables. Just take the woman you want and leave the rest of us be."

"No!" the young woman's husband yelled.

"From where I'm standing I see three pocket watches, two brooches, and several guns. I'd say we're going to have ourselves a good payday. Now shut up, all of you, and let us get down to our business. I don't have time for your prattle." He chuckled. "Besides, the sooner we're gone, the fewer of you I'll have killed."

"We can't let them take her," Rosellen whispered.

"We can and we will. It's not our problem."

Cason listened to the man but remained perfectly still. It didn't bother him to give up his money or his gun. Rosellen was the one he was worried about. She wasn't called a hellion because she sat quietly in church on Sunday mornings and listened to everything the preacher said without question.

Dammit, if she tried anything he'd be forced to help her, and he wasn't ready to get killed.

This new feeling stunned him. He didn't want to die? When had his attitude changed? He'd set charges of dynamite for years, knowing every time he lit a fuse or a line of powder he could have been blown to bits. He'd been buried in mines by fallen rocks, and twice he'd been shot by claim jumpers. Never before had he worried about dying. When he was thirteen he had buried his mother beside his father, and since then he had never cared whether he lived or died—until now.

For the first time in years he had a reason to live. He had to exact for revenge for his father's death.

He had the money he needed to destroy Poppy for what the townspeople did to his family, and he now had the name of a man who could clear his father's name. And, dammit, he didn't want Rosellen Lattimer to take that away from him by pulling some foolish stunt and forcing him to save her life.

"Now listen good. I'm only going to say this one time, and anyone who doesn't follow the rules had better know how to pray. We're going to do this nice and orderly. My partner here is going to walk down the aisle with his sack. There's five guns pointing at you. I'm going to walk behind my partner here, and if I think you've tried to hide anything I won't ask any questions. I'll just shoot and take whatever I want off your dead body. I want every coin, every ring—everything." He laughed again.

"They can't bully us like this," Rosellen said in a hushed whisper.

"Accept it, Rosellen."

"It's not in my nature to give up my gun without a fight. I won't do it."

Cason remembered a hard-and-fast rule that Buster had taught him when they first teamed up together:

Don't butt into another man's business, no matter what kind of business it is, unless he asks you to.

Damn her hide. She was so determined to be tough that he wondered if she had beans for brains. Keeping his gaze on the leader, Cason said to Rosellen, "You can't get the drop on four men. If you start any trouble, I'll shoot you myself."

She huffed. "Who do you think you're trying to scare?"

"You—and, dammit, I mean it."

"You wouldn't shoot me."

"In a heartbeat," he said between clenched teeth, his lips barely moving. "Those men will shoot to kill. I'd only wound you, and I'll do it if you try anything."

"I should have known you'd give in like a weak-kneed granny at the first sign of trouble."

"It's called staying alive, and I aim to do that. You can't fight every goddamn time there's trouble. Your murdering father should have told you that."

"You leave my father out of this," she said, forgetting she was supposed to whisper.

Cason held his breath, thinking one of the robbers must have heard her.

Rosellen would get herself killed for sure. He shouldn't have cared, but somewhere deep inside him, dammit, he did.

In a whisper he said, "If you get yourself killed, I'm going to prop your body up outside the train and let everyone stare at you."

She gasped. "You wouldn't dare do that."

"Of course I would. That's exactly what your father did to mine, and I'd consider it an honor to repay your family in kind." He was surprised at how smooth his voice sounded with his teeth clamped so tightly shut.

"You bastard," she hissed.

"This isn't your fight. Stay out of it."

"Stop talking," the head robber ordered. "I hear talking. The first person I see talking gets my next bullet. Who's it going to be? Speak up. Don't be shy. I promise to make it painless." He laughed. "A bullet to the heart doesn't hurt for as long as one to the gut." His gaze darted around the car. "No takers for my next bullet?"

Cason wasn't interested in being a hero, and he hoped he'd persuaded Rosellen not to do anything crazy and get herself or him killed.

The lanky thief shoved his gun into his holster and opened his burlap sack wide. He started at the other end of the car and quickly moved from person to person, frisking every one of them, including the woman named Nadine.

Cason kept his eyes on the robber as one by one the passengers gave up their valuables. He studied the face of each thief. Only one looked as if he knew how to use a gun.

The other three robbers fanned out, closely watching the passengers. The young woman who'd given herself away was the only one who showed any emotion. Cason's gaze followed the man with the sack as he moved down the narrow aisle.

When he made it to Cason, the thief looked him over carefully. Tense and trying to remain as cold as the icy streams he'd panned in, Cason threw his money and his gun into the sack, then moved aside, putting Rosellen in full view.

When the robber saw Rosellen, his eyes sparkled with amusement. "Hey, Smally, look over here. This woman is dressed like a man, and she's wearing a gun, too."

"You dumb-ass fool! How many times do I have to tell you not to use our names. What the hell do we care how she's dressed? Grab her damn gun, get her money, and let's get out of here."

Cason kept watching Rosellen. She did exactly as she was told. She remained rigid, hands held over her head. The young man came dangerously close to fondling her breasts, pretending to look for valuables. Cason expected Rosellen to ram her knee up into his groin and let him have it, but she stayed calm and let the young man search her pockets.

"That's it," the young man said, turning back to the robber he'd called Smally.

"All right," the leader said. He headed down the aisle, stopping in front of the pretty young woman dressed in a dark blue traveling jacket and matching bonnet. She held her hand over her mouth and cried softly as she shrank behind her husband.

"You're coming with us," he grabbed her arm and pulled her into the aisle beside him.

"No!" she screamed. "Guthrie, help me! Don't let them take me."

"Get your hands off her!" the husband yelled and grabbed for her. The robber slammed the handle of his pistol into Guthrie's forehead, knocking him down onto the seat.

"I'd shoot you, but I'm going to need somebody to send the ransom note to."

"No, please stop. I don't want to go with you." Mellie continued to cry as the robber took a short length of rope from the pocket of his duster and tied her hands behind her back.

Her lips trembled, and tears rolled down her cheeks. Cason felt sorry for her. He hated to see a woman cry. It reminded him of his mother and gave him that sick, helpless feeling in the pit of his stomach. But now wasn't the time to try to help. He'd have to wait.

"We need the money you can bring us, darlin'. Get on up there." The robber shoved her toward the door. Two other thieves caught her between them and held her arms. She struggled to get away, but they held fast.

Suddenly Rosellen pushed Cason aside and stepped into the aisle. "Let her go. She's not the woman you want."

Rosellen's voice was as calm as Cason had ever heard it, and that scared the hell out of him.

"I'm the rich lady you're looking for."

Chapter

→ 13 ←

"I'm the woman you want," Rosellen repeated as the murmurs on the train quieted.

"You don't look like no rich woman to me," one of the robbers proclaimed.

"The lady you have is Mellie, my hired companion. Whenever we travel, she pretends to be me, and I dress like this, hoping to avoid exactly what you intend to do. You're holding the wrong woman."

Cason clenched his fists. He'd been afraid that Rosellen would do something rash. He just hadn't known what. She was tougher than any woman he'd ever met. Despite himself, he felt his admiration growing and swelling inside him. She was trying to save the young woman and putting herself in danger.

He wondered if the people of Poppy knew exactly how rare a person they had in the woman who wanted to be their next sheriff. Seeing her this strong and brave, he wondered how she could be Henry Lattimer's daughter.

Mellie continued to sniffle and struggle against the

two men holding her, but she didn't confirm or deny Rosellen's claim. Guthrie hadn't bothered to speak up, either. He was too busy trying to stop the flow of blood from the deep cut over his eye.

Cason could tell by the leader's eyes that he was considering Rosellen's claim. Like any man, he could obviously see that, even dressed in old brown trousers, Rosellen was prettier than Mellie.

Staring at Rosellen, Cason wondered if she felt as brave as she looked, or was she already trying to figure out how to get away from the outlaws? Why did he put up with that cocky attitude of hers?

One of the robbers pulled back the hammer on his gun and pointed the barrel at Rosellen's chest. Cason moved forward and found himself facing the other robber's gun.

"We don't like people who think we're stupid," the heaviest outlaw said. "The boss ain't gonna fall for a story like that, so shut up and get back."

"Why would I say I'm someone I'm not?" Rosellen answered calmly. "You aren't the kind of men a woman would want to run away with."

Someone in the train snickered.

Cason tensed again. Her smart mouth was going to get them all killed.

"Maybe you're one of those women who can do some of that fancy shooting. You're dressed like they do, and you had a gun strapped to your hip."

Cason saw that this man was the only one who had sized Rosellen up correctly, and that worried him plenty. Cason hadn't actually seen Rosellen draw or shoot, but he'd heard enough stories to know she was a crack shot. Damn her reckless courage. Let her get herself killed if she didn't have better sense than to put herself up for more trouble than she could handle.

"She's right," Cason spoke up, keeping his hands held high. Rosellen didn't know it, but she had committed both of them. He couldn't let her stay out on that limb by herself without trying to help.

"She and I are the couple you're looking for. Tell me how much money you want and where and when you want it. I'll see you get it. Nobody needs to get hurt."

"He did have a lot of money on him, boss," the robber with the loot bag said. "More'n that man you hit over the head. Could be they're telling the truth."

"Of course it's true," Guthrie spoke from behind the bloodied handkerchief he was mopping his face with. "Why would she lie about something like that?"

Cason glanced at the sniveling little man. It was clear his wife was frightened to death, but at least she'd had the decency to remain quiet and not implicate them.

"How will we know for sure?" the heaviest outlaw asked.

"That's the trouble. We don't," said the man who'd doubted Rosellen's story from the start.

The leader's eyes darted around the railcar. "That's why you boys need me to do your thinking for you. I'll tell you what we're going to do. We're going to take both women with us. That way I'll be sure to get the right one."

"Get on up there with the other woman." He shoved Rosellen toward the front of the car. "See if you can stop her from crying. If you can't, I'll shut her up. Let's get out of here, boys. We've been on this train too long."

Cason was seething with tension, but on the outside he remained as calm as Rosellen. Her shoulders were squared. The determined expression didn't leave her face. He remembered what she'd said about committing herself. She wouldn't back down.

Just last night she had said she didn't need his help. She'd gone to great lengths to tell him she could take care of herself. He hoped that was true, because she'd just bought herself a whole lot of trouble.

His conscience speared him. She'd probably get mad at him for even wanting to help her. The way he saw it, he'd lose either way. What was the use of going after her when she wouldn't want him to?

"W-wait a minute," Guthrie stammered. "You— you didn't tell us how much money you want or where to take it." Blood trickled down his face and stained the collar fastened to his white shirt.

"We want fifty thousand dollars by the day after tomorrow. Send it with an old man on a mule to where Saddlebrook Creek flows over the Mammoth Rock. If you don't want the women to walk back, have him bring two horses. If I see signs of anyone following us when we leave this train, I'll kill both women, and I'll leave their bodies where you can find them. Now get down on the floor, all of you. If I see any heads pop up, I'm going to shoot 'em off your shoulders." He laughed again. "And I'm a damn good shot. Let's go, boys."

Rosellen was snatched around and forced out the door behind the other woman.

The last robber to leave the train fired his gun over the passengers' heads, and they all ducked behind the safety of the velvet seats.

As soon as the shooting stopped, Cason jumped up and, taking care not to get his head blown off, peeked out the window nearest him. He couldn't see a thing. "Damn!" he swore and quickly crawled to the other side of the train and looked out that window.

"Somebody check on the man who was shot," Cason barked. "See if he's dead."

"We've been robbed," the voice of an older man called out into the quiet. "What are we going to do?"

"The robbery isn't important," Guthrie shouted. "They have my wife!"

"Where are the conductor and the engineer?" someone else piped up. "They'll know what to do."

"There's no use in looking to them," Cason reminded them. "If they haven't helped us by now, it's because they can't. We're on our own."

"This man won't be any help to us either," Nadine's husband said. "He's dead. I'll go check on the crew. One of them might be alive."

"Be careful, Walt," Nadine said. "The robbers might still be around."

"Those murdering outlaws killed our bodyguard and took my wife! What are we going to do about that?" Guthrie demanded.

No one answered.

"Aren't you going after them?" Nadine asked Cason, her red-rimmed eyes searching his face for an answer. "They took your wife, too."

"Yeah, aren't you going after your wife?" another man asked.

"Maybe he doesn't want to go after her," a middle-aged woman said. "They were arguing last night. I heard them. Maybe he doesn't care about her."

"You hush that kind of nonsense talk," Nadine said. "Of course he's going after her. She's his wife. I saw them last night too, and they weren't arguing. When I saw them, they were kissing."

"That's right. I saw it, too," an elderly woman said. "I saw the kiss."

Cason was forced to listen to the inane conversation when what he needed was two minutes by himself to think and plan what to do.

"Hey, which one of you men is really married to the rich lady?" one of the other men asked.

Guthrie pushed his way over to Cason. The man was agitated and obviously didn't know that at a time like this he needed to remain calm and think rationally. The men who had kidnapped Rosellen and Mellie weren't just robbers. They were killers, too.

"My wife is the one they're after. Those bloody outlaws will figure that out soon enough."

"You're the one who's bloody," Cason said. "And it doesn't matter which woman has the money. They took both of them, and I don't plan on letting the bastards keep either one of them, do you?"

The man blinked rapidly. "Of course not. I love my wife, and I want her back unharmed."

Cason looked out the window again and in the distance saw Rosellen and the other woman riding double with two of the men. He felt as if a fist had plowed into his chest, robbing him of breath.

Then it struck him. It wasn't just that he didn't want the outlaws putting their hands on Rosellen. He didn't want any man touching her. No matter how tough she was and no matter how hard he tried to convince himself otherwise, for some reason he hadn't yet figured out, Rosellen mattered to him.

All that stuff he was thinking about her taking care of herself was bullshit. He was already planning how to find and rescue her.

A cold lump of fear formed in his chest. He wished he had told her with his eyes that he would come after her. He wished he'd told her to trust him and not take any unnecessary chances with her life. But even if he had, he wasn't sure she trusted him enough to believe any of those things.

He had no time to examine these new feelings for Rosellen. He only knew that everything had changed between them after their kiss.

He checked the landscape again. There were only four horses hightailing it. Whoever had been sent to kill the conductor and engineer must also have been shot. The only men riding away were the ones who had held up the passengers.

Rosellen had spoken up to save Mellie. She had considered that her job. Rosellen was smart but reckless. He would have bet on her escaping if there'd been only one or two men holding them, but since there were four, it would be nearly impossible for her get away.

Cason turned his attention back to the confused people milling around him.

"What are we going to do?" asked Nadine as she stepped up to Cason.

"Yeah, I sure don't know how to drive this train," a man said.

"Who does?" the oldest man asked as the other six or seven men and three women gathered around Cason and Guthrie.

"Forget about the train," Guthrie said. "Don't you understand that's my wife those bastards took? I'm going after her."

"On what? There aren't any horses on this train," one man said. "I was told it's only carrying passengers and cattle."

"There are horses in one of the cars," said the portly man in the bowler hat. "I saw the cowboys loading them myself just before we pulled out. I don't know if you'll find any saddles, though."

"I'll ride bareback if I have to. How about you?" Guthrie asked Cason.

"I can do it. But if there are horses in one of the railcars, it would be my guess there's a saddle or two somewhere close by."

"What about the ransom money?" Nadine asked.

"We're not planning on needing it," Cason said.

"All right, who else is going with us?" Guthrie asked, looking from one man to the other.

As Cason suspected, no one volunteered.

"All right, we'll do it by ourselves." Guthrie turned

to Cason. "Let's go. We don't have any time to waste."

"Hold up," Cason said, remembering the time he and Buster had chased some men who'd stolen their stash of nuggets. "We need to stay far enough behind them so that they can't see us. We can't do anything until dark any way. Traveling fast, four horses will make an easy trail to follow."

"It might be too late by the time it's dark. The bastards might have put their filthy hands on Mellie by then."

"But she probably won't be dead, and there's a good chance you will be if they see you coming after her. When dusk hits, we'll be able to travel fast. They won't see us until we're on top of them. If we're lucky, they'll be comfortable enough to build a fire and lead us right to them."

"You sound as if you know what you're talking about." The distressed young man mopped his forehead again with his already soiled handkerchief and asked, "You ever chased robbers before?"

"Not train robbers. Claim jumpers. I don't figure there's much difference. By the time we get the horses out of the car and saddled, the robbers should be far enough ahead so that they won't spot us trailing them."

"What are we going to do for weapons? We don't have guns."

"Check the passenger who was killed. I don't remember anyone picking up his gun."

Guthrie pushed through the people surrounding them to look for the weapon while Cason took down his satchel from the overhead rack. He still had his single-shot derringer, which was better than no gun at all.

"I have a pistol in my bag too," the elderly woman said, and everyone turned and looked at her.

The woman had to be seventy if she was a day and couldn't have weighed more than one hundred pounds fully dressed. Cason couldn't believe she was carrying a gun.

"It's up there in my carpetbag." She pointed to the overhead rack.

A man grabbed the bag and handed it to Cason. He opened it, and the spirited woman reached inside and pulled out what looked like a brand-new gunmetal six-shooter with a carved ivory handle. It was the most handsome firearm Cason had ever seen. The revolver must have cost a fortune.

He looked at the old lady. "Where did you get this?"

"I bought it," she said with a gleam in her eyes. "I went into the general store and told the clerk I was going to Denver to see my granddaughter and I needed some protection—just in case, you know."

Cason took the gun from her. "And he sold you this?"

Anger flared inside him that someone would have taken advantage of her. There's no way the woman could hold the heavy gun, let alone aim and fire it.

"Well, I sure didn't steal it. He tried to sell me one of those little guns that shoot only one bullet. He said it was all I needed." She waved her hand dismissively. "I told him I wanted a real gun. I bought the biggest one he had in the store. I knew a gun like that would save somebody's life, if not mine."

Cason looked from the gun to the old woman. This was just what he needed to save Rosellen. "Tell me where you'll be, and I'll send it back to you."

She handed him a box of bullets, which she pulled from her bag. "If it will help you get the women back, you can keep the gun. The store clerk was right. I don't need a gun like that."

"No, but you do need one like this." He took her

hand and laid his derringer in her palm. "What do you say we call it an even swap?"

The woman smiled and winked at him.

"I have found the dead man's gun," Guthrie rose from the floor where he'd been looking and proudly displayed the revolver. "Let's go get the horses."

"Wait a minute," the man in the bowler hat said. "How are the rest of us going to get to town?"

"We've got to clear the tracks first," another man said. "Then we'll worry about that."

Cason strode out the door, listening to the men argue about how to clear the tracks and get the train running. He was glad he didn't have to depend on any of them to get to the next town and send help. He had a feeling he'd be waiting a long time. And come dark, Rosellen and Mellie would run out of time.

Chapter

→ 14 ←

$\mathcal{R}$osellen sat cross-legged on the ground with her hands tied behind her back, watching the man named Boddie build a campfire in the fading twilight. Mellie hunkered down quietly beside her. Two of the other men were taking care of the horses down at the stream, and not far away was the man named Hall, keeping watch to make sure no one from the train had followed them.

All day her thoughts had kept going back to the expression on Cason's face before she was shoved out the door. He seemed to be trying to tell her something, but she didn't know what. She had expected to see a satisfied smile and a twinkle in his eyes at the thought of getting rid of her for good.

She had threatened to be a constant thorn in his side. How could she even consider the possibility he'd come help her? But she had. After the tongue-lashing she'd given him last night, he'd be a fool to try to help her, but that didn't keep her from hoping he would.

During the long ride, she had looked behind her

and to either side so many times her neck hurt from straining, trying to detect any speck of movement that would tell her if anyone from the train was following them. She hadn't even seen a sign of dust floating in the air.

As the sun crept from east to west and the sky darkened to dusk, her hope faded that Cason or anyone else was out looking for them. He was getting rid of her, and that was exactly what he wanted. She felt angry with herself for hoping Cason would come to her aid as he had before.

At every opportunity Rosellen had picked and pulled on the tight rope binding her wrists. She had twisted her hands until her skin was rubbed raw, but the rope was so tight that she couldn't maneuver the knot around to where she could work on it.

When her wrists became so sore she could hardly move them, she had to admit that maybe her brothers had made allowances for her when they used to tie her up. When she finally realized she couldn't untie her hands, she started thinking about other ways to escape.

Reynolds was the name of the man she rode behind. It irritated her that he was so confident she couldn't get loose that he rode with his gun in his holster, right in front of her, instead of stuck down the front of his waistband. She'd tried desperately to free her hands so she could grab his gun and show him what a dunce he was.

She'd have bet a hundred dollars that she was a better shot than any of the men holding them captive, including the braggart Smally. Resigning herself to the fact that she wouldn't get to outshoot the robbers, she put her mind to outsmarting them. Her fear was that the outlaws had no intention of letting her and Mellie go, because the men now had no qualms about using their names.

It would have been so much easier to get away if she'd had only herself to worry about, but Mellie was the reason she was in this predicament. One look at her frightened face had told Rosellen the young woman wasn't capable of caring for herself under normal circumstances, let alone at the hands of four roughneck robbers.

Rosellen hadn't really thought about the consequences of her actions. All she knew was that Mellie was in trouble and needed help. But even now Rosellen was thinking that maybe the better plan would have been to let the outlaws take Mellie and then help with trying to rescue her.

They'd ridden hard all day, stopping only to water the horses and heed the call of nature. That was the only time her hands had been untied and the only opportunity Rosellen had had to talk to Mellie.

Rosellen had told Mellie her name, that she was there to help her, and that when the time came she would have to be strong and do whatever Rosellen told her to do. Having grown up wrestling with her brothers, Rosellen was used to being pushed and shoved around, but the young heiress whimpered if one of the men even looked at her.

From the back of Reynolds's horse Rosellen had studied the four men and tried to learn as much about them as possible. She'd learned that Smally, the leader, was the smartest and meanest of the bunch. The way he laughed after almost every sentence had her nerves strung tight. Mellie had ridden behind Boddie, the youngest and friendliest outlaw. He talked and whistled, mostly to himself, because no one seemed to listen to him. Rosellen had concluded that he'd be the easiest to manipulate into making a mistake.

Hall was short, surly, chunky in build, and looked to be strong as an ox. He hadn't said anything to her and very little to the other men.

Reynolds looked to be about the same age as the leader. He seemed to be brooding about something, and Rosellen had a feeling it was his realization that she'd bluffed them into bringing her along. Reynolds had seen through her story the minute she'd blurted it out.

Rosellen was smart enough to know that as soon as the meal was cooked and their bellies were full, the men's appetites would turn in a different direction. Rosellen and Mellie had to be prepared either to run or to fight.

The twigs caught fire and a big smile appeared on Boddie's face as Hall walked over and tossed a drawstring bag on the ground beside him.

"See any sign?" Boddie asked.

"There's not even an aspen leaf moving out there. I told Smally there wasn't no use in looking. I think Reynolds was right when he said there wouldn't be any horses on that train."

Boddie smiled at Rosellen and Mellie. "Then that means we have the women all to ourselves."

Hall knelt down beside Boddie and opened the sack. "Smally said we got those women for money and nothing else. We'll have to wait until we get to Mexico and find ourselves a dark-eyed senorita."

"I don't know if I can wait, Hall. I'm a-hurtin'. You know what I mean. Besides, one of them ain't even going to bring us any money. It ain't our fault we don't know which one to poke, is it?"

Hall looked at Rosellen and Mellie and rubbed his chin thoughtfully. She wanted to tell him she'd flip him over her shoulder and give him a body slam if he came anywhere near her, but she'd already decided she couldn't give them any reason to think she wouldn't be cooperative. Otherwise, they'd never untie her.

"I reckon we could look at it that way, but, hell, we got to eat first."

"I don't want to eat. I just want to lay down between the legs of one of them women."

Mellie made a strangled noise in her throat, then whispered to Rosellen, "I'm so glad you're here with me. I don't think I bear this alone. I'm so frightened."

Rosellen nodded once. She didn't want Mellie to know it, but her throat was clogged with fear too.

"It ain't good and dark yet," Hall said.

"So?"

"I don't like showing my ass to anybody but the moon. I say we wait."

"Hell, it's almost dark now. Besides, I wasn't going to do it right here. I was going to take her up there to the hills."

"And let her escape."

Ain't no woman gonna escape from me."

"Go on and talk to Smally about it. You know it's his decision. As for me, I'm gonna eat first so after I get through with the woman I can go right to sleep."

Boddie scrambled to his feet, and Rosellen knew she had to do something soon. She wasn't going to sit around hoping someone would rescue them. That wasn't going to happen, and she didn't plan on being any dirty man's woman for the evening without putting up a good fight.

"What do you have in that sack to cook?" Rosellen asked Hall.

"Beans and salted fatback," he said pulling the makings for coffee out of the sack.

"Who's cooking, you or Boddie?"

"I usually do the cooking. None of the rest of them can cook worth a piss."

Rosellen glanced at Mellie and tried to tell her with her eyes to play along with her. "That's because cooking is woman's work." She looked at Mellie again and mouthed, "Tell him I'm a good cook."

Mellie nodded once and cleared her throat. "Ah, why don't you let one of us prepare the meal? Rosellen is an excellent cook. I've eaten the food she's prepared many times."

"What's a rich lady know about cooking?"

For a moment the fear left Mellie's eyes and she lifted her chin. "Everything. It's one of the first things that's taught in finishing school. Cooking is very important in the management of a household."

Hall looked up at Mellie, then over to Rosellen. "That so?"

"Yes, of course. But I'm sure you know all about what women do."

He nodded, but she could see he didn't know. "The key to making tasty beans is in how you cook the fatback. You should fry it first."

"Fry it?"

"Yes, if you'll untie my hands, I'll show you how."

"I can't do that."

"Of course you can. You're not afraid of me, are you?"

"Hell, no."

"And who has the gun? You or me?"

"I do, but—"

"Well then." She turned her tied hands toward him as Boddie walked up with the food. "You and Boddie can sit there with your guns aimed at me if you're afraid I'll try to run away."

Boddie looked at Hall. "Is she trying to talk you into untying her?"

Hall nodded.

"Hey, you don't have to do it if you're afraid of me," Rosellen goaded.

"Ain't none of us scared of no woman, but I don't know what Smally will say."

"Once he tastes my beans he'll be glad you untied me. Now, come on. Everyone's hungry."

Hall looked toward the stream, then back at her hands. "All right, but if you try anything, I'll shoot you."

It worked. The chunky man released her hands, then rose and stood a few feet away so he could watch her.

Rosellen immediately set to work preparing the meal. She put the coffee and water in a pot and set it on a bed of hot coals, which she raked out of the fire. She filled an iron pot with water and beans and set it on the fire to boil. Next she set the iron skillet on some coals and threw in several chunks of the fat and waited for it to sizzle.

The busywork was good for her. A plan started forming in her mind.

Boddie and Hall continued to laugh and talk about getting under Mellie's and Rosellen's skirts.

"Come closer to the fire where I can talk to you," she whispered to Mellie, and the young woman obeyed.

"I'm going to get us out of this," she said softly to Mellie.

"How?" Mellie mouthed.

"I'm not sure yet. But if boiling coffee and simmering beans are the only weapons I have, I'll use them. Don't worry about that right now. Somehow, I'm going to untie you and when I say go, you pick up your skirts and run as fast as you can in the direction of those boulders over to your left at the base of that hill. Can you see them?"

Mellie looked, then nodded. "It's already dark over there."

"That's the idea. Run fast and hide quick so they won't be able to find you."

"Until morning."

"We can't worry about tomorrow. At least if we get away tonight it will buy us some time."

"Where will you be?"

She glanced at Hall and Boddie. "Either behind you or ahead of you, depending on how fast you can run. I'm not planning on hanging around here."

The frightened look appeared again on Mellie's features. "My husband will come for me. I know he will."

"He might not be able to. He took a nasty blow to the head," Rosellen reminded her.

Mellie's eyes watered instantly. "You don't think he's dead, do you?"

"No, of course not," Rosellen assured her, knowing she had to be careful what she said to Mellie. The least little thing would make her start sniffling again.

"Don't cry anymore. Say to yourself right now, 'I won't cry.' You have to help me help us. You have to be strong if you want to see Guthrie again."

Mellie nodded. "I will. I promise to be strong. And I promise to pay you for helping me if we get out of this alive."

"What are you talking about?" Rosellen turned the sizzling fatty bacon.

"I know that you came with me so I'd give you money."

Rosellen sucked in her breath. "First, it's *when* we get out alive not *if.* And second, I don't want your money. I spoke up because I knew you were frightened and you needed help."

Mellie's eyes softened again. "Do you mean that?"

"Of course I do."

"Nobody has ever done anything for me without wanting money. Even my husband married me for my money." Mellie lowered her eyes. "He doesn't realize that I know, but I do."

Rosellen's heart lurched with compassion. Before her eyes Mellie had changed from a frightened girl to a sad woman. "What would make you say that? I'm sure it's not true."

"I'm not very pretty, and Guthrie is a handsome man. He could have married any woman he wanted."

"And he chose you," Rosellen said and realized that for the first time in her life she was enjoying girl talk. "I think you're wrong about why Guthrie married you. After your bodyguard was killed, he stood up to those men and tried to save you, didn't he? They could have shot him instead of hitting him. He wouldn't have done that for a woman he didn't love."

Her eyes brightened. "Do you think so?"

"I'm sure of it. I bet that right now he's riding hard and fast to rescue you."

A grateful smile lifted the corners of Mellie's mouth. "Maybe Guthrie loves me as much as your husband loves you."

Rosellen knew she shouldn't have lied about being married to Cason, but he'd made her so angry she wanted to somehow get back at him. She was sure that Guthrie would come after Mellie, but in truth there wasn't a reason in the world for Cason to help her, and she'd have been foolish to count on him.

In the distance Reynolds's and Smally's voices grew angry, unsettling Rosellen. Trouble in the ranks wouldn't bode well for anybody. Boddie walked down to the stream to join them and Hall returned his attention to Rosellen.

"Sounds like they're arguing over there," Rosellen said to Hall.

"Naw." He sat down and crossed his legs not far from the fire and yawned. "They're probably trying to decide how to divide up Jed's take."

"Jed?" she questioned.

"Yeah. We didn't take time to check, but he never joined us on the train. Guess he took a bullet from one of the train crew," he said, then yawned again.

Hope fluttered inside Rosellen. Hall was sleepy. She stirred the beans and started humming. She pressed a finger to her lips to signal for Mellie to stay still and quiet. The coffee had started bubbling, so Rosellen took the pot off the coals but kept it near the fire so it would stay hot.

Hall's eyes closed, but his head jerked up a moment later. Rosellen pretended not to see and kept humming and stirring the beans. When his eyes closed again she motioned for Mellie to come closer.

With her free hand Rosellen reached behind Mellie and fumbled with the rope binding her hands together. At first Rosellen was so fearful of getting caught that her fingers wouldn't work. She inhaled deeply, trying to calm down.

All she had to do was think of Walter calling her a sissy, and within seconds she'd found the center of the square knot. She inserted her finger into the small opening and worked the rope loose. Her pulse raced as the rope fell away from Mellie's wrists.

Rosellen turned to Mellie and whispered, "Keep your hands behind your back and be ready to run like the devil when I give the word."

At the thought that they might actually escape, panic set in, robbing her of breath. She glanced at Hall, then at the others, about twenty-five yards away. No one seemed to have noticed that they were both untied.

Rosellen looked around. This was the perfect time to make a run for it, while there was enough light to climb into the mountain of boulders. Her breathing became shallow as she uncrossed her legs. She looked at Mellie to tell her to run and her foot hit the pot making a noise.

Hall's eyes popped open.

Rosellen's heart slammed against her rib cage

"Is the grub ready?" he asked.

She nodded slowly. "Why don't you go get the others?"

He rose and took a step. Rosellen prayed he'd go down and get the others, but he stopped and called, "Come to the campfire. Grub's ready."

Rosellen's heart plummeted. What was she going to do? She started shaking. It was now or never. Once the other men made it to the camp, she'd have to fight all four of them, and she knew she wouldn't stand a chance.

She looked at Hall's back, then down at the bubbling food. In one flowing motion she rose to her feet and yelled to Mellie, "Run!" and at the same time she pushed Hall in the back as hard as she could.

The solidly built man stumbled but didn't go down. She turned to run but he swung around, grabbed her hair, and yanked her back to him as she tried to flee.

"You crazy little bitch!" he snarled. "I ought to kill right now for that."

Out of the corner of her eye Rosellen saw Mellie running. Hall pulled hard on her hair, forcing her toward the ground. She winced with the pain and threw her arm down to catch herself. Her hand struck the coffee pot. She grabbed the handle and flung the hot coffee into Hall's face.

The man shrieked and covered his eyes at the same time she realized some of the scalding coffee had splashed onto her.

She saw the other three men racing toward her, guns drawn. Rosellen turned and took off. At first her legs moved like wooden boards. She didn't think she was covering any ground. In the distance ahead of her she saw Mellie's outline.

"Keep running!" Rosellen yelled to Mellie as the first bullet whizzed past her ear. Several more shots followed quickly behind it.

Mellie screamed.

Rosellen's heart jumped up in her throat, and she could no longer see Mellie. "Double damn!" she swore under her breath, thinking the young woman had been shot.

She tried to run faster so she could get to safety before a bullet struck her own back. Her foot slammed down on a rock. Her ankle twisted. Rosellen gasped and hit the ground with bruising force. A bullet plowed into the dirt beside her and she jumped.

Quickly she rolled onto her back and saw Reynolds grab his chest, drop to his knees, then fall face down into the dirt. Two more shots rang out, and Smally and Boddie hit the ground. Hall pulled his gun from his holster and started shooting wildly. Three bullets struck him in the chest.

Rosellen's eyes widened in shock, then relief, as Cason and Guthrie walked into camp with their guns drawn and smoking. She started shaking violently and rolled onto her stomach. Face down she rested her forehead on her arm. It was the first shoot-out she'd ever witnessed, and she realized she didn't like seeing men die, even men she knew were trying to kill her.

"Guthrie!" she heard a scream as Mellie rushed past her, but Rosellen was too overcome to move. She needed a moment to assess what had happened.

What kept singing through her mind was that Cason had come for her. He'd come for her! Relief, satisfaction, and something softer, warmer, more pleasing filled her, and she smiled.

All of a sudden she was whipped around and cradled in strong arms against a hard body. An open palm ran over her chest and down her side.

"Rosellen, where are you hit?"

She opened her eyes and saw Cason staring down at her. Concern flooded his eyes. He was trembling. She felt it in his strong arms. Her ear rested against his hammering heart.

"I'm not hurt. I'm all right."

"Are you sure? I saw you fall."

Rosellen shivered, knowing how close she had come to taking a slug in the back. "I stepped on a rock and turned my ankle. I was running so fast it tripped me. I felt the bullets hit the dirt beside me."

His arms tightened around her; his breathing was harsh, excited. "Don't think about it. It's over. You're safe now."

"Is Mellie all right?"

Cason looked behind him. "Looks like she's fine. She's with Guthrie."

"The robbers. Are they all dead?"

"I think so, but Guthrie was going to check to be sure. I didn't take the time. I thought you'd been shot when I saw you fall."

"Thank God their aim was lousy."

"Damn, that scared the hell out of me!"

His words made her heart flutter. It surprised her that he admitted he'd been worried about her, and it shocked her even more that she believed him. "I didn't know if you'd come to help us," she said, reluctant to get up and leave his warm embrace.

She didn't know how to cope with what she felt for Cason Murdock. She was grateful to him for saving her life, but there was much more than that. From the moment she first saw Cason, she'd felt different about him than she did for any other man. She couldn't put him in a category with her brothers or her father.

"You wanted me to come for you, didn't you?" He raked his open palm over her head, across her shoulders, then down each leg, checking for injuries.

She made a grumbling noise low in her throat. "Hell, yes. What took you so damn long?"

Cason chuckled lightly and drew his hand back up to her face and let the tips of his fingers rest on her cheek. The gentle touch was all she needed to wash away the last of her fears.

"I wanted to see if you could take care of those outlaws by yourself first. And you almost did. You were able to get yourself and Mellie out of the way so we could shoot those men without having to worry about killing you, too."

Held tightly in Cason's arms, Rosellen felt safe. For the first time she could ever remember, she didn't feel that she had to be in charge. She could rely on Cason, and that gave her a rare feeling of contentment.

"I guess I should thank you for helping us."

"A little gratitude for saving your life would be welcomed," he said with a hint of amusement in his expression and his voice. "Or you could thank me the way Mellie is thanking Guthrie with a—"

"Hold it right there, mister."

Cason froze.

Chapter

⇒ 15 ⇐

Rosellen tried to move, but Cason held her tight. "Be still and stay quiet," he muttered. Then in a louder voice he asked, "Who am I talking to?"

Cason heard of boots crunching on rocky ground. A tall, heavyset man with a bushy beard stepped into view. The barrel of his rifle was pointed directly at Cason's chest. Cason knew he wasn't one of the robbers, but that didn't mean he wasn't dangerous.

Night had fallen quickly, but the dark sky was brightened by a large summer moon and millions of twinkling stars. Cason was glad that the man's widened eyes had zeroed in on him and not Rosellen.

"I'll ask the questions. Now, both of you get up nice and easy and walk over there where your partners are. Any sudden moves will make me pull this trigger."

"Don't get itchy fingers," Cason said calmly. "We've had enough trouble for one day."

"I've had enough of being ordered around by men with guns to last me a lifetime," Rosellen remarked, glancing at the intruder as she pushed out of Cason's arms.

Cason saw that the fear was gone from her eyes. He wondered if that could possibly mean she trusted him to take care of her. "Let me handle this, Rosellen," he said and carefully let her go. He raised his hands into the air and slowly rose from the ground.

Rosellen scrambled to her feet and stood beside him.

"What do you want from us?" Cason asked.

"I want you to walk over there and stand with the others so I can keep an eye on all four of you." He motioned to Mellie and Guthrie with his rifle.

Rosellen huffed loudly, but to Cason's surprise she remained quiet as they walked over to where Guthrie and Mellie were standing, arms wrapped around each other. They broke apart as the three approached them.

"What's going on here?" Guthrie asked, moving Mellie slightly behind him.

"He's the one asking the questions," Cason said. "Not you."

"Do whatever he says, Guthrie," Mellie said in a pleading voice. "I don't want any more trouble. I can't take it."

"Don't fret, dearest. I'll take care of you now. No one's going to hurt you."

"First, tell me who you are," the man with the rifle said. "Then tell me why I see all these dead men lying on the ground."

Cason relaxed and lowered his arms a little. If they were in immediate danger from this man, he wouldn't be concerned about the corpses

"My name's Cason Murdock. The dead men are train robbers. They killed the conductor and driver, robbed the passengers, then kidnapped these two women. They said they were going to hold them for ransom."

"Among other things," Rosellen added in an impatient voice. "And they tried to kill us, too."

The mountain of a man glanced over at Mellie and asked, "You agree with that story?"

Mellie stepped out from behind Guthrie but kept both hands clasped around his upper arm. Tears pooled in her eyes. "Of course it's true," she said. "This is my husband, Guthrie Wilkerson. He came after me because he loves me." She glanced at Rosellen before looking back at the gunman. "Please don't hurt us. We've been through too much already."

Cason looked at Rosellen. Even in the moonlight he could see that her face was dirty and her hair was a tangled mess, but he liked what he saw in her eyes. Unlike Mellie, Rosellen wasn't frightened. She was angry and ready to get even with someone.

He took a deep breath and relaxed some more. Working the claims and prospecting hadn't given Cason a reason to be around a lot of different kinds of women. Once or twice a month, depending on how close the nearest town was to their latest digging site, he and Buster had stopped panning long enough to buy supplies and pay a visit to the nearest sporting parlor. Sometimes, if they were near a tent city or a mining camp, the women would come to them.

Over the years Cason had been with more prostitutes than he could count, but he'd never been with a more courageous woman than Rosellen. He was beginning to wonder if she was afraid of anything.

After a moment's hesitation, the man lowered his rifle. "My name is Beck. What can I do to help you?"

"Help us find their gunnysack," Rosellen said, walking away from the group and toward the horses. "It has what they stole from everyone on the train in it, including my pistol."

Cason turned his attention from Rosellen to Beck. He wasn't ready to turn his back on the man just yet. "How about telling us what you're doing out here in the middle of nowhere."

"We're not in the middle of nowhere. There's a small town just over that rise, and the city of Pueblo is not too much farther east. I have a cabin on the other side of that stand of cottonwoods. I grabbed my rifle and came running when I heard the first shot. But everything was quiet by the time I got here."

"Oh, Guthrie, there's a town nearby, and I'm so tired and dirty. Let's go so I can rest. Now, please," she said shaking his arm.

"Won't do you no good," Beck said. "There's no lodging unless you want to sleep on the saloon floor. That's about all that's there. The rest of the town burned down about five years ago. Most of the people just up and left. There's a few houses still around, but most folks took up closer to Pueblo."

Mellie looked at one of the dead men lying close by. "I don't care if it's a saloon. I just want to get away from these horrible men."

"Can we stay at your cabin?" Guthrie asked. "I'll pay you if you'll let my wife have a bed for the night."

Beck looked over at Rosellen. "I reckon I can do that, but I only have one bed. The women will have to sleep together. The three of us men can sack out in the barn, if you want to do it that way."

Cason nodded. The sleeping arrangements were fine with him. He didn't plan on hanging around anyway. This was the perfect chance to lose Rosellen. The way he felt about her was making him nervous.

She was tenacious to a fault. She'd promised to tail him. He admired her. He wanted her. What more reason did he need to put as much distance between them as possible?

"What about these men?" Beck asked, pointing to the dead outlaws.

"They're animals," Guthrie said. "Let the wolves have them."

"These animals might be worth money," Cason said to Beck. "You might want to take them to a sheriff and see if there's a bounty on any of them. If they robbed one train, chances are they've robbed something else."

"You don't want to take them in?" Beck asked, looking from Cason to Guthrie.

Cason shook his head. "We're through with them. If you want them, take them."

"Much obliged."

"The only things we'll take with us are the possessions they stole from the passengers," Guthrie said. "We'll give them to the authorities."

"How do I know I can trust you to do that?" Beck asked.

"You don't," Cason answered.

"You can trust me," Rosellen said, coming up from behind them holding the loot sack. "My father was the sheriff of Poppy for twenty years, and I aim to take his place soon. I'll return the stolen property." She dropped her gun into her empty holster and snapped the safety in place.

"You want to be a sheriff?" Mellie exclaimed.

"I aim to be."

Mellie turned to Cason, her big brown eyes wide. "You'd allow that?"

"It's fine with me," Cason said as he glanced at Rosellen. "She has a mind of her own, and she's not afraid to use it. She's already shown that she's not afraid of anything. You were a stranger but she risked her life to help you."

Rosellen looked up from the gunnysack and stared at Cason with beautiful shining eyes. Slowly her lips relaxed into a soft smile of appreciation. She was surprised by his compliment, and it made him feel good to know he'd pleased her.

Cason acknowledged her gratitude with a smile of his own, but what he really wanted to do was pull her into his arms and kiss her.

He had to get away from her. Fast.

"Thank you for your vote of confidence," she said.

"You're a courageous woman, Rosellen. I hope you get your wish," Cason said.

"If that's what you want," Mellie said, "then I hope you become sheriff too."

Blushing, Rosellen returned her attention to the sack. "Guthrie, tell me how much money you and Mellie put in here, and I'll count it out for you."

"I'm not sure, and it doesn't matter. I just want enough to pay Beck for his bed and to get Mellie back home." He looked at his wife. "That's all I need to make me happy."

Mellie smiled at him, then turned to Rosellen. "My wedding ring is in there. I must have that and the brooch Guthrie gave me for my birthday."

"Come over by the fire," Rosellen said. "I'll help you find them."

The two women walked away. Cason took his hat off and brushed his hand through his hair. He turned to Guthrie and said, "You handled that gun pretty well." That was as close as he would come to telling the man that he could watch his back anytime.

"We did what we had to do to save our wives."

Cason nodded. He kept forgetting that the people on the train thought Rosellen was his wife. And for some reason he didn't understand, that idea didn't bother him as much as it had when Rosellen first made the announcement.

Another reason to hightail it.

He was getting in too deep. Cason knew he had to

get away from Rosellen. He was finding too much to admire about her. He had a job to do, and he knew she wasn't going to like the outcome. If he wasn't careful, she could make him lose sight of his goal to find the man named Dodge. It would be best to cut his ties with her right now before he did some foolish, crazy thing like take her in his arms again.

"I don't see any reason to stand around here wasting any more time," Beck said. "Come on with me. I'll get you settled in my cabin; then I'll come back in the wagon for these poor souls."

"You go ahead with the women, Guthrie," Cason said. "Beck can tell you where to pick up the train again tomorrow."

"Aren't you going back to the cabin with us?" Guthrie asked.

Cason glanced at Rosellen. It was dark, but he could see that she and Mellie were busy digging through the gunnysack. An unusual feeling of longing simmered inside him.

He shook his head. "I'm going to head on out tonight, but I'd appreciate it if you'd keep an eye on Rosellen."

Guthrie studied him for a moment, but Cason couldn't worry about what the man might be thinking. Rosellen could explain why her so-called husband was leaving her without saying good-bye. She had talked herself into being married; she could talk herself out of it.

"Of course we'll look after her. I'm indebted to her for helping Mellie."

"Much obliged."

"I don't understand why you're not going with us. You haven't even talked to your wife."

"She'll understand." He looked at Beck. "Is Pueblo the nearest train station?"

"Sure is."

"East?" Cason asked and Beck nodded. Cason stuck his hat on his head and headed for his horse. He didn't owe Rosellen anything, not even a good-bye. This was the best way to handle their separation.

"Cason, where you going?"

Cason swung into the saddle and looked over at Rosellen. He couldn't see her features in the darkness, but he heard confusion in her voice. He shook off the odd feeling that gave him.

"Maybe I'll see you when I get back to Poppy, Rosellen," he called to her and turned the horse around. He gently nudged the mare with his heels, and the animal took off at an easy canter.

Cason held himself in check and wouldn't allow himself to feel anything as he rode away into the darkness. He forced himself not to look back even when he heard her calling his name. He couldn't think about her at all. He had to do what was best for him. And that meant getting away from Rosellen Lattimer.

"Why would your husband leave you like that?" Mellie asked Rosellen.

"He's not my husband," Rosellen said through gritted teeth as she tightened the strings on the gunnysack, then slung it over her shoulder. "And I don't have time to explain. I'm going after him."

"Wait a minute. You can't go off in the dark by yourself."

"Of course I can. I don't need any man to take care of me." She made the statement with unusual harshness. She realized that Cason's running off hadn't made her angry. It had surprised her. Dammit, it had hurt her.

Furious at herself for turning her back on Cason, Rosellen marched over to Beck and Guthrie. "Did he say where he was headed?"

Beck scratched his head in confusion. "He asked if Pueblo was the nearest depot and if it was east."

Rosellen inhaled deeply. Her insides were shaking. Damn Cason Murdock. He'd told her he'd lose her. Why hadn't she believed him? Because he'd fooled her by coming to help her, by holding her in his arms, and by showing concern for her safety. He had lulled her into trusting him.

Why had she been so susceptible to him?

Dammit, she'd find him, and she wouldn't be fooled again. She'd never turned away from a challenge and she wasn't going to forgo this one, either.

"To Pueblo," Rosellen said. "Which direction is it?"

"That way." Beck pointed east.

Rosellen walked over to one of the horses the outlaws had been riding and saddled it.

"What do you think you're doing?" Guthrie asked Rosellen.

"Exactly what my father would have done. I'm going to catch up with that no-good Cason Murdock, and then I'm going to give this bag of money and jewelry to the sheriff at Pueblo."

"Are you going to just take that horse," Guthrie asked, walking over to her.

"I don't think any of those dead men will need it." She threw the strings of the gunnysack over the saddle horn. "Besides, I'm not going to keep it. I'll leave the mare at the livery." She glanced back at Beck. "I'll tell the authorities you'll be bringing the outlaws in later."

"You can do that tomorrow. You can't take off in the dark by yourself. Cason will be way ahead of you by now. You'll never catch him."

"I'm sure that's what he thinks, too," she muttered, slipping the toe of her boot into the stirrup. "Look me up if you ever get to Poppy," she told Mellie, then turned the horse around and galloped away.

The near full moon lighted her way, but it took only a couple of minutes for Rosellen to realize she was alone. When she looked into the distance before her she saw only darkness. The shadowed outline of the trees and mountains had been engulfed by the night.

She shivered and looked behind her. There was no sign of smoke from the campfire she'd left behind. She must have ridden faster than she thought. She was sure she was heading in the right direction, but she should have asked Beck exactly how far she was from Pueblo.

With the ease of years of experience in the saddle, Rosellen rode the unfamiliar horse. It was dangerous to keep up the fast pace, but she wasn't being reckless and she was eager to gain ground on Cason.

She had to do this. This was the kind of thing she'd be expected to do when she became sheriff of Poppy, so she might as well get used to it. Sure, she was afraid, just as she had been when she faced the hardscrabble prospector, but she had to overcome the fear and do her job. She wasn't going to let Cason get away from her.

As the night deepened, the temperature fell, and she wished she had Cason's strong, warm arms around her again. She shook her head. Why was she thinking about Cason? She needed her buckskin jacket and felt hat to keep the chill off her bones, but she had left both garments on the train. Why had Cason even entered her mind when she thought about warmth? But she knew the answer to that question. She'd felt safe and secure for those few moments when he'd held her close to his chest. It touched her heart and softened her to know that he had come to rescue her and Mellie.

But that was over. Now she had to remember he was an enemy out to destroy her town, and she was the only one who could find him and stop him.

Why would she want to see him again? He was trying to pin two murders on her father. And as far as she was concerned Cason's running off without her strengthened her conviction that he would do anything to verify Gayla's story.

Rosellen shivered again and knew none of that had mattered when he'd kissed her, when he'd held her in his arms at the campsite. It was a violation of her memory of her father, but when she was in Cason's arms she forgot everything—the past, the present, and the future. Nothing but Cason mattered.

Rosellen shook her head, clearing her thoughts. Being the next sheriff of Poppy should be the only thing on her mind. Once the townspeople heard how she'd helped Mellie and how she'd returned the passengers' stolen goods, she should have no trouble getting the job.

Of course she'd have to minimize Guthrie's and Cason's roles in handling the entire incident. She might even be able to beat Walter if he was serious about wanting the position. A pang of something she didn't quite understand hit her. What was wrong with her? She'd always competed against her brothers. Why should running for sheriff be any different? But suddenly something inside her didn't feel right when she thought about that.

Rosellen pulled back on the reins and slowed her horse. If she was going to catch Cason, she would have spotted him by now. What would she do if she didn't catch up to him? Would she be able to find him in Denver, or would she never see him again? Of course she'd see him. It would take too long to make the journey to Denver on horseback and most of the stagecoach lines had gone out of business since so many railroad tracks had been laid. No doubt if she didn't catch him tonight, she'd see him at the depot tomorrow.

The night air had made her hands and cheeks cold. She would come across the town of Pueblo soon enough, but it bothered her to know she was completely alone.

"Poppycock," she whispered. But as she stared into the tunnel of darkness ahead of her, the lonely feeling increased instead of dissipating.

She'd been outside after dark so many times her mother had grown weary of being worried. The only difference was that she'd always known her way back home, and she'd always known someone would come looking for her if she didn't show up for supper. She had no such certainty this time.

There was no reason to be frightened, and she wouldn't be. Her brothers had taught her not to be afraid of the dark or of what was in it. She didn't need anybody to look after her. What was she thinking? How could she be the sheriff of Poppy if she was afraid to ride off into the dark after an outlaw?

"You're not frightened, you silly goose," she admonished herself out loud.

She would just think about something pleasant or exciting. Like the exquisite tremor she'd felt deep in her soul when Cason held her in his arms and kissed her so passionately. Or she could think about how she'd felt when she climbed through the window of the saloon and saw his magnificent nude body. Forgetting her vow not to think about him, she settled into the saddle and vividly brought Cason to mind.

A noise that sounded like thunder roaring in the distance distracted her, and she looked up at the sky wondering if the muffled rumbling was a sign of an approaching storm. It was just her luck that it would rain when she didn't have an oilskin or a heavy jacket.

"Whoa." She tightened the reins and stopped her horse.

The sound was coming from behind her. She held

her breath and listened. The pounding came closer and closer, but all she could see was pitch darkness.

The sound she heard was horses' hooves on hard-packed ground. Her heartbeat kept time with the pounding on the earth. She peered into the distance, searching the night until she saw a shadow, the figure of a man and a horse racing toward her.

At first she thought it was Cason, but the man wasn't slowing down. Her horse snorted, stomped, and shied away from the danger bearing down upon them. Fear rose up inside her. The horse was at a full run.

He didn't see her!

He was going to run over her. She spurred her mare to get out of the way, but the animal bucked. She screamed above the sound of the horse heading straight for her.

An arm snaked out and knocked Rosellen to the side, snatching her from the saddle.

Chapter

→ 16 ←

She struck out at the heavy weight pinning her to the hard ground. Her knuckles connected with a hard jawbone.

"Rosellen, stop fighting me. I'm trying to help you."

"Cason?" She stopped struggling and took a moment to breathe deeply and refill her lungs with the cool mountain air.

"What the hell are you trying to do? Kill me?"

"Are you all right?" he asked "Are you hurt?" His words were hardly more than a gasp, and he was laboring for breath.

"You bastard." She pushed at him, but he didn't budge. She knew she might as well give up trying to stop cussing and swearing as long as Cason Murdock was around. He had a knack for bringing out the worst in her.

"Damn you, Murdock, you ran me down like a wild boar. You could have killed me."

His heavy breath fanned her eyelashes and cooled her heated cheeks as he said, "I had to stop you."

"What are you talking about? I *was* stopped. You almost took my head off when you threw me from the saddle. Why did you do that?"

"I was riding so fast I didn't see you until I was on top of you. I was hoping to break your fall."

She shoved at his chest again with both her hands, trying to push him away. Instead of rolling off her or letting her go, Cason slid his arms under her shoulders and pillowed her head with his open hands.

"When I saw you riding like the wind, I went crazy. I—I haven't been so frightened since—"

Realizing Cason was trembling, Rosellen calmed down and asked, "Since when? What are you talking about?"

"You rode right past me, Rosellen. You didn't know where you were going. You were just riding blindly into the darkness. I was afraid you were lost."

She heard a remnant of fear in his voice and saw it in his eyes. He had been truly frightened for her. She sensed his desperation to find her in the tautness of his prone body. A thrill shimmied through her. His troubled state filled her with concern for him and softened her to his feelings and to his body.

"What do you mean?" she asked. She locked her gaze with his. "I wasn't lost, Cason. I was trying to catch up with you."

"I saw you ride past me. I called to you, but you didn't hear me. It was like that night when I couldn't find my way. I thought—" He stopped.

She didn't understand what he meant, but compassion for him crept inside her chest and burrowed there like a fox in its hole. There was much more going on inside him than what had just happened. "You thought what?"

"You should have listened to me and gone to Beck's cabin with Mellie and Guthrie."

"Since when do I listen to you?" she snapped, still feeling a tiny bit of anger.

"You scared the hell out of me."

"Why?" she asked, knowing that something had upset him greatly.

"Just promise me you won't ever run off in the dark like that again."

In the moonlight she saw his handsome face just above hers. He needed a shave. His lips were moist. Very kissable. A spiral of odd feelings curled inside her, low in the pit of her stomach.

Suddenly she was aware that Cason lay between her spread legs. His manhood rested snugly against her womanhood. Her mind flashed the vision of Cason standing naked before her in the saloon. Heat flooded her face so hotly she thought she must be glowing like a blazing fire on a pitch-dark night, but she didn't try to push him away again.

The weight of his body pressed heavily, easily, wonderfully upon her. His muscular chest lay intimately against her breasts and her midriff, but she didn't want to push him away.

He was desperate for her to promise him. She saw it in his eyes, heard it in his voice, but Rosellen never made promises. She'd learned early that every time her brothers forced her to promise something she either regretted it or broke it, so she had stopped making them.

"Why? Tell me why you want me to promise."

Cason remained quiet, staring down into her eyes. The ground was hard and cold against her back, but the way Cason was making her feel gave her all the heat she needed. He'd come to help her so many times now she'd lost count.

Another thing her brothers had told her was always to return a favor. It was her turn to help Cason. She wanted to know what had spooked him. "What frightened you, Cason?"

A heavy sigh passed his lip. "I was lost in the dark once and couldn't find my way. I didn't want that to happen to you."

"Tell me about it," she said, in her mind seeing a little boy of three or four wandering alone at night.

"No." He shook his head and looked away from her. "I was a kid. I don't want to talk about it. I don't ever think about it again."

She knew that wasn't true. He was thinking about it right now. "How old were you?"

"Thirteen."

His age surprised her. So he wasn't a little boy, as she'd suspected. That intrigued her. Why was a young man already in his teens frightened of being lost in the dark? But looking into Cason's eyes with their glassy, faraway expression, she knew there was much more to the story than he was telling.

With open hands she gently cupped his face and brought his attention back to her. His growth of beard tickled her palms. The sky was so bright she easily made out his troubled features. She took the time to really look at him and saw a tortured soul living inside the handsome, hard-hearted man.

The tension between them mounted slowly as they studied each other. She wouldn't pressure him any more about the past right now. She had something else on her mind, and she would have bet a twenty-dollar gold piece that Cason was thinking the same thing. But later she intended to find out what had happened to him.

Her harsh feelings toward him melted away. A need to comfort him surged inside her. And then with no thought to stopping herself, she lifted her head and placed her lips on Cason's.

At first the kiss was merely contact of two pairs of

lips. Neither of them made a move to make more out of it. She expected him to deepen the kiss and make it come alive like the one they'd shared on the train platform, but he remained passive.

Rosellen's heart hammered, then fluttered. She lowered her head a little and swallowed hard. Their eyes held fast on each other. She let go of his face and rested against his arm again.

Cason bent his head and covered her lips with his. The kiss was short, tentative, questioning. It was as if he was asking if he'd read her invitation right, did she know what she was doing?

Hell, yes.

Forgetting everything except the body covering hers, Rosellen let instinct take over and slipped her arms around Cason's shoulders and pulled him to her again.

She didn't want to think. She only wanted to feel.

Instantly his lips grabbed hungrily at hers. His lower body pressed eagerly against hers. She welcomed him. A hot shooting fire of desire flamed inside Rosellen. Her lips parted, and Cason's tongue darted deep inside her mouth.

He slipped one arm out from underneath her head and caressed her cheek with his fingertips before making a trail down her neck to her chest. He flattened his hand and pressed his palm into the soft firmness of her breast. Rosellen softly moaned her acceptance and arched her body off the ground to meet the demand of his hand.

Their kisses turned frantic as his body pressed harder against her. She met him with equal force. With jerky fingers he unbuttoned her shirt and tore it away from her shoulder. She pulled open the buttons on his shirt as Cason yanked the wide strap of her cotton chemise aside. Her breasts sprung free of the restraining garment, and instantly his mouth covered one dusky pink nipple.

A thrilling shock shimmied through her. She gasped at the delight that sailed through her. His wet tongue tweaked the small nubbin while his lips pulled on the nipple, causing delicious sensations to skyrocket through her lower abdomen. She wiggled her bottom, trying to satisfy the urgent need that was building inside her.

When Cason lifted his mouth from her breast and kissed her lips again, the cold air peaked her nipple, sending shivers of desire shooting through her. As his lips plundered hers, Cason again found the tight peak of her breast and rubbed it between his thumb and finger.

He moved his mouth back to her breast, then quickly returned to her mouth, driving her crazy with a need she didn't understand but knew she didn't want to be without. Rosellen felt as if she were on fire, but she didn't want the flames to stop burning.

Cason pulled at the buckle on her gun belt and quickly unfastened it. He yanked her shirt free of her trousers and worked the silver buckle on her belt. With nimble fingers, he unbuttoned the front of her trousers, then struggled to free himself of his own clothing.

Rosellen couldn't take her hands off him. She allowed her open palms to explore his shoulders and back. His body was so firm, his skin so smooth. She'd wanted to touch him like this ever since she saw his magnificent body in the saloon. She reached up and kissed his chest, letting her tongue rake over the small nipples.

"Oh, God, I can't believe you're this hot," he whispered as his tongue laved her earlobe and sucked it into his mouth for a moment before letting it go. "I can't believe you're making *me* this hot."

"I've never felt this way before," she admitted honestly.

Cason moved down her body and quickly did away with her boots. His fingers caught her waistband and slid her trousers and drawers off, then gently shoved the clothing under her backside.

"I want you so bad I don't want to take time to pull off my boots."

"Don't stop," she answered and pulled him down her to her lips again.

Fervent kisses inflamed their passion to a white-hot intensity. One hand cushioned her head and the other slowly slid down her side, across her hip, and over to the center of her of her womanhood.

Rosellen gasped with pleasure as he lifted himself slightly so that his hand fit between them. He cupped her. His fingertips inched forward and parted the soft flesh to find that secret part of her. He stroked her pearl of desire in a soft, slow circular motion.

Without thinking any further than his touch, Rosellen allowed Cason to spread her legs with his knee and guide his shaft to that secret womanly part of her that yearned for his touch. At first there was an intense, burning pressure but it quickly subsided to a thickness, a fullness, that she sensed was a natural part of what they were doing.

Cason growled low in his throat as he pushed against an unyielding force. His moan of protest, but he continued to shove against her innocence. Rosellen didn't try to restrain him.

"Dammit, I didn't know you were a virgin," he whispered in a ragged voice as he lifted his head and looked down into her eyes. "You should have stopped me before we got this far."

"I didn't want to. Do you want to stop?"

"No. Hell, no." His voice was more of a pant. "I can't stop."

"Me either, Cason. I like the way you make me feel."

"You're not ready for me," he whispered.

"Yes, I am. Don't stop now, Cason. Don't tell me no. I know what I'm doing, and I'm old enough to make my own decisions."

For a moment Rosellen thought his protests might make him stop. She slid her hand down to his firm buttocks and cupped them, holding him to her, urging him to sink deeper inside her.

She needed him to push harder, faster. She knew she would cry out in pain if he stopped. Nothing mattered except what they were doing.

Rosellen lifted her bottom and met Cason's thrust. His large shaft drove inside her tight space.

She winced, afraid to let him know she'd felt a little pain for fear he'd want to stop again. She inhaled deeply, then said, "Now I'm not a virgin. You don't have to worry about that anymore."

Cason groaned and kissed her lips again before nipping at them gently with his teeth.

He moved his lips over to her ear and blew his warm breath on her. "I knew you'd be this passionate the first day I met you," he whispered. "I knew you'd know how to enjoy a man's touch."

"Cason, I feel as if I might explode. Am I supposed to feel this way?"

"Oh, yes, I feel that way too, but we won't explode," he managed to say in a comforting voice. "Just ride with me to the end, Rosellen."

"I don't want this to end."

"When it does, you'll be glad it did."

His mouth came down hard on hers. His pumping became smoother, easier. She matched him movement for movement, ride for ride. He pressed deep, hard, rocking against her womanhood. All the new sensations he'd created inside her mounted into a giant ball.

She was going to explode.

A shocked cry tore from her lips. She dug her fingers into his muscled back and moaned with the sheer delight of the strange sensations that left her gasping for breath and as weak as a newborn kitten.

A few moments later Cason shuddered softly, then eased his chest back down on her bare breasts. Breathless, he pressed his nose into the crook of her neck.

It was over far too soon. Her body tingled and wanted to move. She needed more kisses, more touches, more caresses. She wanted Cason to start at the first kiss and do it all again.

She looked into his eyes. "Does it always happen so fast?"

"No. There are ways to make it last all night."

"Hmm. Then let's do it again, Cason. Don't stop. Make me feel that way again—all night."

He chuckled. "You're so damned eager. I can't believe no one has dipped into your passion before."

"I've been kissed before. More than once."

"But you've never done what we just did."

She liked the way his eyes were sparkling. "No. I never wanted to until I met you. I like the way you make me feel when you kiss me."

"Oh, God, don't tell me that, Rosellen."

"Why? It's true."

"Because it makes me want to take you again, and I don't want to hurt you."

Rosellen cupped his face and planted kisses on his whiskered cheeks, his nose, and his lips. "You didn't hurt me. I felt things I've never felt before. I want to feel them again. Touch me here again, Cason. Kiss me like that again." She laid an open palm on her exposed breast. "Don't stop until I say stop."

Cason couldn't remember a time when he'd wanted a woman again so soon after such a satisfying completion. He looked into Rosellen's guileless eyes, then saw her hand touching her breast, asking him to love her, and his body shot to full erection immediately.

He couldn't believe it. He didn't think that had ever happened to him before. Not even at eighteen, when lying between a woman's legs was always on his mind. He doubted if five full minutes had passed since his climax, but Rosellen's innocent candor had him as hard as granite and throbbing to go again.

Cason smiled down at her as he started moving within her. She was tight, slick. Oh, God, he was in heaven. She was a wonderfully delicious woman, and her innocence made him want her all the more.

He'd lain with many women on the cold ground. Camp followers, sporting women, and prostitutes were all alike. If he wanted a second go, he had to pay again, but here was Rosellen, asking him—no, pleading with him—to love her again, and her innocence touched his heart in a way that no other woman had.

Suddenly it struck him that he couldn't remember ever having a woman he hadn't paid for. He'd made love to just about every kind of woman there was. He had lain with light- and dark-skinned women. Those who spoke English and those who didn't know a word. He'd been with women of every size—tall, short, fat, and thin. It had never mattered to him because there was no emotional connection. He only wanted to satisfy the woman if she was interested and to be satisfied himself.

Of all the women he'd been with, not one had come close to making him feel the way Rosellen had just now. Something about her felt right. It was more than just gratification, but whatever it was, it was too scary to think about right now.

Rosellen wanted him. Him—Cason Murdock. That was all that mattered, and it made him feel good.

Later he'd have to figure out how they'd progressed

from despising each other to him being embedded so deep inside her he didn't want to come out. Desire curled low in his belly. But now wasn't the time to sort out his muddled thoughts. He could do that when the sun was on the rise.

Right now he was going to give her what she wanted—what he wanted. He was hard and ready for her. He wouldn't disappoint her. Prospecting had taught him patience, but he would need that trait tonight. Now that he was over the excitement of having her for the first time, he would wait to satisfy himself again until he'd given her a thorough loving.

"I like the way it feels when you move inside me, Cason. I like the way your chest grazes mine."

If he hadn't known better, he'd have thought someone had schooled her on what to say to push a man over the edge and make him spill his seed before he was ready.

He inhaled deeply and nuzzled the soft skin on her neck, snaking out his tongue to taste her. "I like it, too," he said, already testing his restraint.

"I'm not sorry we're doing this, Cason."

"That's good, considering we didn't plan it."

"I guess it took us both by surprise."

He lifted his head and stared down at her. "No, I wanted you the minute you strode into the saloon, even though you looked as if you were gunning for trouble."

"You caught my eye, too," she admitted. "I was wary of you right from the start, but I was interested, too."

"I could tell by the way you entered the room that you wouldn't be afraid of a man's loving."

"Does that make me a bad woman?"

"No." He smiled. "It makes you every man's dream woman."

"Really?"

He nodded and kissed her lips.

"Everyone thinks I know more about being a man than I do about being a woman."

"I know that's not true." He looked down at the moonlight bathing her white breasts with their dusky brown centers. "There's nothing manly about you right now, Rosellen."

She smiled her appreciation, then arched up and kissed the base of his throat, then moved along his neck and back down to his flat nipples.

Cason sucked in his breath. "You don't know what you're doing to me."

"I'm doing what feels natural."

Oh, God, what a wonderful woman.

He pushed deep inside her. To hell with worrying about hurting her. He was the one in pain. "Keep doing that," he whispered into her ear.

"I don't understand it, Cason. How can I enjoy this—you inside me—knowing how you feel about my father?"

"Because right now none of that matters. Only you and I matter, and how good we can make each other feel."

"Is it always this exciting? I mean, if we make love a hundred times, will it still feel this good?"

"Oh, yes. If it's done right."

"Does it—does it always feel the same, no matter who you're with?"

His eyes met hers, and the rocking movements of his pelvic slowed. "No. Special people make it feel special."

Cason bent his head to her breast again and pulled the rosy tip into his mouth and suckled the delicious taste of her. He palmed her breast and pushed it up to give him better access to the tight little bud. With his other hand he shoved the rest of her shirt away from her shoulders and yanked down on the underwear beneath her shirt.

He pushed deep inside her and heard a soft moan.

"Did you say 'Stop'?" he teased.

"No, you bastard. You better not stop."

He slid both arms underneath her and rolled her on top of him.

"Oops! Cason, what are you doing?"

"I've pressed you into the hard ground long enough for one night. Now it's your turn to be on top."

He rubbed his hands over her buttocks and brushed away the dirt and gravel that clung to her skin. She placed her hands on his chest and rose up over him.

"Hmm." She laughed softly. "I guess it does work this way, too."

Cason chuckled. "Don't even think about stopping. I have a lot of things to show you."

She looked down at him and smiled. "I don't want to stop."

Over her shoulder a bright summer moon shone against the dark velvety sky behind her, bathing her in a silvery glow. Damn, she was beautiful. Her hair lay soft against her shoulders, glimmering in the moonlight. The men's clothes she wore and the rough-and-tough talk hid the fact Rosellen Lattimer was a desirable woman.

With one hand he caressed her soft yet firm buttocks, but with the other he covered one breast. He slid his hand from one to the other, feeling their sweet heaviness and their taut tips. He'd been so eager, so hungry, so in need before that he hadn't taken time to touch her properly, to look at her and get to know her body. But now he had time.

They had all night.

She wanted this.

He wanted it.

There wasn't a soul around to tell either of them no.

"I don't know if I can do this with me on top," she said, supporting herself with her hands spread on the ground beside him.

"Sure you can." He settled his hands around her waist. "Just start moving your hips."

"Like this?" she asked, squirming her bottom around and from side to side.

"Oh, yes. Like that, only harder. Lift yourself up and then down."

"How's that?"

"It's killing me," he whispered.

A confident chuckle passed Rosellen's lips. Cason smiled and closed his eyes for a moment to enjoy the movements of the beautiful woman on top of him. He knew he'd never felt this good with a woman.

"I'll be able to do this better once I've had more practice."

"Keep practicing. After we finish this time, I'll get the bedrolls. You must be cold."

"I don't feel anything but heat."

She made soft, sensual noises low in her throat. He pressed into her harder, wanting to please her as much as she pleased him with her body and her words.

"Am I hurting you?" he asked, knowing he wasn't taking it easy on her.

She tilted her head back and looked up at the star-filled sky. "No. It feels so wonderful I think I might fly up to heaven."

"Go ahead and fly, Rosellen. Fly."

He began to rub her buttocks with one hand, gently, lovingly squeezing and massaging her breasts with the other, moving constantly. He could have spurted inside her so easily, but he held off releasing himself even when she climaxed and shuddered heavily on top of him.

He counted the seconds and let her rest on top of

him one minute, then whispered. "Start moving again, Rosellen."

"No, I can't. I have no breath left."

Cason smiled to himself. For the first time in his life he didn't want the night to end. He didn't want to leave this woman. A strange feeling of distant doom trembled through him at that thought. He shook it off and kept moving.

"Either start moving or tell me to stop," Cason whispered against her ear.

Rosellen lifted her head from his chest and looked into his eyes.

He smiled at her.

She started moving.

Chapter

→ 17 ←

Daybreak illuminated the horizon and cast a purplish glow on the eastern sky, outlining the majestic faraway mountain peaks. Fir, spruce, and aspen trees stood watch over the green valley like proud soldiers protecting their land.

Early morning. It was Cason's favorite time of day.

A comfortable breeze ruffled his hair as he built a fire. The night sounds that had earlier roared in his ears like a distant waterfall had faded with the darkness, and only the occasional chirp of morning birds and hawks broke the peaceful silence.

Sometime during the night Cason had taken the bedrolls from the horses and spread them wide for him and Rosellen to lie on.

Rosellen.

Every few seconds he glanced at her. He'd never met a woman like her. The taste of her was on his lips. The womanly scent of her was on his skin.

She remained quiet, thoughtful, as he added twigs to the small fire. Usually, at sunrise, the crisp chill in the air left him feeling invigorated, but not after last night. Rosellen had worn him out—more than once. He knew she had to be bone-weary and as hungry as a bear after a long winter, but she hadn't offered a word or a moan of complaint.

He'd checked the saddlebags on both horses, hoping to find something to eat, but he'd found only a half-empty bottle of Five Jack whiskey and a silver flask— probably stolen from one of the passengers—that was filled with more liquor.

There was no way that hard stuff would sit still on their empty stomachs, but they needed to moisten their dry throats and replenish thirsty bodies.

Cason heard the popping and crackling of the tinder as it had caught the flames, and he added more twigs and small sticks to keep the fire going.

Rosellen had managed to straighten her clothing, a task that took some doing, considering how careless he had been with their clothes. He'd been so eager and frantic to see her and touch her that he'd almost torn the blouse off her body. He was surprised it was missing only one button.

She sat with her legs bent and her arms wrapped around her knees. Occasionally he noticed she sipped from the flask. But mostly she watched him, and he didn't mind.

The chill in the air didn't seem to bother her. Maybe, like him, she was heated from their lovemaking. And maybe, like him, she was wondering what in the hell they were going to do now that the cold light of day had cooled their passions and they were facing the reality of opposing goals.

He was astonished when he thought about what had happened between them. He'd never spent an entire night with a woman before. Never wanted to until last evening.

Over the years he'd certainly been with more experienced women, but he'd never been with a woman who was more excited and eager to explore his body and to have him search every detail of hers. They had satisfied each other time and time again and had wanted more when the sun peaked above the horizon. Not once had she asked him to stop. Rosellen was indeed every man's dream woman.

Cason couldn't figure out what made him feel differently about Rosellen than he had any other woman he'd been with when just the opposite should have been true. He hadn't wanted to get up and walk away from her after their first time together—or their second or third. They'd be lucky if either one of them could sit a horse.

It wasn't just Rosellen's pretty face, her intelligence, or her courage that drew him to her. He was attracted to the way she took control and charged after life. As far as he was concerned she only had one flaw but damn it was a big one: she was Henry Lattimer's daughter.

That alone should have made her repulsive to him, but when he looked at her, when he touched her, when he thought about her, that bastard Henry Lattimer never even entered his mind.

"Tell me what happened when you were lost."

Cason jerked his head up and stared at her. That wasn't the first thing he expected her to say when she decided to speak. He'd been thinking she might be angry with him for not showing any restraint last night, but it sure as hell never crossed his mind she might want to bring that forbidden subject up again.

He returned his attention to the fire and stared into the flames. "No."

"Where were you lost? In the woods, in a town, or in the mountains?"

Cason threw another handful of twigs onto the fire. "It's not something I discuss with anyone."

"How long were you lost?"

She was pressuring him. That should have upset him, but for some reason it didn't. The story was about *his* mother. It was *his* fault. And *he* didn't talk about it.

"It's none of your business, Rosellen." He glanced over at her. She was so beautiful. How could he be angry with her for wanting to know? He would want to know if their roles were reversed. "Drop it," he said and turned away.

Cason opened the bottle of Five Jack. He took a long drink, then a deep breath to cool the burning in his throat. His night with Rosellen had left him feeling . . . different, odd. He couldn't allow himself to get attached to Rosellen. He needed the strong drink to put him on the right thinking track again.

"Were you lost before or after your parents died?"

He liked the way air chilled his skin and the fire warmed it. And he liked the fact that Rosellen knew, despite his protests to the contrary, that he suddenly felt an overpowering need to tell her everything.

But he resisted. "It's not a story you want to hear, or one I want to tell."

"Why do you think that? I wouldn't ask if I didn't want to know."

"Because it's an ugly story. Because what happened involves the people of Poppy," he said, thinking that would stop her questions.

"How did you get lost in Poppy?"

"I didn't. I was lost because of the people there. I know you think about the town the way you do about your father. You don't want to hear anything bad about the people there."

"You're wrong. I want to know."

Cason glanced at her again. Her expression was serene. Her eyes held a look of innocence. The breeze stirred her long hair and blew a golden strand across her soft cheek. He believed her. He shouldn't want to talk about it, but for some reason he did. What had his night with Rosellen done to him?

He stretched out comfortably on the blanket, propping himself up on one elbow setting the whiskey bottle in front of him. Instead of looking at Rosellen, he looked into the dancing flames. The past rose up before his eyes, and he remembered every small detail of that time.

"I would have been all right if I'd waited until morning. I blame myself for that. I started out in the middle of the night, not really knowing where I was going. I just took off and started riding like the devil was after me. When you rushed past me, last night not even seeing me, it brought all those helpless feelings back. I took off after you without thinking clearly."

"That's why you were so frightened I'd be lost? Because you were?"

"Yes. When I saw you ride hell-bent past me, that long-ago night came rushing back to me as if it were yesterday instead of fifteen years ago. I was so wild with fear for you that I didn't see you until I'd almost run you down."

"When you were thirteen, what made you strike out on your own in the middle of the night?"

She wasn't going to let him forget the past, and he didn't want to anymore, but there were some things he couldn't tell her—like how he'd woken up in the middle of the night hearing his mother's screams and seeing his father propped up outside the jail with flies swarming around the bullet hole in his head.

God, no! He couldn't tell her about the times he'd gotten falling-down drunk, trying to erase those haunting images from his mind. The memories cut him like a razor, would always hurt him so bad that not even revenge on the town and on Henry Lattimer's family could make the pain go away.

Maybe he wanted her to know the story because she was so insistent, or maybe it was because for just a few moments he wanted her to feel the pain of what happened. Maybe he wanted her to know for both reasons a little of what he'd been through.

"My mother . . ."

"You told Gayla that your father's death caused your mother's death, too."

"Yes, but Mama started dying long before my father was killed. She had buried five sons. Three before their first birthday and the other two when a fever hit. I was the only child to survive.

"My God, how horrible for her, for all of you."

She moved closer to him and laid a gentle hand on his leg just above his knee. He wished he hadn't felt so much comfort from that one little movement. He wished he hadn't felt so damn good when he was inside her last night. There was no future for him and Rosellen. He knew that, yet he continued as if he had no doubts.

"Mama never got over the loss of her children. The laudanum she took helped her forget for a time, but as the effects of it wore off each day she would remember her babies and cry well into the evening. My father moved us to Poppy to get her away from their graves, thinking that would help her get better."

"Did it?"

He shook his head, remembering the afternoons he'd come home from school to find her passed out on the floor.

"Nothing made her feel better except that damn medicine. It calmed her and allowed her sleep, but it didn't end her grieving. When Papa was killed, Mama started taking more of the laudanum. We were frugal with our food, but it soon gave out, and so did Mama's medication. She was either screaming like a mad-woman or crying so pitifully it—" He stopped.

She squeezed her eyes shut and whispered, "It must have ripped your heart from your chest."

"Something like that," he admitted, remembering the pain. "I had already gone to town several times trying to find a job. No one would hire me because of what they thought my father had done."

"The bank robbery and killing?"

"Yes. No one would even hire me to wash the spittoons and piss pots at the saloons. I couldn't get even the lowest-paying job at the mine."

He took another swallow of whiskey, then corked the bottle. He'd learned a long time ago that liquor, like his mother's medicine, hid problems for a only short time. When he sobered up the memories would still be there.

"What did you do?"

"I saw a drunk passed out in an alley, so I robbed him. I took every coin he had."

Cason didn't look at her. Dammit, he hated admitting that to her. She'd expect him to do something like that, because she thought his father was a robbing, murdering outlaw. How many times in town when he was begging for work had he heard people whisper behind his back, "Like father like son."

"For your mother's medicine?"

He was grateful he didn't hear accusation in her voice. Cason nodded as frustration mounted in his chest and tightened in his throat. Goose bumps peppered his skin, but he kept talking, telling Rosellen what he'd told only one other person. "I'm sure it doesn't surprise you that I stole his money."

"You were trying to help your mother. I would have done the same thing."

He appreciated Rosellen's attempt to make him feel better about what he did, but he didn't need her sympathy, and he damn sure didn't want it. "The respectable sheriff's daughter? I don't believe that."

No one would ever really know how desperate he was to save his mother. He would have done anything.

A bitter chuckle flew past Cason's lips in a rush. "I finally had some money, but the doctor wouldn't sell me the laudanum. I begged him. I hit him with my fists, but he was bigger and stronger. He bloodied my nose, then picked me up and threw me out of his office.

"Doc Harmon?"

"He locked the door behind me. I knew the nearest town was over thirty miles away, but seeing the state my mother was in and not knowing what else to do, I took off in the middle of the night, thinking I could be back by the next evening. All I knew was that Mama needed that medication. She had to have it."

"But in the dark you got lost." Her voice was husky, compassionate.

He nodded. He wanted to end the story there. Cason didn't want her to know the rest, but something made him continue.

"I couldn't find my way out of a grove of trees I'd ridden into. I thought I was going to die. I wanted to die, but then I'd remember that Mama was counting on me, so I kept riding. I kept searching. It took me two days to get to the town."

"But you got the medication?" she asked.

"Yes, not that it did any good. By the time I made it back home the inside of our house had been destroyed. The furniture was broken, the curtains were pulled down, the dishes were broken and thrown all over the room. It was as if Mama had gone mad. She lay on the floor in front of the fireplace, jerking. At first I didn't recognize her. She was so white, her lips so pale. Her eyes were wild, sunken, and dark. I don't think she knew I was there."

"Oh, God, no," Rosellen whispered.

"I forced some of the medication down her throat, but it was too late. Sometime that night her heart just stopped beating. I buried her beside Papa and left town. It took me years to get over it."

He said the words, but he knew they weren't true. He wasn't over it. Sometimes he'd wake up in the middle of the night with the shakes, drenched with sweat, remembering how desperately he'd wanted to help his mother and how devastated he was when he failed her.

"I'm sorry," she whispered, moving a gentle hand up to grasp his and hold it tight. "I'm so very sorry about your mother."

Cason tore his hand away and looked directly into her eyes. "Yeah, that's why I don't tell anyone what happened."

"I mean it, Cason."

"Save your pity for the town, Rosellen. No one felt sorry for me fifteen years ago when I needed help and compassion. I sure as hell don't need anyone feeling sorry for me now."

Chapter

➤ 18 ◄

Rosellen sat in stunned silence while Cason stuffed the whiskey bottle back into the saddlebag. Her chest was so heavy with sorrow she wanted to cry. She wanted to comfort Cason. She wanted to pull him into her arms and hug him, but she understood why he didn't want her comfort.

She thought of her own father, how sad and grief-stricken she and her whole family had been for months after his sudden death. She could only imagine how Cason had felt as he carried the guilt of not being able to help his mother when she needed it. And he had no one to share his sorrow with.

It was an unbelievable story, yet she knew that every word of it was true and that the experience must have been much worse than he'd said.

"You never went back to Poppy?" she asked.

"Not until three days before I met you."

"So all these years you vowed to take revenge on Poppy."

"No. That's the hell of it. I never wanted to set foot in the town again."

"What do you mean?" she asked, knowing that he planned to shut down the mine.

His expression took on that faraway look again. She wanted to brush his hair away from his forehead and kiss away the pain she saw in his dark eyes, but he'd made it clear that he wanted no sympathy from her.

"Revenge never crossed my mind at that time. When I left Poppy that late summer day, I wanted to die. My brothers were dead. My parents were dead. I thought I should be dead, too. I couldn't figure out why I was alive. I didn't want to be, but I didn't have the courage to kill myself."

Her breath caught in her chest, strangling her for a moment. "Did you ever try?" she whispered before she realized she didn't really want to know the answer.

He nodded. "I put a gun to my head more than once."

The pain in his eyes was so real it frightened her. "Cason," she whispered softly, torn apart by his honesty, searching for a way to respond to him.

"That was before I met Buster, but for a long time after we teamed up together, I thought about killing myself."

Disbelief flooded her again.

"Don't look so shocked, Rosellen. And don't you dare feel sorry for me."

"I don't." She lied to comfort him, but she knew he could hear her sympathy for him in her voice.

"I'm over it. It's all safely buried in a past I no longer think about."

Rosellen swallowed past a lump of sadness for the man she'd met a few days ago. She saw the flames of the campfire reflected in Cason's eyes and knew that was only part of the fire burning inside him. "I'm glad Buster helped you get over the feeling of wanting to die."

"Buster did more than that. He gave me a reason

to live. He never would have taught me how to use dynamite if he'd had any doubt that I wanted to live. He knows better than anyone how dangerous dynamite can be. I knew that he trusted me completely when he let me light the first charge. Since that day, I've never wanted to disappoint Buster."

"Is that how he lost his arm? Using dynamite?"

Cason nodded. "That happened before I met him, but it didn't keep him from digging and panning as hard as any man with two arms."

"I can tell you have great respect for him."

"He's a true friend. He convinced me that one day we'd hit a mother lode and I'd be rich enough to go back to Poppy, buy up the town, and shut it down—not that he ever expected me actually to do it."

"Revenge gave you a reason to live."

"It grew on me. I finally decided if I wasn't going to die I'd destroy the town that had killed my parents." He pierced her with a deathly calm expression. "It's your town I want to destroy, Rosellen. If your father were alive today I'd kill him. Are you glad Buster saved me?"

The lump of sadness in her throat grew. "I wouldn't want you dead, even if my father were alive today."

"I'm not so sure you're telling the truth. I saw you there that day."

Suddenly the wind chilled her. "What are you talking about? Where did you see me? When?"

"Outside the jail fifteen years ago. You were looking up at your father with adoring eyes while the townspeople stood around laughing and clapping him on the back."

A vague memory skittered across her mind. "You saw me? I was there for only a minute or two before my mother grabbed my hand and hurried away with me. I had broken away from her to run over to see what had happened. I saw people congratulating my father. I heard loud talking. I didn't see your father."

He took a step toward her. "Maybe you should have. At least then you'd know why I wish your father were alive today so I could kill him."

Rosellen shook her head. She couldn't think properly. This was the man who'd touched her soul last night. They had laughed together. They'd joined their bodies and become one time and time again. They had shared something exciting and special. Now he talked of destroying her town, killing her father, and all she could think of was that she wanted to comfort the young man who couldn't save his mother.

"Cason, I don't know what to say except I'm sorry. I can't believe that no one helped you. I can't believe Doc Harmon wouldn't sell you that medicine."

His gaze stayed on her face. "It's true. No one at the mine would even talk to me about a job. Mr. Carmichael at the general store wouldn't sell me a sack of flour."

"It's just so hard to believe."

"Why, Rosellen?" His voice was harsh and demanding. His expression threatening. "You didn't have any trouble believing my father committed robbery and murder, but you have trouble believing Mr. Carmichael would deny a starving boy and his mother food. Why?"

Startled, she gasped. "I—I didn't know your father. I've known Doc Harmon and Mr. Carmichael all my life. I know most of the people at the mine. They're good people. You couldn't help what your father did. You had nothing to do with the crimes. I don't understand why the townspeople wouldn't help you and your mother."

"You're blind, Rosellen." He picked up the saddlebag and placed it over the horse's rump.

Rosellen jumped up and followed him, her hands

clenched into fists of agony. "What are you getting at? You're hurt, and you're being mean."

He glared at her. "Isn't that what you expect from me? I told you I robbed a man. You think I'm the son of a murderer."

"No."

"No what? No, my father wasn't a murderer?"

"Don't twist my words."

"You don't want to see your father's flaws or anybody else's, do you?"

"I haven't been given enough of a reason to look for any," she snapped.

"It's time you woke up to the truth. The world is full of people who don't give a damn about others."

"You're wrong."

"Think back to when you stood in the street facing that prospector. Where were Mr. Carmichael and the rest of the townspeople then? On the sidelines, watching. No one stepped up to help you because no one cared whether or not you got shot."

Her whole body stiffened with outrage and with a hurt she didn't understand. How dare he suggest that *her* town didn't care about her? "You're not only wrong, you're a liar to boot. The townspeople didn't help me because they knew I didn't need them. I'm the best shot in town, and I know how to take care of myself."

"I wouldn't care if you were the best shot in the world. I wouldn't let you face a gun by yourself, and neither should any other self-respecting man. And listen to this, Rosellen. Your so-called respectable father was the one who did the killings that day in Poppy."

"No! No, you're wrong." Her voice was almost a whisper. Anger burned white-hot inside her as she sought to make sense of the abrupt change in Cason's attitude.

"And as far as I'm concerned your precious town killed my mother."

"You're not over your mother's death. You said it took you years to get over it, but you haven't even begun to heal. That's why you're seeking revenge, and that's why you want to destroy the town."

His eyes were wild with conviction. "And why shouldn't I?"

She opened her mouth to speak, but nothing came out. Suddenly she felt uncertain. She would have wanted revenge, too, if she'd been through what Cason had. She would have wanted to kill someone, too.

A tremor shook her. Somewhere inside her a change had occurred. For the first time she wondered if Cason could possibly be right. She pressed her hand to her chest in an attempt to slow her racing heartbeat.

What was she going to do?

She had to repress her disloyal thoughts. She needed to convince Cason that she was right.

Rosellen thought she must be going daft or getting soft. Only a woman would fall for a sad story like Cason's. She had to suppress the womanly feelings Cason had created inside her last night and be strong.

"Well." She took a deep breath. "I'm glad to see our goals haven't changed just because we've been lovers."

"Are you truly blind, Rosellen?" A smug smile appeared on his handsome face.

"What do you mean?"

"We weren't lovers. We had an itch and we scratched it. It just took us all night long to make it go away."

His words hit her like a fist to her stomach. Tears sprang to her eyes and spilled out so fast she couldn't turn away before he saw them.

"You bastard," she whispered and rubbed the back

of her trembling hand across her cheek. "But thank you for correcting me. What happened between us was no more than two animals rutting on the ground."

He flinched, but it didn't make her feel any better to know she'd wounded him as he had her.

"I never would have touched you last night if I'd known you were a virgin."

He had already told her that, but now his voice held more conviction than it had last night. He was truly sorry they had come together. That realization wounded her deeply, but she tried to hide her pain.

"Why did you assume I wasn't a virgin?"

"Because you have a reputation in town for being wild. Most girls who are allowed as much freedom as you had have their first man before they're fifteen. Because you're called the town hellion I assumed you'd been with a man."

His words cut her. She hadn't caused any trouble for over a year until she jumped Delta—but he'd witnessed that. No wonder he thought she was a hellion.

"I'm not wild," she declared, remembering that her own mother had said many times, "Rosellen is too wild for me to handle."

"Tell that to the people who told me you were the town hellion. The sheriff let his hellion of a daughter get away with murder is because he got away with it himself."

"Stop it, you bastard. I hate you for calling me that." Her voice broke on a sob. "I'm *not* a hellion. Don't call me that. And leave my father out of this."

"No, Rosellen. If I'm the son of a murderer, then you are a hellion."

She felt as if something had trapped her and she couldn't get away from it. "I just wanted to do everything my brothers did. I wanted to show them I was as strong as they were. When they grew up and went to work in the mines, I knew I had to grow up, too, and I have."

"Who are you trying to convince?"

Tears continued to spill from her eyes, but she didn't bother to wipe them away as she stood before him. The hurt went too deep. What had happened to the man who had made her feel like a woman for the first time in her life? She and Cason had shared too much for her not to be affected by his words, his tone.

"I've changed, damn you." She was desperate for him to understand, desperate for him to believe her. "I don't do the things I used to do anymore. I'll be a fine sheriff, just like my father. And your saying otherwise won't make it true."

A hint of a grim smile touched Cason's lips. "Haven't you figured it out yet, Rosellen? You can't live down a bad reputation. All the good behavior in the world won't clean up a bad past. And one sentence of gossip will ruin a spotless reputation forever."

"Stop it, you dirty rotten bastard! You don't know what you're talking about. Why are you saying these horrible things?"

She tried to hold back the tears, but they only came faster and harder. She especially didn't want to cry in front of this man, but she couldn't stop. Cason had wounded her too deeply. "Stupid, stupid tears," she said. "I hate you for making me cry."

Rosellen dropped to her knees, buried her face in her hands, and sobbed—and not just because Cason thought she was a hellion.

She cried for a young man who had desperately wanted to save his mother and who couldn't find anyone to help him. She cried because she didn't know what to believe about her father anymore. She didn't know what to believe about her town. She hated Cason for forcing her to look deeper into the lives of people than she wanted to.

Her shoulders shook until they hurt. Her heart felt as if it were being ripped from her chest, and her hands filled with tears as she cried for all the times she'd wanted to cry in front of her brothers and wouldn't allow herself to show that weakness.

Cason knelt beside her, but she shoved him away when he tried to take her in his arms. "Don't touch me."

"Let me hold you, Rosellen."

She sobbed until she was too weak to hold herself upright. Then she turned and curled into his comforting embrace like a small frightened child. She had too many things to cry for, and once the tears started, it seemed to take forever for them to subside into controllable sniffles.

He brushed her hair away from her face and rubbed her back and shoulders with a gentle hand. "I didn't mean to make you cry."

His voice was soft, gentle. She believed him but mumbled a muffled, "The hell you didn't."

"I didn't realize you were so sensitive about being called that name."

She hadn't been, until she realized Cason considered her a hellion, too. Especially when she'd been trying so hard to change and gain the town's respect. Maybe she couldn't change. Maybe she would always be a better man than a woman.

"Look, Rosellen, we don't need to be together like this anymore. When we get to Pueblo I want you to head back to Poppy."

She looked up at him and dried her wet face with her sleeve. Through a stuffy nose she said, "You're not getting rid of me so you'll be free to go to Denver and hire someone to pose as Dodge."

"Look. We've already made love once."

"Once? Don't you know how to count?"

He raked a hand across his mouth and chin,

scraping across his heavy stubble. "All right, dammit, it was a hell of a lot of times, and the truth is I'd do it again right now if you'd let me, but one day I'm going to walk away from you, Rosellen, and I don't want to worry about leaving any babies inside you."

She blinked back her surprise that such a thing would even occur to him. "It's too late for that. But don't worry about me or any offspring. I wouldn't let you touch me again if you were the last man on earth."

He walked over to where she stood by the fire and grabbed her, pulling her up against his hard chest. "You issue more challenges than any woman I've ever met. You tempt me, Rosellen. If I wanted to, I could make a liar out of you in about thirty seconds."

"Just try it," she ordered, trying to push away from him but not succeeding. "My trousers are buttoned tight, and they're going to stay that way."

"That's what you say now, but what will you do if you find yourself in my arms like this, feeling my hardness for you like this?" He thrust his pelvis forward and rocked against her womanhood.

Oh, God, he was right. She was weak when it came to the way he made her feel, the way he made her want him. She didn't know how, but she remained motionless and passive in his arms when every muscle in her body was taut, crying out to move with him.

"Nothing," she whispered, hoping he would think that her voice sounded funny because she'd been crying and not because it took all her willpower to withstand the erotic pressure he was applying to her body.

"Don't you find it exciting, Rosellen?"

Her body wanted to move in time with his so badly it was painful. "I hate you," she whispered.

A faint chuckle rumbled in his throat. "Knowing you hate me, knowing what I think of your father and your town, you want me right now as hungrily as I want you."

"No," she lied past a throat tight with rigid pride.

"Yes," he bent his head and murmured softly against her ear as he blew his breath warmly against her skin. "You want to touch me right now."

"No."

She was melting. Her legs no longer wanted to hold her. She was seconds away from begging him to stop pressing against her so she wouldn't break down and give in to the desires flooding her, sapping her power to control her feelings for this man.

He kissed her temple, the side of her face. He inhaled deeply the scent of her. "You want me to touch you here." The backs of his fingers grazed her cheek. "And here." He ran his hand down her chest and over the swell of her breast. "Admit you want me to touch you."

Admit you want me to touch you.

How many times had her brothers held her arm behind her back until the pain shot up through the top of her head, trying to get her to admit something. Somewhere inside herself she'd always managed to withstand the pressure. She had to find that kind of strength right now and deny her heart's desire for Cason.

"I want to be touched again." She slapped his hand away from her breast and spun away from him. "But next time I'll get a different man to do it."

His eyes narrowed, his breath became heavy and harsh. "If you let another man touch you, I'll kill him."

Chapter

→ 19 ←

Rosellen sat on the slow-moving train staring at Cason. He watched out the window as the city of Denver came into view. The tall buildings were a big change from Poppy, which only had two main streets, but Rosellen had too much on her mind to appreciate the scenery.

The ride from Pueblo to Denver had been long, because they'd stopped in every little town along the route, and it had been hard, because her body was tired, sore, and acutely aware of Cason. They had traveled in silence, because she and Cason had spent most of the time sleeping. Now she was rested, and she was thinking.

The whistle had awakened them a few minutes ago, but they had continued to remain quiet, uneasy, and unsure with each other.

Rosellen had wanted to make it to Pueblo before the train left for Denver so she could return the passengers' belongings, but they arrived too late. When the disabled train from Poppy didn't arrive in Pueblo on time, a work crew was sent out immediately to find out what had happened. They soon had the train running again and the passengers safely delivered to their destinations.

She and Cason turned in the bag of loot and picked up their own satchels, which had been left for them at the depot. They spent several hours talking with the authorities about the outlaws and the man who would be bringing them in later for any bounties or rewards that might be offered on the gang.

Rosellen had wanted to wash, eat, and sleep but there was no time for any of that if they were going to take the next train to Denver.

She'd had just enough time to send a telegram to her mother, keeping the message simple, saying only that she was fine and would send word again from Denver. Rosellen knew her mother would worry about her. Evelyn always had.

Now for the first time in Rosellen's life she felt sorry for all the heartache and worry she'd caused her mother over the years. She decided that when she returned to Poppy she would find a way to make it up to her mother. She would be a good daughter.

As if realizing she was staring at him, Cason turned and looked at her. She quickly glanced away. His jealous, possessive words rang in her ear. Why had it thrilled her, angered her, shocked her, to hear him say he would kill any other man who touched her? She didn't know why he had said such a thing or why at times she wanted to believe he meant him.

She was astounded to recall how wanton she'd been with Cason, how much she'd enjoyed their night together. And why? She should be horrified, but she wasn't. How could she be so attached to this man who wanted to destroy all she held dear? How could she be so attracted to him that even now with him sitting opposite her, she wanted to reach over and touch him?

She wanted to tell him that she was sorry for what had happened to his mother, and that the townspeople had been wrong to not to help him after his father was killed. She wanted to say she was sorry his father's body had been put on display for the townspeople to jeer at. She wanted him to know that some of her tears had been for the suffering he'd been through. But now wasn't the time to tell him all those things. And her fear was that there might never be a time. She had no assurance that Cason would be a part of her future.

The only thing Rosellen could do was shore up her courage and not allow herself to fall under his spell again. She had to accept that what happened between them was just something she had needed to experience, like smoking, drinking, and firing her revolver.

But when she thought about it like that, she felt empty inside. A part of her wished she could just walk away from him and never see him again, but another part was telling her this man was different from all the others she'd known.

The train came to a complete stop, and the passengers rose from the velvet-covered seats. Cason took her carpetbag off the brass rack and handed it to her. She avoided his eyes, as she had done ever since they rode into Pueblo.

Cason moved aside so she could step into the aisle in front of him, but she said, "You first," wanting to keep her eye on him at all times. She didn't trust him not to try to lose her again.

She followed him out of the train and onto the platform where they had to wait their turn to disembark. Rosellen couldn't believe the great number of people milling around the station. There must have been more than one hundred people in front of her. Cason stepped down onto the crowded boardwalk.

Rosellen took her eyes off his back in order to make

sure she hit the steps, and when she looked up, he was nowhere in sight. A prickle of fear stung her. He'd disappeared into the thicket of people. She glanced right and left, but she saw only strangers hurrying past.

Frantic and afraid she'd lost him, Rosellen quickly climbed back up on the platform so she could see better and searched the crowd for Cason's black hat with the fancy beaded hatband. When she finally spotted it, her heart lurched with relief. He was heading east and walking very fast.

"Damn him," she muttered and jumped down onto the boardwalk.

He *was* trying to lose her. With her bag swinging from one hand she pushed people aside without care and started running in the direction she's seen Cason walking. She didn't slow down until she spotted him and eased up beside him, letting her long legs fall into step with him.

He turned his head and glanced at her. "What took you so long to catch up? I thought I'd lost you."

"I'll bet you did," she complained tersely. "I'd lay down a twenty-dollar gold piece you were deliberately trying to get away from me again."

"You shouldn't throw your money away on foolish bets."

"As if you'd care. I shouldn't waste my time on you, either, but that's exactly what I'm doing."

"Go home. I told you I don't need your help to find Dodge."

She pushed herself to keep up with his longer stride. "And I've told you I'm not looking for Dodge. I'm keeping an eye on you."

"Then keep up. I don't mind you watching me, but don't hinder me."

They remained quiet for a few minutes as they walked through busy streets crowded with all kinds of vehicles, from fancy brass-trimmed carriages to old beat-up wagons that looked ready to fall apart. Rosellen had never seen so many horses of so many different sizes, colors, and breeds.

Some of the buildings were old and weathered. Others looked brand-new, with fresh coats of paint and brightly colored signs. There were single-story buildings and structures of five and six stories, but at Cason's pace there was no time even to peek into the shop windows they hurried past.

As they walked, she saw men and women dressed in fine clothes and others dressed in old work clothes. Some people chatted as if they were taking a leisurely stroll about town, and others hurried past them as if they were going to be late for an appointment.

Rosellen had heard of the bustling city of Denver all her life, but Cason wasn't giving her a chance to stop and take note of any of it. One thing she was aware of as she walked along the streets beside Cason, however, was that her feet no longer hurt. Her new mule-ear boots had finally been broken in.

"Where are we going?" she asked after they'd been walking for at least ten minutes.

"The hotel."

"We've already passed three hotels, one inn, and two boardinghouses."

"I'm going to the one where I stayed the last time I was in town."

"You were in Denver? You never told me that."

"You never asked."

She fell behind him to let a group of elegantly dressed women pass, then quickly caught up with him again.

"I didn't have a reason to ask such a question," she said as she hurried up beside him. "From what you told me about your past, I thought you spent all your time prospecting in the mountains."

"I did. Most of it anyway. But when we struck it rich we came here to contract with an established company to actually do the work of extracting the gold from the mountain and to—" He stopped.

"To what?"

"To make sure all the papers were legal for me to purchase the mine in Poppy. The company that used to own it is based here in Denver."

She stiffened. Why hadn't she remembered that he was shutting down the mine when she was purring like a kitten in his arms? She should have been appalled by her behavior with him, but for some reason she wasn't. She prayed her family never found out what a traitor she'd been.

"So you're familiar with Denver," she said.

"I wouldn't go so far as to say that. I know some men in town. Most of them are prospectors Buster and I have met over the years who've had the kind of success we had."

He didn't know it, but he'd just given her another reason to stay on his tail. She'd heard her father say that wealthy men had a way of getting what they wanted.

Cason stopped in front of a leaded glass door with large brass handles that were so shiny Rosellen would have been afraid to touch them. And the owners must have been afraid too, because a portly man dressed in a uniform and wearing white gloves opened the door for them.

Rosellen followed Cason inside. Her steps faltered as she looked around the most lavishly appointed room she had ever seen. She could never have imagined something so grand. Her eyes slowly scanned the room, taking in the opulence.

The center of the highly polished floor was covered with a floral-print rug that looked as if it had never been stepped on. Flocked and embossed paper covered walls that were lit by intricately designed crystal sconces. From the high ceiling hung a brilliantly lit chandelier that sparkled and glimmered as sunshine from the open doorway struck it, throwing prisms of pink, blue, and green light around the room.

Strategically placed around the perimeter of the room were several small settees and wing chairs upholstered in expensive brocade and velvet in vivid shades of emerald, ruby, and topaz. Rosewood and satinwood side tables flanked some of the larger pieces.

The women who milled about the room were dressed in frilly satin and velvet. The plumes, feathers, and ribbons on their hats matched their clothing perfectly—and they were all staring at her.

Rosellen grabbed her hat off her head and crushed it to her chest. Her long braid fell to her back. She glanced down at herself and was horrified at how rumpled and unkempt she looked. Her dark brown shirt and trousers were wrinkled and smeared with dirt. And it was no wonder her new boots felt like her old ones. They *looked* like them, too.

She'd never felt out of place dressed as she was in Poppy, but in this room even her gun belt and holster seemed too tight around her hips.

It didn't make her feel any better to know that, with his three-day growth of beard, Cason didn't look any more reputable than she did. She followed him to the front desk and set her satchel down while they waited for the clerk to return.

A door at behind the counter opened, and an immaculately dressed man with his hair greased away from his forehead started toward them, giving Cason the once-over.

She had nowhere near enough money to stay in a place like this, even if the clerk with the string tie and fancy brocade waistcoat would give them a room. No one but the very wealthy could afford to stay in this hotel.

"It will be a cold day in the secret caverns of Hades before we get a room here," she murmured to Cason.

"We'll get a room," he answered confidently.

Rosellen cleared her throat. Already her stomach rumbled because she hadn't had a proper meal since she left Poppy. What was she thinking? She hadn't had a good meal since she'd met Cason Murdock!

How could she have allowed a man to upset her life to the point where she was standing in a rich man's hotel, in a big city she knew nothing about, with only a few dollars in her pockets?

The clerk stopped in front of them and planted a smile on his wooden face, clearly recognizing Cason once he was closer to him. "Welcome back, Mr. Murdock. If you're looking for a room you've arrived here just in time."

"Two rooms," Cason said. "One for me and one for the lady." He turned and looked at Rosellen.

Forgetting she was supposed to be upset with him she gave him an appreciative smile for the compliment. No one could look at her right now and know she was a lady.

"The lady?" the man looked past Rosellen, and then, not seeing anyone else, his gaze fell on her. He cleared his throat. "I'm sorry, Mr. Murdock, but I was about to tell you that we have only one set of accommodations left in the hotel. We have that one vacancy only because a guest left this morning. I'm sorry. Maybe a nearby hotel can accommodate the young lady."

"We'll take the suite," Rosellen said, stepping up beside Cason. She couldn't keep an eye on him if he was in one hotel and she another.

Cason gave her a questioning look.

"I'll pay for my half," she told him. "And I'll sleep on the sofa in the sitting room."

"Ah, I—I'm not sure we can allow that, miss," the clerk said, stumbling over his words and looking at Cason for help.

Cason ignored the man as he took the pen from the stand and signed his name in the guest book. "The lady says we'll take the suite. Send up bedclothes for the sofa and hot water for the lady to wash. Can you do that?"

"Yes, sir. I'll have it taken care of immediately." He reached behind him and grabbed a key off a shelf. "Your room is on the first floor, Mr. Murdock. Down the hall to the left. Number five. It's a large suite. You should have plenty of privacy."

As she walked beside Cason, Rosellen couldn't help but feel that someone somewhere was looking out for her. The only way she could afford to stay in this hotel was to sleep on Cason's sofa.

The door opened into a large sitting room with a pair of camel-back settees in its center and a larger sofa over by a window. That one would be a perfect bed for her. Several chairs and small tables were scattered around the area. She would be fine.

"You can have the bedroom," Cason said, placing his satchel on the floor at his feet.

"Thank you, but no," she said. "I'd rather stay between you and that door."

Cason took off his hat and dropped it on a small table. "If I had wanted to get away from you, Rosellen, I could easily have lost you at the train station. In a city this size you would never have found me."

What he said was true. "How do I know I can trust you not to slip away from me again?"

"You don't. But sometimes you just have to have faith. And I want you to forget your ridiculous notion that I want to hire some old man to pose as Dodge.

I've had enough lies to last me a lifetime. I'm looking for the truth."

A calm feeling washed over her, and she knew she could trust him. She wasn't sure exactly when it had started or why. She only knew she did.

"What if we find this man and he says he knew my father but he doesn't know anything about a robbery or a murder? What do you plan to do then?"

"Don't think I haven't thought of that possibility. I don't expect any man to own up to a crime. I plan to find out everything I can about him and his way of life. If he showed up in Denver fifteen years ago with a lot of money in his pocket, he'll have a tough time making me believe he wasn't involved in the robbery."

"Maybe he was a prospector who struck it rich, like you and Buster."

"Then he'll be able to prove it."

"All right," she conceded. "I'll take the bedroom."

"Now that that's settled, we have other plans to make. If you want to help me look for Dodge you're going to have to dress like a woman."

His gaze raked her body. She needed to wash her face and brush her hair. Dammit, why did he make her care what she looked like?

Rosellen gave him a sharp look and said, "A woman?"

"Yes. That means you need dresses, petticoats, and bonnets. Ever heard of those things?"

"Of course," she snapped. "I know how a woman dresses."

He didn't say a word, but his expression told her he had his doubts.

She tapped her booted foot. "My mother has made me wear a dress to church every Sunday morning since I was old enough to walk. I know how to dress, and it so happens I have three frocks at home."

"All right, we'll get you some."

She brushed an errant strand of hair from her face and plopped down on one of the settees. "I don't have enough money to buy ready-made dresses, and I never learned how to sew. Looks like you're out of luck."

"I'll pay for them."

She jumped up. "You most certainly will not. I can't allow you buy me clothes as if I were your wife or mistress."

"Then look at me as your partner, because you don't have a choice in this, Rosellen. I'm willing to have you go with me to look for Dodge, but you will have to wear a dress. You can't go around town wearing trousers and a gun. You might look fine in a small town like Poppy where everyone knows you and you've dressed like that for years, but you're in a big city now and you're going to have to dress and act like a lady."

Rosellen huffed. She didn't want to feel as if she didn't measure up to his standards. She tried to deny that strange feeling of wanting to please him. Why did her body betray her?

A little smile played on his lips. "If you're going to be my shadow, you have to be a properly dressed shadow."

Rosellen had never liked it when her brothers backed her into a corner, and that was how she felt right now. Win or lose, she'd always fought them to the bitter end, but she didn't want to fight Cason on this. What he proposed was reasonable.

"All right. Where will we be going and what will we be doing?"

"We'll be going everywhere and asking questions. I plan to search every public place, from the opera house to the saloons to the graveyards."

"That could take weeks!" she exclaimed.

"I'm not in any hurry, are you?"

She had thought she was, but she wasn't so sure anymore. "I'm staying here as long as you are."

"I know some miners who live here, and I plan to visit them to see if they know anything. If Dodge has lived the life of a wealthy man, one of them will have heard about him. I'll concentrate on the scar on his hand rather than his name. It would have been easy for him to change that, as any smart man would have done."

"If there is such a man he could have squandered all the money long ago," she offered.

"That's a real possibility. That's why I'll also be hitting the streets to talk to the drunks and the hoboes who loiter in the alleys. They have memories like elephants when it comes to anyone who'd buy them a free drink. And they are always looking for whiskey money and would sell their mothers for a bottle."

She shook her head and sighed. It wasn't like her to give in to anything. "Why do I suddenly feel like a slave to everything you want?"

He walked closer to her and touched her chin with the tips of his fingers. His touch heated her like a fire licking along her skin. "Because you're the one following me." Lowering his voice, he said, "It's not too late to change your mind. You can still go home. Right now."

Rosellen's stomach fluttered expectantly at his touch. She listened to his words but knew he was saying more in the way he looked at her with those dreamy eyes. She knew exactly what he was telling her. They would be sharing a room and very probably a bed, too. He was giving her a chance to keep that from happening.

She looked at him, and a quiver of longing shivered through her, followed by something even more powerful. Rosellen felt warm, safe.

This situation was dangerous, foolhardy, but she wasn't leaving.

"I'm staying."

He nodded once, then picked up his hat and settled it on his head. "I'll tell the man at the desk to send a seamstress over with some clothes and have them fitted to you."

A nervous prickle skimmed her spine. "Wait a minute. What are you going to do?"

He raked his hand over his chin and cheeks. "I'm going to get a shave and then go down to the bathhouse while you clean up here. Last time I was in town I ordered some clothes. I'll have those sent over and change there so you can have privacy. I'll meet you in the dining room downstairs at six. That should give us both plenty of time. Tomorrow we start our search." He turned to walk out.

"Cason," she called, and he faced her. "I guess I should thank you again."

He gave her a curious look. "For what?"

She wasn't any good at this sort of thing. "You know. For helping me with the outlaws."

A warm gleam shone in his eyes, and he smiled at her. "Don't bother. I like the idea of you owing me."

Chapter

⇒ 20 ⇐

Rosellen felt different as she walked out the door to meet Cason in the dining room. She'd told him the truth when she said she wore a dress to church every Sunday, but she'd never felt as if she belonged in a dress. For as long as she could remember, she'd wanted to have as much freedom in her clothing as her brothers had.

But as she had twirled in front of the mirror in the beautiful dress she now wore, she felt different, she looked different, she *was* different. Now she didn't want to take off the gorgeous striped skirt and blouse and step into her dark brown trousers and shirt.

The silky blue blouse buttoned up the front to a high collar and a white satin bow. The long sleeves had wide tight cuffs with tiny covered buttons that ran halfway up her forearm. The blouse nipped in at the waist and then flared gently over her hips. The skirt was full and draped in beautiful folds down to the tops of her new kid shoes.

The seamstress and her two helpers had spent all

afternoon with Rosellen, measuring, cutting, and hemming clothes to fit her. Luckily the seamstress made most of her clothes to fit tall, well-shaped women. She told Rosellen she could always make a dress shorter or smaller, but it was difficult to make them longer and fuller.

Rosellen had balked at all the clothing the seamstress wanted to fit to her, but the woman insisted she had orders to completely dress Rosellen, from corsets and petticoats to nightgown and robe. She gave up telling the woman no and allowed herself to be pampered.

Now as she rounded the corner and walked into the beautiful lobby, which was filled with elegantly clad people chatting quietly, Rosellen didn't feel at all out of place. To her astonishment she felt completely comfortable dressed as a lady.

The man who had registered them into the hotel was behind the desk. She walked over to him and said, "I'm to meet Mr. Murdock in the dining room. Would you point me in the right direction, please?"

He looked her over with appreciation, and a genuine smile lifted the corners of his mouth. "Please allow me to escort you to Mr. Murdock's table." He rushed from behind the counter and held out his arm for her.

Rosellen wasn't sure that she'd ever been properly escorted anywhere in her life, but she gently touched the crook of the man's arm and walked with him. She caught the eye of a man she passed. He smiled and nodded to her. She returned the greeting. But just as quickly she saw another man smiling at her and then another before she made it into the dining room and saw Cason rising from his chair at the small white linen–draped table.

His shining brown eyes swept her up and down, causing a tingling of expectation to prickle her skin. His expression seemed to be filled with the promise of something wonderful. When she approached him, he reached for her hand, lifted it to his lips, and kissed the back of it.

Rosellen gasped softly. She was so stunned she didn't even hear what Cason said to the desk clerk. No man had ever kissed her hand. Breathless, she sank onto the chair he held out for her.

"You are very beautiful tonight, Rosellen, very womanly." He seated himself opposite her.

"Thank you," she answered, her voice sounding more natural than she felt at the moment.

All of a sudden she understood why she'd never cared about dressing like a woman: she'd never met a man who made her feel like a woman; she'd never met a man she wanted to dress up for, until Cason.

"You are very handsome tonight, too."

"I'm afraid Buster wouldn't approve."

"Why is that? It looks as if your tailor did a fine job on your clothes."

"He did, but Buster would be upset that I don't have on a starched collar and necktie. He considers it the mark of a gentleman to know how to tie those damn things and to wear one every day."

She laughed softly. He returned her smile and made her stomach flutter. His brand-new white shirt with banded collar was buttoned tight. His clean-shaven face looked smooth. If they had been in their room she would have leaned forward and kissed his cheek. "I think you look like a gentleman."

"When I first saw you shouldering your way into the saloon with your gun strapped to your hip, it was easy for me to believe you'd never been courted. Most men are afraid of a woman who knows how to use a Colt, but if you look like this every Sunday morning, I'm surprised the preacher could keep his mind on the sermon."

Rosellen blushed at his compliment. "Cason, that's sacrilegious."

"It's the truth."

"I have to admit my Sunday dresses aren't made of such fine a material or so well stitched as this one."

His gaze lingered on her face. "I'm not talking about your clothes. You make the clothes beautiful. The men in Poppy don't deserve you if they haven't shown up at your door at least once a month demanding to court you."

Rosellen beamed at his praise. It was the best compliment he could give her. She was delighted to know that she was tough enough to intimidate someone when she was dressed like a man but soft enough to look like a woman and catch a man's eyes when she wanted to. If Cason liked her better in these clothes, then she wanted to dress this way and please him.

That thought startled her. When had she started caring what Cason thought of her?

"From time to time I've had offers from men who wanted to come courting, but I was never interested."

Until Cason came along, she had never met anyone who made her feel this way. She had never wanted a man to touch or kiss her, never wanted to lie with a man, until she met Cason.

And looking at him now, she was beginning to understand why she felt the way she did. She couldn't possibly be falling in love with Cason, could she? All of the signs were there. The way she had responded to his lovemaking. The fact that she wanted to look pretty for him. The way she had cried over what happened to his mother.

She hadn't planned on falling in love with Cason Murdock, and she didn't know what she was going to do about her feelings for him.

A pang of worry nipped at her heart. How could she face her family knowing how she felt about the man who was going to destroy her town? Would they understand if she told them that he was really a good man and it was only what had happened in the past that drove him to seek revenge?

Even if she could explain her feelings to her family, what about Cason. There was no way he could fall in love with the daughter of the man he believed had murdered his father. He had already warned her that they would have to part one day.

That wasn't fair. It broke her heart. But their destiny been ordained by their fathers years ago.

She looked at Cason. He was motioning to a woman in a little white lacy cap who wore a matching starched apron over her dress.

Rosellen might not have Cason in her life forever, but she had him tonight. A smile touched Rosellen's lips. She hadn't ever run from anything in her life, and she wouldn't run from fate, either.

"Are you ready to order dinner?" the waitress asked.

Cason looked at Rosellen and saw her smiling. He turned to the woman and said, "We'd like to start with a bottle of your best wine."

Cason had called it right when he considered Rosellen Lattimer trouble with a capital *T*. He'd been hungry when he walked into the dining room, but he couldn't keep his mind on the deliciously rare steak or the fine wine for thinking about Rosellen and how much he wanted to lay her on that soft bed in their room, gaze at her beautiful body, and make love to her all night long. And judging from the way she kept looking at him, he suspected that she was thinking the same thing.

He'd been hungry for her since he looked up and saw her walking across the dining room toward him. She needed to put on dresses and wear her hair up all the time. He was dying to kiss that soft skin just below her ear. And if Rosellen were his wife, he'd never let her wear brown or trousers. Cason mentally shook himself. What the hell was he thinking—if she were his wife?

A cold dose of reality hit him, and he sipped the last of his wine. He'd told the truth when he said he'd kill any man who touched her.

Rosellen belonged to him. He truly cared about her. That was the reason he hated himself when he made her cry. That was why there had been a wrench in his gut at the train station when he thought he wanted to lose her until he looked back and couldn't see her following him.

He'd felt it again when he was told there was only one room. He could have taken the room and forced her to go elsewhere, but he wanted her with him. When she told the clerk they'd take the room, he had been relieved.

Even though he'd tried to deny it many times, things had changed between them, and Rosellen knew it too. They were no longer fighting their attraction.

He wanted to be with her.

He wanted her with him.

Always, not just at this hotel, not just in Denver, but forever. But what were they going to do about the past? It stood between them like a gorge as wide as any he'd ever seen. He had to find Dodge. The man had to be alive, and Cason needed to find him and put to rest the demons that had possessed him. And the town didn't deserve to thrive. The people of Poppy should be scattered like leaves before a vagrant wind.

Cason looked across the table at Rosellen, who was enjoying her apple pie. Caring for a woman was such a new feeling for him that he wanted to run it around in his mind and make sure it was a lasting feeling.

Maybe he was just thinking this way because she was so beautiful tonight or because he'd drunk the wine and there was a convenient bed nearby. He didn't want to be separated from her right now, but maybe he would feel different tomorrow.

Either way, nothing would change between them. They weren't going to change their minds about their fathers.

"Why are you so quiet?"

Cason blinked to clear his thoughts. "I was letting you finish your apple pie."

"Delicious."

She ran her tongue over her lips and made a light smacking noise that sent shivers of desire up Cason's back. He ached to feel her lips upon his and to dip his tongue into the sweetness of her mouth. He didn't know how he was going to get through the night without touching her.

"I'm glad you enjoyed the meal." He laid his napkin beside his empty plate and wished he hadn't finished the wine. He could have used one more glass.

"What were you thinking about?" she said.

"That I've never sat in a dining room with a beautiful woman before."

"Really? But you said you and Buster had been to Denver before and— I mean, I assumed you'd courted women when you were here. After all, you're handsome, wealthy, and available."

He gave her a crooked grin. "You don't take the local saloon girl out to dinner. Other than you, that's the only kind of woman I'm familiar with. I've never stayed in one town long enough to court a woman."

"I guess we've both missed out on some things in our lives and gotten a late start on . . ."

He smiled when she blushed. For all her rough talk, she didn't want to say "making love." And he didn't want to tell her he'd been with more women than he could remember.

"Being here with you like this, I don't feel as if I missed out on anything," he said.

She lowered her dark lashes over her clear blue eyes. "That was a nice thing to say."

"It's the truth."

Rosellen was a woman of rare inner strength. And the more he was with her the more he wanted to be with her.

Her heavy-lidded gaze wandered over his face. "What are you going to do once you've—" She stopped.

"Made Poppy a ghost town?"

Frustration clouded her eyes. "Closed the mine," she countered.

"I don't know," he answered truthfully. He'd been tortured inside for so long he didn't know what he'd do once his revenge was complete.

He looked around the elaborately decorated room. It was almost deserted. They'd stayed late. Maybe it was best she'd brought up the subject. Discussing it might give him some perspective on their relationship.

A lump formed in his chest. "The truth is that I never really believed we'd strike it rich, so I never planned beyond going back to Poppy and shutting down the mine, but I like Denver. I might decide to settle here and open some kind of business."

"What is Buster going to do?"

She seemed unusually calm. He wouldn't have expected that, considering what they were talking about.

"He'll probably do whatever I do. I've tried to get him to go back east and visit his family, but I don't know if he ever will. For some reason he resists the idea of going home."

A touch of sadness settled on her face. "Do you

think it's because he lost his arm? Maybe he doesn't want them to know."

"Could be."

"I guess we all have things about our lives that we don't want our family to know about."

Cason felt an unexpected sharp pain in his chest. "You don't want your family to know we made love, do you?"

Her eyes widened. "No . . . yes. I mean, I wouldn't want them to know because it's none of their business, not because of who you are, if that's what you're thinking."

"You're lying, Rosellen."

"Don't accuse me."

Tension knotted in his throat. "You wouldn't want your mother, your brothers, or anyone else in your precious town to know that you made love to the man who's going to prove Henry Lattimer was a murderer and destroy the town of Poppy. Admit it."

She leaned forward. "I'm not ashamed of what we did."

"Yes, you are. And you should be."

Cold blue eyes pierced him. "Stop it. You don't know what you're talking about. Making love to you isn't the first bad thing I've ever done."

He'd caught her. "See, you do think it was bad."

She clenched her teeth to keep her voice from rising. "No, dammit, you're twisting my words."

"How can you be considered for the job of sheriff if you've slept with an outlaw's son?"

She opened her mouth to speak, then stopped and stared intently into his eyes. She settled back in her chair and calmed down. "You're trying to pick a fight with me, aren't you?"

"No," he lied.

"Yes, you are."

This time he leaned forward and softly punctuated

every word. "Then listen to me, Rosellen. What I'm saying is for your own good."

She remained relaxed and in control, showing her strength. "I never listened to my parents or my brothers when they told me that, and I don't intend to listen to you."

"I'm giving you an out here. You should listen to me and take it."

"No, you're issuing a challenge, and I never back down from a challenge."

"You need to this time, Rosellen."

He needed some help from her. He wasn't made of stone. He remembered how she'd felt beneath him, how he'd felt when she touched him. He hadn't wanted to make love to her because of who she was, but he hadn't been able to stop himself then and he couldn't now.

Did she know what she was doing to him? Didn't she know he was trying to be chivalrous? Didn't she know he was aching to take her back to the room and love her all night long?

"It's not going to work, is it?" he asked.

"What? Your challenge?"

"No. You and me not wanting each other. Staying away from each other."

Her eyes met his and held fast. She shook her head.

"Can I take that as an invitation?"

She nodded.

"Do you know what's going to happen between us if we go back to that room together with you looking at me the way you are right now."

"I know."

His heart skipped a beat. He didn't need to be convinced. "Then let's get the hell out of this dining room."

Cason felt her heat when he touched the small of her back as they left the table. After all he'd said to her, after the way he'd treated her, she still wanted him. The lobby was a blur as they walked through it. All he knew was that he couldn't wait to get Rosellen inside that room.

They stopped outside their suite, and he unlocked the door. She walked inside. Cason stepped in behind her, closed the door, and immediately took her in his arms and crushed her to him.

Rosellen fell against the door as their breath and then their lips met in a long, hard, hungry kiss that was meant to stir their already heated passions.

They were charged by a wild awakening and neither of them wanted to let go.

"I've been wanting this all evening," he whispered into her mouth.

"Me too." She started unbuttoning his shirt.

His lips left hers, and he kissed the soft skin underneath her jawline and down to the top of her collar, then back up to that delicate spot behind her ear that he'd wanted to touch all night.

She arched her head back to give him access to wherever his lips wanted to go. With frantic fingers he pulled the end of the ribbon that circled her throat, untied it, and let it fall to the floor at their feet. He worked on unfastening the tiny buttons running between her breasts while he pressed her against the door with his body.

Cason heard her heavy breathing and knew that she didn't want to wait for sweet words, loving touches, or lingering kisses. When he had the front of her dress open, he reached inside her corset to free her breasts for his open mouth.

A soft moan of pleasure wafted past his ear, and Cason became more desperate to plunge inside her hot wetness. He didn't want to take time to undress and possibly lose the unbanked fires burning inside them.

Sucking gently, he savored the exquisite taste of her breast while he unbuttoned his trousers with one hand and shoved them down past his knees. He gathered up the skirt and petticoats that billowed around their legs and lifted them up around her waist with one hand while he stripped her drawers down her legs with the other.

Unable to wait, he found her center and, with one single motion, drove himself deep inside her. Rosellen jerked but held him closer to her when he tried to back away.

"No, don't stop," she whispered as her hands cupped his buttocks, pressing him to her. "Please."

That was all Cason needed to hear. He kissed her forehead, her eyes, her lips. He whispered her name softly in her ear over and over again. He couldn't have loved her more than he did at that moment. He vowed to find a way to make her his forever.

He was breathless, but he wasn't ready to bring this to an end. He needed Rosellen again and again. He'd never been with a woman who enjoyed his touch as much as Rosellen did.

She clung to him and moved with him until she let out a pleasurable cry of completion. Her fingers dug into his back with enough force to cause an exquisite form of torture that sent his own climax exploding through him.

Their union was so powerful he couldn't have remained standing if Rosellen had not been braced against the door. He rested against her bosom, loving the taste of her, the feel of her in his arms.

"I shouldn't have taken you this way," he mumbled, breathless.

A soft, short chuckle passed Rosellen's lips. "Let's do it again."

He raised his head and looked into her smiling face.

"You mean you're not mad I didn't take my time and make love to you properly?"

She inhaled deeply, a contented expression on her face. "What wasn't proper about it?"

"It was hard and fast."

"And I loved it." She touched his cheek with an open palm. "You enjoyed it, didn't you?"

"Hell, I loved it." *I love you.*

God, yes, he loved her, and he wanted her to know it. He squeezed his eyes shut and rested his head against her forehead for a moment, calming down after the heat, the exhilaration, of their out-of-control passion. But he couldn't tell her until his business with her father was settled. Like it or not, he'd made one hell of a mistake: he'd fallen in love with Rosellen Lattimer.

That thought sobered him. He had been foolish to think anything between them could work. When the mine closed and her brothers had to move to find jobs, she would hate him. He dropped her skirts, then reached down and pulled up his trousers, covering himself.

"Cason."

He looked up at her.

"Will you sleep with me?"

He shook his head. He was filled with passion and desire, but he was also humbled. After all they'd said to each other, after all that was between them, she wanted him to come to her bed. "I have no right to continue to make love to you."

"You make me feel wonderful."

He cupped her chin. "Yes, right now, but what about later? What about next month? What about next year, when there's no one left in the town of Poppy?"

He saw the pain flash across her face, and hurting her wounded him.

"Don't make me think about that, Cason."

Her words were so earnest he couldn't ignore them.

"I shouldn't have taken you with your back pressed against the door. I shouldn't be standing here with you like this, wanting you with every fiber of my being. You're a fine woman, not an upstairs whore. Men don't just sleep with women like you. They marry you first."

"I'm not asking for marriage."

"I know." *But you should be.*

"Cason, I've never let propriety keep me from doing something I wanted to do. I don't plan to start now. Sleep with me."

He looked at her with her hair tumbling from her chignon, her blouse unbuttoned, baring her beautiful breasts, and he knew he loved her too much to reject her invitation. He would have liked to convince himself that she was like all the other women he'd been with, but his heart and his head wouldn't let him. She was special.

He loved Rosellen. He was sure of that.

His throat ached to tell her he loved her, but he merely said, "Come here." He pulled her into his arms and kissed her tenderly for a long time. They had mated. Now they were going to make love.

Cason took his time and undressed her there in the sitting room, leaving her skirt, blouse, and petticoats scattered in front of the door. He left his own clothes there, too. Then, sliding one arm around her back and the other underneath her buttocks, he lifted her in his arms and carried her to the bedroom.

The wall sconces had been lit and burned low. A lamp on the bedside table cast a pale yellow light upon the small room. The covers had been turned back to reveal gleaming white sheets. He laid her on the bed and carefully straddled her, keeping his weight off her legs with his knees, looking at her.

Since he was fifteen years old he had sat around campfires and heard men talk about begging their wives to let them touch them, forcing their wives, and finally giving up and going to prostitutes. Cason knew that would never happen with Rosellen. She enjoyed lovemaking as much as he did.

She ran her open hand over the crest of his shoulder, across his upper chest, and down his other arm. He was acutely aware of her every touch.

"Your muscles are so big and firm," she said. "It's no wonder you can hold me so tight."

His senses came alive to her praise. "I'm softer than I used to be. Working a mountainside with a pickax and shovel day after day gives a man all kind of muscles. I've got to start working again, or I'm going to go soft."

Rosellen smiled and dropped her gaze to below his abdomen. "I know one place you won't go soft."

His throbbing desire for her showed in the glowing light and made him all the harder. His muscles tightened under her touch as her fingertips grazed the length of his shaft.

"Rosellen . . ."

Pleasing Cason gave Rosellen a deep feeling of satisfaction. He whispered her name over and over as she loved him. She wasn't gentle, and she knew he didn't want her to be. Their relationship was too volatile for that.

He stretched his arms up over his head and allowed her to have her way.

"You're pushing me over the edge," he whispered.

Go, her mind answered, content to give him enjoyment.

But Cason wasn't ready for that.

He changed places with her and pleasured her with his lips and tongue until she cried out with shuddering gasps of delight. Only then did he lower his strong body over her and stretch out his legs.

Rosellen loved the way his chest flattened against her breasts and fueled the fire of burning desire inside her. She didn't think she would ever get tired of making love with Cason.

They kissed and caressed over and over again, enjoying the taste and the feel of each other. Relishing the heaviness of his weight upon her, she let her hands glide over his chest, across his flat nipples, over his shoulders, and down his arms to the soft skin on the underside of his wrist. She didn't want to miss tasting and touching one square inch of him.

He supported himself with one hand while he caressed her breasts with the other. He let his hand glide down to her narrow waist and over her shapely hip.

She was sensitive to his every touch, the slight roughness of his beginning stubble as it scraped against her skin. His lips left feathery tickles of moisture across her skin that made her nipples harden and stand erect, ready for his mouth to cover them with its warmth.

He shifted his body and nudged her legs apart with his knee. She accepted his hardened arousal as he slipped smoothly inside her.

Chest to chest, abdomen to abdomen, he buried himself deep inside her. Without effort, a natural familiar rhythm took over, and they moved together as one. Heat built in the pit of her stomach and in the valley between her legs. She couldn't suppress her soft cries of pleasure.

Her fingers and the palms of her hands squeezed and kneaded the muscles of his back and the planes of his shoulders and hips.

As she moved eagerly beneath him, Cason constantly stroked her until her senses could no longer resist what her body cried out for. She let herself fly, arching toward him, pulling him closer, letting love take over and guide her to completion.

Cason cupped the back of her head and pulled her to his chest until his own body was racked with shudders, and then he relaxed upon her.

"My beautiful Rosellen, I've never been with a woman like you."

She lay as content as she could be, knowing that she loved him and that he saw her only as one more woman in a long roster of women, knowing that one day they would have to part.

Her mind went back in time to something she remembered her father telling her brothers when he thought she wasn't listening: "Men don't love the women they have sex with before they marry. They just use them. Then they marry the good girls."

Rosellen moistened her lips and smiled to herself. She'd decided early in life that the "good girls" didn't know what they were missing. Swimming in a pond, racing on a horse, smoking, and shooting bottles off a fence post— that was a hell of a lot more exciting than sewing, knitting, and cooking. Why should boys and men have all the fun?

A sadness gripped her. She wished she could have more time with Cason. She knew Cason was worried about her, and she appreciated that, but she'd been doing things her own way too long to stop now. Now that she knew she loved Cason, being here with him like this was all the more special. Tomorrow they would look for Dodge.

"Rosellen, you wear me out," he whispered.

"Is that good or bad?" she asked.

"That's very good." He smiled then kissed her tenderly on the lips.

A noise awakened Cason, and he stirred in the bed. The room was bright with morning light. There was muffled shouting and banging on a door.

Rosellen rose up on her elbows. "What's that?" she asked when the loud knocking continued.

Cason gave her a sweet, brief kiss on the lips. "Probably some drunk trying to get into the wrong room. He'll go away when he realizes his key won't fit. How do you feel this morning?"

"I could sleep for a few more hours. You kept me awake too long last night."

"Mmm. I don't remember hearing you ask me to stop."

"Why would I want to do that? I enjoyed making love."

"So did I. Come here and we'll start all over again." He pulled her into his arms and kissed the warm skin behind her ear.

"Not with that noise going on." Rosellen listened for a moment to the muffled shouts. "It sounds as if the banging is on our door."

"Could be. You stay here. I'll take care of whoever it is and send them on their way." He rolled off the bed and headed for the sitting room to get his trousers.

"Good-looking backside," she called out to him.

"I'll let you see it again sometime." Cason turned around and grinned at her, then kept walking.

Taking orders was something Rosellen didn't know how to do. She rose from the bed and put on her new robe. Whatever was going on, she wanted to know about it.

Cason opened the door as Rosellen walked into the sitting room, tying her sash. Two large men plowed into the room and charged Cason.

Chapter

⇥ 21 ⇤

Cason ducked and missed the first punch, but a second meaty fist caught him under the chin, snapping his head back. Another quick fist plowed into his stomach and bent him double.

"Walter, Jarred, Stop!" Rosellen yelled.

Cason groaned. Pain splintered his chin and shot up to his eyes, but he came up fighting and landed a powerful blow on a hard cheek. He caught a glancing fist under his jaw, and his head snapped back painfully again.

He threw a forceful hard right that landed in a large gut. Someone stopped him cold with an arm strike across the throat. Cason lost his breath and fell backward, knocking a chair over on top of him.

"Stop, you big oafs! Dammit, stop this!"

Cason heard Rosellen yelling, but he was too winded to speak or rise from the floor. He looked up with blurred vision and saw Rosellen riding one man's back and boxing his ears. Fear for her safety spurred him to help her. Coughing, he tried to rise, but a large foot landed on his chest and stomped him down.

"Stay put."

Rosellen was gently deposited on the floor, but the man held on to her arm.

"You idiots make me sorry I ever had brothers," she yelled. "Get your foot off him and help him stand," she snapped.

Cason's eyes widened. These big apes were her brothers? No wonder they were so damn mad.

The foot left his chest. Cason brushed away the arm that offered help and held his throat, struggling to breathe as he climbed to his feet. He wanted to smash his fist into their faces again, but he knew it would be futile to tackle those two big men again.

He hurt in too many places to count as he straightened. He wiped blood from the corner of his mouth with his fingertips. Thank God Rosellen didn't embarrass him by rushing over to ask him if he was all right. He wasn't, but he didn't want anyone in this room to know it. His jaw ached, and his mouth felt swollen.

Rosellen brushed her hair away from her face and straightened her robe. She looked over at Cason. Her expression seemed to tell him to back off and let her handle this. He wanted to tear into her brothers again, but Rosellen's cool composure kept him silent. If she wanted to take care of them, out of respect for her he'd let her do it—up to a point.

"Cason, meet Jarred, my oldest brother, and Walter, the youngest brother."

Rosellen's two brothers were giants. They were stockier and heavier than Cason, and after he'd spent most of the night making love to their sister, they were much stronger than he was.

He blinked rapidly, trying to clear his eyes, and realized part of the problem was sweat from the heated fight running in them. He wiped his forehead and eyes with the back of his hand and focused again on Rosellen and her brothers. He saw a mixture of shock, confusion, and anger in her eyes. Her cheeks and neck were flushed.

"What the hell are you two doing here?" she asked.

"Looking for you," Walter remarked angrily. "Why did you run off like that?"

"I left a note telling Mama where I was going and what I was doing. Why did you come after me?"

"How could we not come after you, Rose?" Jarred said. "You're our sister."

"Yeah, we came after you all right," Walter piped up. "But it looks like we got here too damn late, judging from the cozy scene I see here." He reached down and picked up her petticoat, then threw it back down on the floor in disgust.

She folded her arms across her chest. "I don't believe this. I can look after myself. You two know that better than anybody. You've never treated me like a sister you had to take care of before. I've always been one of the brothers. Why have you changed now?"

"We've been trying to get you to dress and act like a woman for the past two years. You wouldn't do it."

"You started too late."

Jarred sighed deeply. "You've done a lot of stupid things in your life, Rose, but you've never run off after a man before."

"I did most of those stupid things because one of you goaded me into it."

"That's not important right now."

"You're right. I'm upset that you thought you had to follow me."

"No, you're upset that we caught you monkeying around with this bastard."

Cason stayed quiet. So far Rosellen was doing fine.

"What's going on here, Rose?" Jarred asked. "Is this what it looks like?"

"What are you missing here?" Walter snapped at Jarred. "Does it have to be rubbed into your face? These are women's clothes," he kicked the skirt up into the air. "And this is his shirt on the floor, too. Dammit, he's made her his whore."

Rage struck Cason. He bent his head and plowed his shoulder into Walter's chest. It was like running into an elephant. Walter stumbled, then fell backward on his rump and grunted.

"Stop this fighting. Cason, don't," Rosellen said, grabbing his arm to keep him from jumping on top of her brother.

Cason stared into her eyes. The air was thick with tension. "I won't let anyone say things like that about you."

"It's all right." Her eyes pleaded with him to understand. "My brothers and I have called each other names for years. I'm used to it."

"I'm not, and I won't get used to it," he said with unwavering conviction.

"You son of a murdering bastard," Walter ground out, struggling to his feet.

"I don't care what you say about me," Cason said in a low voice, "but keep your filthy mouth shut about Rosellen."

"You can't tell me what I can say to her. She's my sister."

Cason's eyes narrowed, and he calmly said, "Leave comments about her out of this or I will kill you."

"You don't scare me, you hunk of dog shit."

"Hold your vile tongue, Walter, and let's try to discuss this calmly."

"You stay calm. I can't. Open your eyes, Jarred, and look around the room. It's clear they were in bed together, and it's clear you don't give a damn, but I do."

"Of course I care, but going crazy over this isn't

going to solve anything." Jarred turned to Cason. "Look, Murdock, she's the reason we're here. We can't leave her out of this."

"That's exactly what you're doing." Rosellen stepped in the middle of the three men. "All of you are talking about me as if I weren't standing right here in front of you."

"Rose, we know what this looks like," Walter said. "Start at the beginning and tell us what's going on here."

"Nothing I intend to explain to either of you. I'm angry at you for following me here. How did you find me, anyway?"

"We took the train the day after you left," Jarred said. "We've been looking all over Denver for your name or his. We thought he might know where you were, but we never expected to find you in his room."

"Or his bed," Walter added. "My God, Rosellen, this is the man who's shutting down the mine and putting all of us out of work, and you're sleeping with him! What's happened to you?"

Cason watched as Rosellen stood straight, her chin held high, accepting her brothers' criticism without flinching. He admired the fact they didn't intimidate her even though she was definitely at a disadvantage. What a hell of a mess he had put her in.

Contrary to what he'd said last night, he'd never really thought about how her family would treat her if they ever found out about them, because he never expected anyone to find them together. He knew Rosellen meant trouble for him, but he hadn't planned on making any for her.

"We were going to take you home, but now I guess you'll have to get married first."

Rosellen gasped. "What?"

Cason stiffened. "What the hell are you talking about?"

"You had no right to touch her." Walter pointed an angry finger at Cason. "Now, dammit, we insist you make an honest woman out of her by marrying her."

"Wait a minute," Rosellen demanded. "This is *my* life you're talking about. I've never let the two of you make decisions for me, and I'm not about to let you make an important decision like this."

"He's ruined you for any other man, Rose," Jarred said. "Now he can marry you. You don't have a choice."

"Of course I do," she answered indignantly. "I don't need you two butting into my life, coming in here and threatening me or Cason. You have followed me for no reason. I know what I'm doing. I think I'm old enough to decide when I need to get married and to whom."

Cason wasn't sure how to help her. He didn't know what she wanted or expected from him. He wasn't about to declare his love her for in front of her brothers. And he was absolutely sure Rosellen wouldn't want him cowering before her brothers under any circumstances.

"No one's getting married just because you say so," Cason answered.

"Want to bet?" Walter pulled a gun from his jacket pocket and pointed it at Cason. "It's like this, Murdock. I could kill you right now and save the mine and the town."

"Are you crazy, Walter?" Rosellen exclaimed.

"No." Walter's gaze stayed zeroed on Cason, and he kept his weapon leveled at Cason's chest.

It wasn't the first time Cason had looked down the barrel of a gun. It happened often in the prospecting business. Claim jumpers were around every bend. But he didn't like what he saw in Walter's eyes. There was more at stake here than his sister's reputation.

"Put that gun away before you hurt someone," Rosellen said.

"That's my intention."

"You can't shoot a man in cold blood."

"Watch me. If I pull this trigger everyone will come running and see that we caught you in his bed."

Rosellen glanced frantically from brother to brother. "You'd hang or go to jail," she exclaimed.

"What jury would convict me?"

"Stop this, Walter."

"To save our jobs and our families, I can do it. It's called survival, little sister."

"What?" She took a step back. "Jarred, say something," she demanded.

"You shouldn't have run off with him, Rose."

"I don't believe this. I don't believe I'm hearing this kind of talk from my brothers."

"The whole town is going to fall apart when the mine closes," Jarred added. "Families are already talking about moving away."

Cason listened carefully to what her brothers were saying, and he saw fear in Rosellen's eyes. But he wasn't going to give in and say he'd marry her, gun or no gun. He didn't like the idea of her brothers thinking they could frighten him into doing anything.

"Either he marries you or he dies—right now," Walter said and pulled back the hammer on the gun.

"What do you really want?" Cason asked. "Do you want me to marry Rosellen or are you trying to prevent me from closing the mine?"

"Both," Jarred admitted.

"We'll settle for one," Walter said.

"That's all you'll get," Cason said. "Which one do you want?"

Cason heard Rosellen's startled gasp. He glanced over at her and saw that she was trembling. She didn't trust her brothers to choose marriage to save her reputation over saving the town.

His heart broke for her. She'd given herself freely to him, often and joyously. It was wrong of him to put her in a position to be rejected by him and her brothers.

"All right," he said quickly. "I'll send a telegram telling Buster to pay off the guards and send them home, and to keep the mine open."

Rosellen didn't look at him. She stood rigid, staring dispiritedly at Walter.

"For how long?" Jarred asked.

"At least a year. You have my word."

"How do we know we can trust you?"

"I'll put it in writing and make it legal. Let's go over to the telegraph office."

Walter turned to Rosellen. "I guess that tells you what he thinks about marrying you."

At the telegraph office while Cason sent the wire and wrote out his agreement, Rosellen paced nervously. She'd told herself a hundred times in the last hour that it didn't matter that Cason didn't want to marry her. She'd understood that from the beginning.

She'd just had no idea it would hurt so much when she was actually faced with the reality. She'd heard women talk about being brokenhearted, but she'd never known what it felt like until now.

Her brothers had dealt her a hard blow, too. When given the choice between her honor and the town's livelihood, they had quickly chosen the latter. But what disturbed her even more was the look in Walter's eyes. For a few moments she thought he really wanted to shoot Cason. Even now she wanted to tell herself that she hadn't seen malice in Walter's demeanor, but she knew he was capable of murder.

At that moment Walter had looked like their father.

Her throat thickened just thinking about what she'd seen, what her brothers had said. Had her father truly moved to the wrong side of the law? Had he justified his crimes the same way Walter wanted to justify killing Cason? Would she herself be guilty of that someday? Her stomach cramped with a fierce pain she'd never felt before.

No!

What was she thinking? How could she doubt the spotless reputation of her brothers and her father? She wouldn't do it. Henry Lattimer was innocent, and Rosellen couldn't let thoughts like that enter her mind again. Her confusion was Cason's fault. He had confused her.

Rosellen had to keep her mind off Cason, herself, and her brothers before she did something really stupid, like break down and cry. It was bad enough she'd cried in front of Cason that day. She couldn't let her brothers see her cry, too.

But she'd come to Denver to do a job, and no matter how much she might want to go home and forget about Cason's vow to find Dodge she couldn't do it.

She was wound up too tight to let go of the past. Her mind went back over the things Gayla had said. She caught Jarred's eye and motioned for him to join her by the window. He was the oldest. If anyone remembered, he would.

"I don't know if I should leave Walter over there alone with Cason," Jarred said, joining her by the window in the small telegraph office. "Those two do not like each other."

"Is it any wonder?"

"No."

"We'll keep an eye on them."

She looked over to where Cason stood at the counter, writing. Her heart lurched. Oh, why had she fallen in love with him? Of all the men in Colorado, why had she taken a shine to Cason Murdock?

She mentally shook herself and turned her attention to Jarred. "Do you recall Papa ever mentioning a cousin or a friend by the name of Dodge?"

He wrinkled his forehead. "Yeah, I remember that name. Haven't heard it in years, though. He was a big fella who came to the house once or twice. I think he stayed mostly at the jail. We didn't have any extra beds so Papa let him sleep in one of the cells. Why?"

The muscles in her neck tightened. All right. So there was a man named Dodge who came to Poppy. That could easily be explained away. Gayla could have remembered his name if he visited her bedroom.

To Jarred Rosellen said, "I don't remember him at all."

"That's not surprising. You couldn't have been more than five or six years old. And like I said, he didn't come to the house but once or twice. But you must remember something about him or why would you be asking me about him now?

Rosellen rubbed her arms as if she felt cold. She didn't want to know any more, but she couldn't stop herself from saying, "Ah . . . yes, I thought I remembered something in connection with his name and money."

"That's right. Some time after he left, Papa said he'd died and left us some money. It wasn't much, but a lawyer sent it to us every month until the money ran out. I remember Papa went to Denver a few weeks later to talk with the lawyer."

Rosellen didn't feel well. Her legs didn't want to hold her upright any longer. Jarred's story sounded too much like Gayla's, but Jarred's story put their father in a better light.

Why would the saloon owner have made up that lie about her father? Maybe she wanted to hurt Rosellen's father. Yes, that had to be it. As sheriff, Henry must have done something to harm Gayla's business, and she was retaliating.

"Hey, are you all right?" Jarred asked. "You don't look so good."

"I'm fine," Rosellen lied, but she knew her voice revealed the truth. She was hurting from Cason's rejection, her brothers' rejection, and their unexpected visit. She was hurting from doubting her father.

"I think you need to sit down."

Rosellen would have shaken her head, but she was too light-headed. "I just didn't expect my big brothers to come to town and start ordering me around. It was a shock, you know."

"Come back home with us, Rose. You don't belong here, living like this—with him. If you believe he will honor his promise and keep the mine open, there's no reason for you to stay. Think about your future."

"I can't go back yet. I have some other things to do."

"What?"

"Things I don't want to talk about right now. I want you to go back and tell Mama and Simon I'm fine. And I am, Jarred. I know what I've done. I know what I'm doing. And I'm not sorry."

"Rose."

"Don't judge me, please?"

His eyes softened. "I'm not. We always knew you were different from most girls. Maybe that was our fault for pushing you to do things you shouldn't have been doing."

"I'll take that as a compliment."

Jarred shook his head. "Cason Murdock is going to hurt you. You know that, don't you?"

She knew, but she couldn't stop herself. She loved him. It was a violation of all she held dear, but even knowing Cason didn't want to marry her didn't keep her from loving him. She hadn't asked to feel this way about him. She'd tried not to, but she couldn't keep from falling in love with him.

"I know. But there's something inside me that won't let me leave him. I've fallen in love with him, Jarred."

"Oh, hell, Rose, what did you go and do that for? He's not good enough for you."

"Believe me, I didn't plan it this way." She hurt inside, but she hid it. "And don't worry about me. He doesn't want me, remember?"

"We can force him to marry you."

"No. No, I don't want that. I couldn't bear it. Can you imagine what it would be like knowing a man was forced to marry you? Don't put me through that."

Jarred nodded but didn't speak.

Rosellen's gaze drifted back to Cason. He handed a piece of paper to the man behind the counter and started writing again. No, she wasn't sorry for anything that had happened between them.

"You know, Jarred, I understand now why Cason wanted to close the mine."

"You're either blind or looking at life through the eyes of love."

"I've been called blind before," she said, remembering Cason's words about the people of Poppy.

"As far as I'm concerned, no reason is good enough to want to ruin a whole town,"

"No, but he has a reason that comes as close as you could get."

"He's got you thinking with your heart—looking and dressing like a woman."

She nodded, then smiled, but she was looking at Cason not Jarred. Even from this distance she could see the swelling at in the corner of his mouth. "Yeah, for the first time in my life I want to wear dresses. How about that?"

"That would be fine if he were worthy of you, but I don't think he is."

"I'm sure you're wrong about him. Even with everything that's between us, it feels right to be with him."

She was unsure of a lot of things, but she was no longer unsure of her feelings for Cason. Whether or not he wanted to marry her, she loved him and would stay with him until they found Dodge or gave up trying.

"What about Mama?" Jarred said.

Her throat clogged with emotion. "Take care of her. I'll try to be a good daughter when I get back."

"Are you ever coming back?"

"Of course. Poppy is my home," she said, although she didn't say it with the conviction she usually felt, and that surprised her. She knew she'd never feel the same way about the people of Poppy now that she knew how they'd treated Cason and his mother.

And she hadn't settled in her mind what Cason had pointed out—that none of the men in town had come forward to help her when she was in danger. But that hadn't bothered her until Cason made her aware of it.

Was he right? Did the townspeople lack compassion and respect? Did the men of Poppy care no more for her than they had for a young man and his sick mother? Or were they content to stay on the sidelines and let her handle the danger because they assumed she was capable of handling the situation? She didn't know who was right anymore.

Cason was causing her to see everything through a different pair of eyes.

"You won't tell Mama about Cason and me, will you?"

Jarred gave her a smile and tapped her chin affectionately with the tips of his fingers. "Did I ever tell on you?"

She took a deep, sobering breath. "Jarred, if Cason

hadn't spoken up and said he wouldn't close the mine, which alternative would you have chosen? Would you have told him you wanted him to marry me?"

He hesitated, looking uncertain, then said unconvincingly, "Yes."

"What about Walter?"

"You'll have to ask him."

She glanced at Walter. No. She wouldn't ask him. He wouldn't lie, as Jarred had, and she wasn't ready to hear the truth.

Walter and Cason joined them, and they all walked out of the telegraph office and stood on the boardwalk in the bright sunshine.

"I have the signed statement," Walter said putting the letter in his pocket. "Come home with us, Rose. Don't do this to yourself."

Rosellen looked at Cason but saw nothing in his face. Damn him. Why didn't he try to persuade her one way or the other?

Because he probably doesn't want you to stay. Run.

"I'm not going home. I have business here."

"Well, my business is finished," Walter said. "Jarred, you got anything else to say before we leave?"

Jarred touched Rosellen's arm, then turned to Cason and said, "She's as strong as a mountain lion everywhere but her heart. You'll have to take care of that for her."

His words made her breath thick with emotion. Maybe Jarred did love her. She watched her brothers walk down the street, but she didn't feel the tiniest urge to join them. She knew Cason was watching her and probably wondering why she was still hanging around, but she couldn't leave him.

She took a deep breath and said, "I'm sorry for what happened. I'm ashamed of my brothers. They shouldn't have attacked you."

His expression remained solemn. "What they did wasn't your fault. Besides, I would have done the same thing if you were my sister. They were right. You should have gone back with them. You don't belong here with me."

Her heart broke as he put into words the rejection that she had feared. He didn't want her with him. She took a moment to catch her breath, then hoped her voice was even when she said, "No, I'm going to see this through to the end. I'll move to another hotel if you want me to."

His gaze feathered lightly down her face. She felt as if he'd caressed her.

"Why would I want you to do that?"

Her throat hurt and her eyes watered. "I thought maybe you were ready to be alone."

"Stay with me."

Her heart soared so fast she gasped. "All right."

His eyes stayed on hers. "Nothing's settled between us. You know that."

"I know."

"Do you want me to explain why I wouldn't agree to marry you."

"No," she answered quickly, knowing that subject had the power to make her cry, and she'd been fighting tears all morning. She couldn't take any more rejection.

"Rosellen—"

"Please, don't. I don't want to spoil what's between us with explanations. You don't owe me any, and I don't want to owe you."

"All right. Let's see if we can find anyone who knows a man named Dodge."

Chapter

⇒ 22 ⇐

Two days later Rosellen sank down on the settee, took off her new shoes, and rubbed her tired feet. She had just broken in her boots when she let that woman talk her into a new pair of high-button shoes to wear with her dresses. Rosellen must have been crazy. She was beginning to wonder what her feet would look like without blisters.

She and Cason had spent two full days walking the busy streets of Denver, going in and out of stores asking if anyone remembered a man named Dodge or a man with a scar on his left hand. They had talked with shopkeepers, hoboes, and to policemen who walked the streets. Occasionally someone would remember the name, but no one knew what had happened to the man.

In a town the size of Poppy it wouldn't have been any trouble finding out about a man who had lived there years ago. In a small town, people remembered, but Denver was a big city. It would have been easy for one man to get lost there.

Rosellen curled her feet up under her and leaned her head against the back of the settee to rest and think about Cason.

She would rather have been with him right now, but he had gone to the Miners Club, which dared to have a rule against allowing women into its headquarters. She had been furious but had finally agreed not to make a scene. She had walked back to the hotel to wait for him.

"Cason," she whispered. There was no doubt in her mind that she loved him. Yes, she wanted to find Dodge and clear up the lies about her father but she also knew that she was still here partly because she didn't want to leave Cason.

She had never given up anything she wanted without a fight, and she wasn't going to give Cason up without a fight, either. Every night when he pulled her into his arms, she was reminded that she didn't want to live without him. And yet she didn't know quite how to fight for the man she loved. Her brothers had taught her how to fight with her hands and with a gun, but she hadn't learned how to fight with her heart.

Oh, God, their nights together . . . They made love until the late hours of the evening, then again before they rose in the morning. It was as if Cason knew, as she did, that they would have to part one day and didn't want to waste a moment of their time together.

As soon as they walked through the door each evening, they ripped off their clothes and made love. They'd tried taking their lovemaking slowly, savoring each touch, but their desire for each other was too urgent. Her lips were swollen, and her breasts ached from his loving, but still she wanted him again.

A knock sounded on the door, rousing Rosellen from her thoughts. It couldn't be Cason. She'd just left him. Deciding it must be the seamstress bringing more clothes, she opened the door without bothering to ask who was there. She was stunned to see a dere-lict, holding a worn hat that he squeezed unmercifully between his wringing hands.

He reeked of rank whiskey and an unwashed body. His freshly shaven face had three nicks, and his greasy hair was plastered to his head. Still, she could see that he'd tried hard to make himself presentable.

"Can I help you?" she asked, feeling no fear, only thinking he must have knocked on the wrong door.

"Name's Pilcher, ma'am. I—I heard on the street someone in this room was looking for a man with a scar on his left hand."

A tremor shook Rosellen. Something inside her told her this man was too nervous to be trying to dupe her. "You have the right room," she said cautiously. "What information do you have?"

"I know where there's a man like that—with a scar like that. It's a far piece from here, but I remember how to get there."

Her breath was so shallow she had to clear her throat. She mentally shook herself. Why was she let-ting this man make her feel so strange? He was obvi-ously a winebibber in search of a quick dollar. He probably didn't know anything.

"I was told you'd pay money," he said and contin-ued to wring his hat. "I wouldn't ask, but my wife's sick and I could use the money for her, you see."

Rosellen wondered if the man really thought she would fall for that story. Didn't he know he smelled like a packed saloon on a hot Saturday night? But as she stared at his disreputable appearance, she knew that even a drunkard needed a bit of pride.

"I understand," she said, "but I can't give you any money until I verify your story."

"I—I can take you there, but I don't have no horse or wagon."

"How far away is this man?"

"A good ways."

Rosellen didn't know if he was just afraid to give her any more information without money in hand or if he really didn't know anything and was hoping to bluff her into giving him enough money for a bottle.

"How long has he been where he is now?" she asked, hoping to elicit enough information to make an intelligent decision.

"I was there 'bout three, four years ago, and I heard a feller mention him not more than a week or two ago."

"Was he a man about your age or was he younger?"

"Same as me, I guess. Maybe a sight older."

She pondered what to do. She didn't expect Cason to return for some time. He could be gone all afternoon. Should she tell the man to come back later, after Cason returned? No, if she sent him away he might find his drink money some other way. If there was any chance that what he said was true she had to trust him.

Besides, this wouldn't be the first time she'd gone on a wild-goose chase. Her brothers used to trick her into doing things like this all the time.

"If I hire horses from the livery, can we make it there and back before dark?"

He wiped a trembling hand across his dry lips. "Don't see why not, if we start now."

Rosellen looked at the man's eyes. He was nervous but not shifty. She was desperate to clear up this whole affair. If there was any chance this man knew Dodge, she had to take a chance on finding him.

She looked back into the room as if searching for an answer. Finally she said, "All right, I'll go with you. Give me five minutes to change clothes. Wait for me at the back entrance of the hotel."

She would not go off with this man without her gun strapped to her hip.

* * *

Rosellen and the derelict left Denver and rode for more than two hours. Rosellen was surprised to find that the man seemed to have a destination in mind and stayed steady on the course. She'd watched for trail signs in case she had to make the trip back by herself or after dark.

She was beginning to worry that the man was indeed leading her on a wild-goose chase when just over a rise she saw a small white house sitting in a clearing with the majestic rise of the Rocky Mountains behind it.

Two men sat on the front porch playing checkers, using the top of a short barrel as a table. Off to the side of the house another man was chopping wood. It was a serene, peaceful picture.

Pilcher stopped his horse. "He lives there."

"With all these other men?" She looked around for signs of horses. "What kind of place is this?"

"It's his church."

"His church?" Rosellen took a closer look at the building, and sure enough, there was a small wooden cross above the door.

"I think he's a minister. He wears a white collar and carries the Good Book around all the time."

She suddenly felt as if she'd ridden all this way for nothing. "You should have told me. He can't be the man I'm looking for."

Pilcher swallowed hard and his Adam's apple quivered. "He has a jagged scar on his hand, just like you were asking about."

Her hopes dashed, she said, "The man I'm looking for once robbed a bank and was involved in a murder."

"It could be him," he offered with more enthusiasm. "I guess what he has here is more of a mission than a church, but he has a scar. I'm sure of that. He took me in one time when I was lost and couldn't find my way back to town. I stayed with him a few days. He was a right nice fellow."

Now that she'd ridden all this way, she had to at least investigate. "All right, let's go."

They rode up to the church and threw their reins over the hitching rail in front of the house. There was a water trough and a bucket with hay in it for the horses. The man obviously knew how to welcome strangers. The two men playing checkers looked up but didn't break from their game.

As they dismounted, the door opened and an old man with a thick beard and a full head of silver hair came out to meet them. He held a book to his chest. The words "Holy Bible" were stamped on the cover in large gold lettering. His left arm hung down by his side. The chess players didn't bother to look up from their game.

"Welcome, brother and sister," he said. "Come in. I always have a pot of coffee ready to quench weary travelers' thirst and the word of God to comfort their souls."

Rosellen searched his face for some resemblance to her father, but found none.

"Is it him?" Pilcher asked softly.

"I don't know." She needed to look at his hand. She needed to ask him some questions, but now that she was here, she was the nervous one and she didn't know what to say to him.

"Will you come in for a spell, brethren?"

Pilcher remained quiet.

Rosellen looked around her. The day was hot, still. The sun hung halfway down the western sky. Rosellen didn't want to be here, but if she hoped to restore her father's reputation she would have to confront the man.

She walked up the two rickety steps and stood before the man under the shelter of the porch roof.

"My name is Rosellen Lattimer. I'm looking for a man named Dodge."

His eyes registered surprise, then acknowledgment as he slowly nodded. He lifted his left arm and placed his hand on the Bible, displaying a wide, jagged scar on the back of his hand. Rosellen felt her stomach turn a somersault.

"So you're Henry's little girl. He must be very proud of you."

Rosellen could only nod. At that moment she realized she had never really expected to find a man named Dodge. And now that she had, what in the world was she going to do?

"Everyone around here has known me as Preacher Jack for a long time. But you've found Dodge. Now tell me, what can I do for you?"

Rosellen could only stare at him. She'd denied his existence for so long that she didn't want to accept that she was looking at him now.

"Ah, ma'am, if he's the person you been looking for, I'd be much obliged if you'd pay me so I can head back into town."

She glanced at Pilcher. "Yes, he's the right man." She dug into the pocket of her trousers and pulled out a twenty-dollar gold piece.

Pilcher's eyes lit up like gaslights on a dark street corner. He closed his trembling hand around the coin. "Thank you, ma'am. I'm glad he's the right man, but I don't feel right about leaving you out here by herself. Do you want me to wait for you?"

"No, you go on. I might be a while. I can find my way back to town."

He hesitated.

"I'll be fine." She touched the handle of her gun. "I have protection if I need it."

"Yes, ma'am. I'm glad you found him." He pulled his reins free and mounted his horse.

"We have some things to talk about," she said.

Dodge nodded. "We can go inside and sit down, but it's cooler out here. Why don't we step over here by the well where we can have more privacy. There are some big ears around here."

Rosellen followed Preacher Jack over to the well, where the men on the porch couldn't hear their conversation.

"Did Henry send you looking for me?"

She shook her head. She was at a loss for words, and she knew the reason must be that she really didn't want to hear what Dodge had to say.

"How is your father?"

"He's dead."

"I'm sorry to hear that. Recently or a long time ago?"

"A year ago."

"May his soul rest in peace."

She had to moisten her lips before she could speak, but she managed to say, "That will depend on what you tell me."

"I'm a man of the cloth, sworn to tell the truth."

"Have you always been a minister?"

He laughed, and Rosellen could see a handsome man beneath his beard. "No, no. I was called to help my fellow man and preach the word of God some eight or nine years ago."

"I see."

Where should she begin? Could she just say, "Did you and my father rob a bank?" Even though she wasn't sure she wanted to know what he had to say, she was determined not to be wishy washy.

"You look a bit like Henry. I only saw you one other time when you were a young thing no more than five or six."

She wondered why she didn't remember his visit. She'd remembered seeing her father being congratulated in town when Cason's father was killed. Dodge must have visited around that same time but she had no recollection of him.

"Something's bothering you that you can't seem to get out," he said. "You didn't come all the way here just to tell me your father had died, did you?"

"No."

"Then tell me what I can do for, Rosellen."

"I want to know what happened fifteen years ago when you visited my father." Her voice shook. "The day the bank was robbed."

His lashes fluttered, and he gazed past her. Rosellen knew he was focusing on the hillside behind her as he looked into the past. He laid his Bible on the board that surrounded the well.

He was quiet for a few moments but finally said, "I guess you know all about that day or you wouldn't be asking me to tell you anything."

Her throat was tight. "No, you're wrong. I don't know. I—I've been told some things I can't believe, and I need you to swear to me on that Bible that they aren't true."

"What did you hear, child?"

Tears sprang to her eyes. She was angry with herself for being so weepy-eyed recently. "I can't say it."

"Then I'll tell you. The Lord told me that someday I'd have to pay a price for my part in what happened that day. I just thought it'd be after I'd done all the work I could do for God. I guess that time's come."

"What happened?"

"To start, me and your pa were never cousins. We were partners. He threw me in jail one night for cheating at cards. Guess I was lucky I wasn't shot. Me and Henry started talking about the big gold strikes that had been happening all around us." His voice turned wistful. "We wanted some of that money so bad. When it came time for me to leave, I asked him if I could stay in jail a while longer. I didn't have anywhere to go, and I was getting two meals a day."

"So you didn't come to our house."

"Only once, I think. And then not for long. We didn't want your mother asking too many questions we couldn't answer."

That explained why Rosellen never remembered seeing him, but he hadn't told her anything about the robbery. "Were you in Poppy when the bank was robbed?"

"I was there. Me and Henry had been talking about how everyone was finding gold and silver in the mountains and how it wasn't fair that some had so much and we had so little. Henry wasn't making much money either. Prospectors were coming into town every day talking about their gold strikes. Me and Henry talked about getting a grubstake and prospecting ourselves, but I said what we really needed was to find somebody who'd give us some so we wouldn't have to work to get it."

"Who'd do such a thing?"

"No one. That's why we hatched the plan to rob the bank."

Rosellen winced and grabbed hold of the railing around the well.

Preacher Jack kept talking. "I'm ashamed of the man I was back then, but even at that, we never wanted anyone to get hurt. Killing wasn't part of the plan."

It was easy for Rosellen to remain rigid. None of her muscles wanted to work, not even her mouth to ask the questions. "Tell me the whole story."

"It was stupid right from the beginning, but we were crazy with gold fever. Getting some of it was all we could talk about. Stealing it seemed to be the easiest and quickest way to get it. Henry thought no one would recognize him if he tied his kerchief over his face and wore some of my old clothes. But the young teller knew who he was, so Henry had to shoot him or risk being caught."

Rosellen shook with denial even as icy fingers of doom crept up her back. She felt hot and cold at the same time. "That's an easy story for you to tell, considering my father isn't here to dispute your word."

Preacher Jack stared directly into her eyes as if he wanted her to look deep into his soul and try to find one tiny shred of malice, anger, or deceit to indicate that he was lying, but she saw nothing but sorrow in the depths of his eyes.

"Guess you could take it that way. I wouldn't even mind if you did, though that wouldn't make it true. I'm to blame, same as Henry. The robbery was my idea in the first place. He wanted us to run off to the gold fields, but I didn't want to work that hard."

She had to ask about Cason's father. She was trembling so hard she wasn't sure he could understand her words. "Frank Murdock. What happened to him?"

"That was another part of our plan that went wrong. We'd gotten away with bags of gold flakes and nuggets. We took a big pile of money that day. When we went back to the abandoned mine to change our clothes there was a man there panning the stream. Henry said he recognized him from the town. When the man walked over to us, Henry had to shoot him, too."

"You're lying," she managed to choke out.

"No one questioned Henry too closely when he came riding into town with that man's body slung over his horse because no one would have suspected the sheriff of robbing his own town. He told the people that the other bank robber got away. I headed up to Denver, just as we planned. Me and Henry had worked out all the details about how I was to put his half of the money in a bank account and have it sent to him a little at a time."

She couldn't stop shaking. "Don't say any more. I can't believe that my father killed anyone." *Please tell me he didn't kill anyone!* "It seems too convenient that my father is dead and you say that he's the one who did both the killings."

"If it will make you feel better, I'll turn myself in and say that I'm the one who pulled the trigger."

"I want you to tell the truth," she managed to whisper.

He picked up the Bible and held it to his chest. "I have."

"How can I ever feel better knowing what you just said?"

"I'm just as responsible as Henry." His voice sounded tired. "The blood of those men is on my hands, too. I don't mind going to jail. The Lord has given me more time than I deserve. I've tried to redeem myself, and I believe I have helped some of God's people. I told the Lord to let me know when He was ready for me to confess my part in what happened. I'm ready to tell the story to the authorities."

She had to leave this man and think. Think? She couldn't think at all. What she needed to do was scream and scream and not stop until the hurt went away.

"My father was a good man. How could he have done such a thing?"

"He didn't set out to kill anyone."

"Then why did he? And why did you suggest robbing the bank?"

"I just wanted the gold, and it satisfied me for a long time. But one night after I'd drunk too much, the Lord told me in a dream to stop wasting that money and build a church. He said I'd hurt enough people and it was time to atone for my sins. He said for me to start helping the needy. Most of my share of the gold was gone, so I took what was left of Henry's and built this house for God's work and I've been here ever since. I heard he came to Denver looking for me, but the men I knew weren't going to tell a man wearing a badge anything."

Rosellen's breathing was heavy, thick. She needed somebody to tell her that this man was a liar, but no one stepped up to aid her. Somehow she had to endure this pain by herself.

"Whenever you're ready we'll go into town and talk to the authorities. My conscience has bothered me every day since the Lord spoke to me. I've been waiting for Him to let me know when He was ready for me to take my punishment. I guess it's time."

Her head was pounding. The bearded man stood with the Bible pressed against his chest. Her stomach rumbled, and she felt nauseated, but she managed to say, "I'll let you know when it's time for you to talk. There's somebody else I have to tell first."

"Would that be your mama? She'd need to know before everyone else."

Her mother—how could Rosellen tell her? But Evelyn wasn't the person she was thinking about. No, there was someone else she had to tell first. "Frank Murdock's son."

Rosellen mounted her horse and rode away from Preacher Jack. The wind whipped her hair into her face and stung her cheeks like pelting grains of sand. When she could hold herself together no longer she stopped the horse and jumped down. She fell against the horse's neck and sobbed into its warmth.

Her chest hurt from the great racking sobs that tore from her throat. Her father had deceived them all. His family. His town. Himself. He had walked the streets as if he were a good man and he wasn't!

"Why, Papa? *Why?*"

She turned away from the horse and cried into the wilderness. Gayla had been right. Cason had been right, and she knew that Preacher Jack was right. But how could she accept it?

Tears streamed down her face, but she didn't bother to wipe them away. Her nose was stuffy and her throat ached. She felt weak and trembly, lacking the strength to mount the horse again.

Her hands made fists and she shook them at the heavens. "Papa, how could you have done this to all of us who loved you so much? You destroyed three lives and for what? Money! You had a loving wife, four children, and the respect of a whole town. Why wasn't that enough?"

Enraged and still sobbing, she looked around for something to throw. She bent down and picked up a small rock and threw it into the sky. Then she threw another and another until tears blinded her and she sank to her knees. She shook her head and cried sorrowfully.

Rosellen had never seen the teller who was killed, nor had she known Frank Murdock and Cason back then, but she had no trouble picturing in her mind the body of a young man lying in a pool of blood on the floor of the bank, his life slipping away from him drop by drop. She could envision a handsome man with a bullet hole in his forehead, propped up outside the jail with flies buzzing about his face. She could picture a young boy holding a gun to his own head, crying and praying for the courage to pull the trigger and end his life. And all she could do was cry.

She stayed on her knees until the sun sank almost to the horizon. An early evening wind rustled the leaves and branches. The sky darkened.

"Oh, Papa," she whispered into the burning glow of sunset, "I wish I could understand why you wanted that money so badly."

She couldn't forgive her father, but she had to consider her mother and her brothers. They had loved him too. They would be devastated. Her mother wouldn't be able to hold her head up when she walked down the street.

What was Rosellen going to do? How could she tell news that would destroy her family?

But maybe she wouldn't have to, she realized. Cason didn't know she'd found Dodge. Rosellen had already paid Pilcher. He would be drunk for days with the money she gave him. No one else had to know the truth.

"Yes," she said aloud, suddenly feeling better. She rose from the ground and wiped her eyes with the edge of the saddle blanket. "Of course. I don't have to tell Cason anything. How can he find out? He will continue to look for Dodge, but even if Pilcher hears about it, there's no reason to think he'll come forward again."

Cason's family had already been destroyed, and he had lived through it. What purpose would be served by ruining her own family as well? Her father was dead and could no longer be punished. Preacher Jack had turned his life around and was doing good work. He couldn't help anyone from prison or hanging from a rope.

Yes, in a few days she'd ride back out here and tell Preacher Jack to forget he ever saw her. No one would ever know she'd found him.

Rosellen climbed back on her horse and rode toward Denver. It was well after dark when she reached town. She wouldn't allow herself to think past the idea of what she had decided to do. She had to deceive Cason in order to spare her mother and her brothers the hurt she'd just gone through.

After returning the horse to the livery stable, she returned to the hotel room. After taking a deep breath she opened the door and walked inside, comfortable with her decision to deceive Cason. She'd convinced herself she would be keeping this from him for all the right reasons. Hadn't her brothers taught her that sometimes it was all right to lie?

There was a light on when the door swung open. Cason swung away from the window.

"Rosellen, where have you been? You've had me worried sick." A frown formed between his brows. "And why are you dressed in men's clothing again?"

Chapter

➤ 23 ◄

Cason had been worried about her. She could see the concern in his face. She'd intended to lie to him, but she couldn't lie to the man she loved. If she did, she'd be no better than her father. Like him, she would always be living a lie.

All of a sudden Rosellen knew she didn't want to be like her father. That realization hit her so hard she staggered. For as long as she could remember she'd wanted to be just like Henry Lattimer. All these years of idolizing him trying to be like him, crumbled away from her. The weight that came off her shoulders tilted her world. She fell backward against the door.

"Rosellen, what's wrong?" Cason rushed to her side and took hold of her shoulders. "What's happened? You look as if you've been crying. What's wrong with you?"

Her strength had been her father's reputation and her dream of continuing his work for the town. She'd wanted to be just like him—until today.

She looked into Cason's concerned eyes and said,

"I have something to tell you, Cason. And it's not going to be easy to say."

"Out with it. I've been half out of my mind with worry."

His hands still held her arms, giving her strength.

"I found Dodge," she said. "You were gone, and I didn't dare wait, for fear of losing the man."

His eyes pierced her. "Where is he? I'll go right now."

"I've already been."

"I bet you have." His voice was harsh. He swung away from her. "It will be a cold day in hell before I believe anything you have to say." He jabbed an angry finger at her.

She didn't blame him for being so angry. She had planned to deceive him. She didn't deserve his high regard.

Her throat clogged with pain as she said, "He told the truth."

He threw her a look of contempt. "So you think that means I'm not going to talk to him. Just because he told you what you wanted to hear. I can't believe you'd think I'd believe that."

For the first time since he'd told his story, she understood how Cason had felt when he said he didn't want to live anymore. Sometimes the pain was just too great. But even as she thought that, she knew she didn't want to kill herself. She just very much wanted to go away somewhere and forget she had ever come to Denver.

She didn't know how she managed to keep her voice loud enough for him to hear her. She didn't know how she was holding herself together.

"He calls himself Preacher Jack. He runs a mission a few miles from here."

Cason picked up his hat and put his hand on the door handle. "Which direction? I'll find it."

"His story was the same as Gayla's. He said my father killed the bank teller and your father."

Cason snapped around and stared at her, stunned. "What? What did you say?"

She remained standing, but she didn't know how. She felt as if her whole world had come crashing down around her feet. Cason could never love her now, knowing for certain she was the daughter of the man who had destroyed his father and his mother.

"Preacher Jack told the story you wanted to hear," she said. "My father was guilty, and your father was innocent."

She saw in his eyes that her words stunned him. He was speechless. He opened the door, then stopped. She felt his tension, his indecision. Did he trust her, or did he want to talk to Preacher Jack himself?

"Which direction?" he finally asked again, but he didn't look at her.

"East." She swallowed hard. "Follow the main road until you come to an old relay station. Take the left fork. You'll see the mission in a clearing."

Cason walked out the door.

She felt empty and alone, but knew she'd done the right thing. She didn't know how she could have considered lying to Cason. She loved him too much to hurt him that way. An innocent man had been branded a murderer long enough, and her father deserved to have his name besmirched in Frank Murdock's place.

She just wished she didn't have to tell her mother and her brothers, but there was no other way to clear Murdock's name to save her family. The lie had to be corrected.

On stiff legs she dragged herself into the bedroom and started packing. Even though she knew it would rip her heart from her chest, she had to go back to Poppy and tell her family the truth.

Then she would be faced with a much greater task: learning to live without Cason.

Cason was crazy with relief and joyous with vindication but also full of pain as he galloped back toward town in the wee hours of the morning. He was afraid for Rosellen. He'd brushed aside her feelings in his mad dash to get to Preacher Jack.

While he was talking to the man once known as Dodge, thoughts of Rosellen had kept flashing across his mind. He'd been too angry with her to comprehend what she must have been going through. But now he remembered how desolate she looked when she told him what Preacher Jack had confirmed.

She hadn't just loved her father; she'd worshiped him. Cason was angry with himself for not realizing sooner what she was going through and what courage it had taken for her to stand before him and tell him the truth. She could have kept the news to herself. In fact, she wouldn't have been the strong woman she was if she hadn't at least thought about not telling him. He should have taken her in his arms and comforted her instead of rushing out to talk with Preacher Jack. He had to get to Rosellen.

So many things had changed for him since he rode into Poppy. But the biggest change of all had been his feelings for Rosellen.

He'd had no thoughts of proving his father's innocence when he arrived in Poppy. His only mission was to shut down the town—an eye for an eye. His thirst for revenge had kept him going when he thought he had nothing to live for. That hadn't changed.

He wanted to make the town pay for not helping his mother when she needed them. He didn't know where that left him with Rosellen. He could tell her he loved her and wanted to marry her, spend the rest of his life loving her, but not in Poppy, Colorado.

Rosellen. He loved her. For now that had to be enough.

Cason made it back to Denver by sunrise. He hurried into the hotel and quietly opened the door, thinking he wouldn't awaken Rosellen if by some chance she was asleep. But she wasn't. He found her dressed and standing by the window.

She turned and faced him. Her eyes were dull with pain. He wanted to rush over and take her in his arms, comfort her. But the unsettled things that lay between them kept him by the door.

"You should be in bed."

"There would be no point. I couldn't sleep. Did you talk to Preacher Jack?"

"Yes, he told me everything." Cason walked farther into the room and noticed her satchel. "You're packed."

She nodded. "There's no reason for me to stay here now. I— We found out what we came for"—she took a deep breath and looked away from him—"and now I have to go home and tell my family the truth. Then I'll tell Mr. Vestly. I'm sure he will be happy to spread the news around town for us. I'll leave it up to him, or you, to decide what needs to be done about Preacher Jack's involvement."

Cason wanted to hold her, but he knew she wouldn't want comfort from him. He hated seeing her like this. His insistence on knowing the truth about their fathers had caused her this pain.

"Rosellen, I can't say I'm sorry things turned out the way they did. I'm not."

She settled her gaze on him. "I don't expect you to be. I certainly wouldn't have been sorry if the story had turned out the way I expected."

"I am sorry for you."

Her lips trembled. He started toward her, but she stepped back. "You once asked me not to feel sorry for you, and now I'm asking you not to pity me," she said. "I'm going to be all right."

She couldn't mask the pain. He saw it. "I know how much you loved and respected your father," he said.

"I now understand that I loved and respected a man who didn't exist. I didn't know the real Henry Lattimer. The man I thought I knew couldn't have killed two men and then lived with a lie for fourteen years."

"I think maybe Gayla was right when she said the gold fever got to him."

"Don't try to comfort me, Cason."

"Rosellen, I saw gold fever every day. I was a part of it. It drove thousands of men crazy. You don't know what it was like before large companies bought up all the claims. Prospectors were killed every day for their stake. Dandies from back east—men who'd never been on a horse or cooked over an open fire—sold all they had and bought a pick, a shovel, and a pan."

"Gold fever doesn't absolve my father."

"No, but the fever struck in different ways. Would a sane man spend twelve hours a day squatting in frigid water, rotating a pan until his arms were numb? Would a sane man endure temperatures of over one hundred degrees in the shade as he picked away at the side of a mountain looking for little nuggets of gold?"

"You did. Buster and many others did. My father could have done it too if he'd wanted gold that badly. He didn't have to kill two innocent men." Her voice was edged with rigid pride.

What she said was true. Cason couldn't offer any other solace.

"My father didn't work hard for that money," she continued passionately. "He stole it. He killed for it. Even if I could forgive him for that, how can I forgive him for leaving me to tell my mother and brothers what a horrible thing he did? Don't you see, Cason, he not only ruined your family but now from the grave he's ruined my family, too."

"Rosellen . . ." He reached out for her, but she stepped away from him again.

"Don't. I refuse to cry any more, and I'm afraid I will if you touch me right now. It would be too easy to lay my head on your shoulder and weep."

His heart broke for her. She was a strong woman, but this news about her father was devastating. "Maybe that's what you need to do."

"No. I'll never cry for Henry Lattimer again. He doesn't deserve one tear."

Cason nodded. He couldn't disagree with what she said about Lattimer, but that didn't keep him from wanting to hold her, love her, and find a way to bring a smile to her face.

"I'm going to the depot to wait for the first train heading south. If you don't mind, I'd like to tell my family before you have Preacher Jack arrested. I don't want the news to get back to them before I do."

Her words stung him. "I wasn't planning on running to the sheriff. I'm going with you back to Poppy."

"I told you I'd tell the truth about what my father did."

"I trust you," he answered. "But I need to see Buster about some things." He didn't want her traveling halfway down the state by herself. He wanted to be with her.

Fear rose up in her eyes again. "Are you going to keep your promise and not close the mine?"

"I gave my word. I intend to keep it." He wasn't going to tell her that he'd thought of another way to ruin the town by buying up the businesses one at a time and then shutting them all down. He didn't want her to know that.

"What will you do now? You have your justice but not your revenge."

"Justice is revenge. The means are different but the outcome is the same. I can live with that."

Rosellen noticed that the end of the day had brought a late summer nip to the air as she stepped down from the platform at the depot in Poppy. She didn't care if she never saw another train. With unexpected delays and numerous stops, it had taken two full days and nights to get to Poppy, but she felt as if she'd been on the train for two weeks. And having Cason beside her the whole way looking at her with such concern in his eyes had shredded her nerves to the breaking point.

She was desperate to get away from him. Looking at him made her want to rely on his strength instead of her own, and she couldn't do that. It was her father, her family, her problem. She had to find the guts to deal with the situation.

She knew Cason would stay in town long enough to see that she told everyone the truth about her father, and then he'd be gone. Just thinking about his leaving made her ache all over. How was she going to learn to live without him, knowing how much she loved him?

There had been no joy when the train pulled into the station. She didn't feel the same way about Poppy as she had when she left, before she learned how the townspeople had treated Cason. Could she and her family stay in Poppy and walk the streets the way they used to? No. There was a real possibility that she, her mother, and her brothers would be ostracized, just as Cason and his mother had been. How could she put her mother through that?

Her brothers could make their own decisions, but what about Evelyn? Just hearing the gossip had upset her mother terribly. Rosellen thought maybe it would be best if she and her mother sold the house and moved away. But where would they go? Their home was paid for.

Probably with money from the robbery.

When Preacher Jack first told her the story she somehow felt responsible for what her father had done. She thought his crimes were hers and she would have to atone for them. But now she was feeling better, and she realized that no one else in her family was responsible for what Henry Lattimer had done. They had nothing to do with that horrible crime, and they shouldn't accept any of the blame or shame.

She turned and faced Cason. "I guess this is where we say good-bye."

"No," he said, and reaching out to take her carpetbag from her hand. "I want to talk to you. I'll walk you home."

"I don't think that's a good idea, Cason." She couldn't keep her lips from trembling. She could live with losing her father, but it was killing her to lose Cason. She didn't know if she could bear it. "We've said all there is to say to each other. I have to talk to my mother now before I lose my courage."

"You lose your courage? Never."

Her eyes watered and she felt silly but said, "Don't try to make me feel better, Cason. You don't know how close I am to losing control. I haven't asked you for anything but I'm asking you to leave me now so I can hold my head up while I walk through town."

"You asked me not to close the mine."

"Dammit, Cason, you can't make me feel any worse than I do right now, so get away from me. Please."

He gently touched her chin with the tips of his fingers, forcing her to look at him. "I'm going to walk you home. Let's go."

It was crazy but sometimes little things meant so much. Just knowing she'd have Cason with her as she walked through town to her house made her feel better. She doubted they'd meet anyone, since this was the dinner hour, but she was grateful he would be by her side for a little longer, giving her his strength.

She looked from one side of the street to the other. The pride she had once felt every time she walked down the boardwalk was gone. In its place was a sad feeling of disappointment.

They were quiet as they walked through town and down the street that led to her house. When they arrived at the white picket fence, Rosellen stopped. She was shaking inside. She didn't want to tell Cason good-bye. She wanted to fight for his love, but how could she?

What her father and her town had done to him had been unforgivable. Cason didn't want to forgive them. She wouldn't ask him to. He wanted to punish them, and she couldn't find it in her heart to believe that wish was wrong. But closing the mine would hurt people who'd had no part in the way Cason was treated fifteen years ago.

She looked up and met his eyes. She saw concern in their depths, and she appreciated it, but she had to get away from him quickly. "I can make it the rest of the way by myself, Cason."

"Wait. There are some things we need to talk about."

How could she talk when all she wanted to do was cry?

"I did a lot of thinking on the train ride to Poppy, Rosellen."

"I know. So did I. And you don't have to worry about me or my family. We're going to be all right."

He looked at the sky for a moment. "The reason I agreed so quickly to keep the mine open is that I knew I could buy up the businesses in town and then close them down one by one until there was no town left. I planned on doing that."

Her heart skipped a beat. "You bastard."

He nodded.

"You fooled us all," she said.

"Even myself. That's what I wanted to do, but I've decided I can't do that to you."

Rosellen stiffened. He was confusing her, and she didn't like it. He was supposed to be telling her it was over between them.

Her fighting spirit returned. "I don't understand, Cason. What exactly are you trying to tell me? Are you going to buy up the town or not?"

"I'm not."

Her breath caught in her throat. She saw in his eyes that he meant what he said. Relief shook her. "Thank you. I know some of the people in Poppy might deserve to be put out of business, but not all of them lived here fifteen years ago."

"I've also decided I don't want you to tell your family what Preacher Jack said about your father."

Rosellen stared at him and shook her head. She didn't hear him correctly. She felt light-headed, confused. "I'm not sure I understand you Cason."

"Let's get out of the street." He led her through the gate and up onto the porch. He grasped her upper arms. "It took me a long time to make up my mind, but I finally decided nothing would be gained by telling your mother and brothers about your father."

"Cason?" She was too stunned to say more. All she could do was stare into his eyes.

He gently squeezed her arms. "I'm not going to destroy the town, and I don't want you to tell the truth about your father."

Goose bumps pebbled her skin. She searched his face. Was he serious? Yes. Her heart leaped for joy. But, no . . . she loved him too much to let him make such a sacrifice.

She swallowed past the lump of gratitude in her throat.

"Your father was an innocent man," she whispered. "He deserves to have his name cleared, and my father deserves to be exposed for the criminal he was."

"They're both dead. I have no family left to be hurt by the truth. You do. It's enough for me that you and I know and that you are *willing* to tell the truth. I don't plan to stay around this town, so the gossip and long glances won't bother me, but your mother and brothers have to live here."

His generosity overwhelmed her. "Why would you want to do that for my family? My brothers attacked you."

"I'm doing it for you, Rosellen. I don't want you to go through the pain of telling them."

Her heart overflowed with love for him. He was such a good man. He was willing to give up his revenge for her. Without thinking about her actions, she reached up and hugged him. Slowly his hands went around her waist and pulled her close. For a second she was tempted to stay there in his arms, but knew she couldn't. Being in his arms felt right, but she had to remember that Cason was giving her this gift of compassion before he told her good-bye.

She quickly slid out of his embrace and backed away before she changed her mind and begged him to find a way in his heart to love her as she loved him.

It was Cason's turn to give her a confused look.

Tears came to her eyes, and for once she didn't care and didn't try to blink them away. She was proud to love this man, and she didn't care who knew it.

"Thank you, Cason, but I can't accept your generous offer. Everyone has to know. I wouldn't feel right about it any other way. Your sacrifice is too great." She took a deep breath and felt good about her decision.

"No. You wanted to do it. That's enough. Think about your mother. Don't put her through the pain you've suffered."

Rosellen was so filled with love for him. "How can I refuse when you ask me not to hurt my mother? But how can I repay you?" A tear ran down her cheek. She lifted her empty hands. "Cason, what can I do for you?"

He wiped the tear away with the pad of his thumb. "You could marry me."

Her breath caught in her throat again.

He stared into her eyes and said, "All the way to Poppy I kept telling myself that I wanted everyone to know what your father did. I wanted to destroy the town and walk away from you without once looking back, but I can't do any of those things. I don't give a damn about this town, but I don't want you to tell anyone about your father because . . . I love you, and I don't want you to be hurt any more."

Rosellen blinked. Her whole body felt as if it had turned to water. "You love me?" she managed to whisper through trembling lips.

"Hell, yes, I love you. That's what I've been trying to tell you."

"You better not be lying to me, Cason Murdock."

He smiled. "Rosellen Lattimer, I love you. You are the only woman I've ever loved. I want to marry you. I want you be my wife and live with me."

"Oh, Cason, I love you, too." She threw her arms around his neck.

Cason wrapped his arms around her waist and twirled her. He kissed her briefly on the lips several times, then set her feet on the porch again.

Suddenly the fear of losing him gripped Rosellen, and she grabbed his arms. "I can't believe this. Cason, how can you want to marry me after what my father did to yours?"

He kept his arms around her and looked deep into her eyes. "I won't lie to you. It took me a while to work that out. I didn't know if I could. But you didn't have anything to do with what happened fifteen years ago. I realized that if I blamed you or your family for what your father did I'd be no better than the people who blamed my mother and me for what they thought my father did. I decided I didn't want to be like those people."

She laid her hand on his chest, needing to touch him. "And you're not. You're nothing like them."

"I know you want to be sheriff."

"No," she murmured earnestly as the lump in her throat grew. "I haven't really thought about being the sheriff for some time now."

"Are you sure?"

A sad smile eased across her face. "Yes. I think I would have been a good sheriff, but I don't want to be the sheriff of Poppy anymore. I wouldn't feel right about it now, even if you hadn't asked me to marry you."

"Listen to me. What your father did has nothing to do with you. You'd be the best sheriff any town could have."

Gratitude filled her. "But that's not what I want anymore. I used to think my father's life was much more interesting than my mother's. He was involved with the town, making decisions. He was out walking the streets, talking with people, helping them reconcile their differences. My mother was always cooking, washing, cleaning, sewing."

He touched her cheek with the back of his hand. "That's what most women do."

"Yes, but I didn't know about the other part until I met you."

"The other part?" he questioned.

"Of being a woman. Most married people make love every night, don't they?"

"Most of the time, I guess. Why?"

"Well, that certainly makes marriage worth thinking about, doesn't it?"

"So you'd recommend it?"

She smiled. "Definitely."

"Is that a yes to my proposal?"

"Oh, yes, Cason. I love you with all my heart."

A shadow of concern crossed his face. "There's one other thing we need to talk about. I won't live here in Poppy. Will you agree to leave your family and go away with me."

"Of course. My life's with you Cason."

"Do you mean that, Rosellen?"

"I do. I was just waiting for you to realize you loved me, too. I was so afraid you were going to say good-bye. You've put me through hell, you know."

"This is a big decision for you to make. I know how much you loved this town."

"I've been thinking of what you said about the townspeople. I never told you, but I was thankful you came to help me that day with the prospector. I was shaking so hard I could barely stand up."

"You didn't seem nervous. You looked very brave."

She looked up the street toward the town. "A few days ago I could have never left this place, but now I can walk away and never look back." She gazed into his eyes. "I love you, Cason. I'll marry you and move anywhere as long as I'm with you."

Cason bent down and gently kissed her lips, sealing their promise to each other.

Rosellen looked up at him and said, "I have to say it one more time, Cason: your father deserves to have his name cleared."

His arms slid around her waist. He pulled her to him. "The rumor is all over town, about your father being the real murderer. Those who want to believe it will, and those who don't wouldn't believe anything bad about Henry Lattimer even if we told the truth. Let it lie, Rosellen. Come away with me, and let's build a home and a family together."

"Oh, yes, Cason, yes."

Cason dipped his head and kissed her passionately.

"Hmm, excuse me."

"Buster," Cason said, breaking away from Rosellen. "How did you know we were here?"

"Ah . . . I didn't." he said, walking up the steps. "Welcome back."

"What are you doing in front of my house with those flowers in your hand?" Rosellen asked.

Buster looked uncomfortable. "Well, Rose, ah . . . I'm courting your mother."

"What?" Rosellen asked, stepping away from Cason. "Since when? I didn't even know you knew her."

Buster stuck his finger down his collar and pulled on it, letting the flowers scrape against his clean-shaven cheek. "She came to see me and asked me if I'd consider not closing the mine."

"My mother did that?"

"Yes, and being a gentleman, I told her I'd think about it—if she'd consider letting me court her. So we worked out an agreement."

Rosellen and Cason looked at each other and smiled as the front door opened. Evelyn stepped out and said, "What's all the talking— Rosellen! You're home, dear!" She threw her arms around her daughter and hugged her tightly. "Thank God you're safe. I've been so worried about you."

"You've always worried about me, Mama," Rosellen said and kissed her mother's cheek.

"I always will." Evelyn stared at her daughter. "Look at you in a dress, and it's not even Sunday. I—

I can't believe it." She looked from Buster to Cason, and her gaze stayed on him.

"Mama, I don't believe you've been introduced to Cason Murdock."

Evelyn's lips tightened, and she stiffened. "No, dear, I haven't."

Rosellen felt a chill. It might take some time for her mother to warm up to Cason.

"I brought these for you, Mrs. Lattimer," Buster said, holding out the boutquet.

She took the flowers. "Thank you, Mr. O'Malley. They're beautiful."

"Why don't we go inside? I think we all need to talk in private," Buster said.

"That's a good idea," Rosellen said. "Mama, you and Mr. O'Malley go on in. We'll be in right behind you."

Evelyn looked at Cason again, but her features weren't as stiff. "All right, dear."

As soon as the front door closed behind them, Cason wrapped his arm around Rosellen's waist and he smiled down at her. "Do we agree that what we learned from Preacher Jack is our secret?"

Rosellen looked at him with all the love she was feeling. "You are such a fine man, Cason. I can never make this up to you."

"And you are a deserving woman, Rosellen. I'm going to do my best to make you happy."

"You already have. You are a very forgiving man, Cason Murdock."

"I have reason to be now. I don't need or want revenge. I have your love, and I don't need anything else."

A bubble of excitement rushed through Rosellen. "Cason, can we go get married right now?"

"What? Right now?"

"Yes. Judge Mack lives on the other side of town.

He's too old to be a judge anymore, but he can still marry people. I want to marry you now, Cason. Before you change your mind let's go to his house."

Cason laughed and hugged her. "I'm not going to change my mind."

"If we don't get married right now, we'll have to sleep alone tonight. You at the hotel and me here at my mother's house."

He kissed her solidly on the lips and then said, "Let's go find that judge."

Chapter

➤ 24 ◄

$\mathcal{M}$r. and Mrs. Cason Murdock walked down the street in Poppy, Colorado, the next morning, boldly holding hands.

It surprised Rosellen that she wasn't sad. She should have been. She was leaving the only home she'd ever known. In a few minutes she would meet her mother, her three brothers, and their wives and children at the train station to say good-bye.

This would be the last time she walked the streets of Poppy. She didn't plan to return, but her family could visit her in Denver whenever they wanted to see her. So she felt at peace.

In her bedroom at her mother's house she had left her trousers and the old Colt her father had given her years ago. She felt all right about leaving those things behind. Her days of wanting to follow in her father's footsteps were gone forever.

She did want to keep up her aim, however. According to Cason, if a woman wanted to shoot in Denver there were firing ranges set up especially for target practice.

She smiled up at Cason. "I hope we have a baby soon, don't you?"

"Well, I'm not in a big hurry. I want all of your attention for a while."

"I want to have a son so I can teach him how to ride and shoot."

"That's my job. You can teach him table manners."

Rosellen pursed her lips. "It might take me a while to figure out all the things a wife is supposed to do."

He smiled. "You haven't had any trouble so far. If you do, I'll help you."

"I was surprised to hear that Gayla died while we were gone."

"She knew her time was short and had made her peace. I just can't understand why she left the Silver Nugget to us even if she did say she loved our fathers."

"I guess she wouldn't have if she'd had any family. What are we going to do with it?"

"We don't need the money," Cason said, "and I don't want to own a saloon."

Rosellen and Cason looked at each other at the same time. "Are you thinking what I am?" he asked.

"What are you thinking?" she asked.

"That we sell the saloon and send the money to Preacher Jack for his church."

His words warmed her. "Cason, how can you want to be so kind to a man who could have helped your father and didn't?"

"Because when you married me yesterday afternoon, you gave me everything I wanted. I can afford too be generous to others."

"That's being more than gen—" Rosellen stopped dead on the boardwalk and stared at a wagon on the opposite side of the street.

"What is it, Rosellen? You look as if you've seen a ghost."

She felt her skin crawl. "Worse. I've seen a devil." Her hand flew to her hip and she looked down. She was wearing a dress, not trousers and a gun belt. *Dammit.* She spun around and looked at Cason. "Give me your gun, Cason."

His brows drew together. "What the hell are you talking about?"

"Please give me your gun."

"Rosellen."

"I don't have time to go back and get mine, Cason, please give me yours."

Without further questions, he pulled his pistol out of his holster and gave it to her, handle first. His faith in her made her question what she intended to do for a second, but she didn't change her mind.

Rosellen held the gun in one hand and her skirt in the other as she stepped off the boardwalk and down into the street. The hem of her dark blue skirt whispered across the dusty road.

She walked about halfway to the other side and pointed the gun at the cargo of a wagon that read "Alford Clark Whiskey Sales." *The man who had spread the gossip about her father—and for money.*

She carefully aimed and fired all six bullets into the wagon so that each bullet shattered several bottles before it was spent. By the time the last bullet was fired, the amber liquor had already started running out of the sides of the wagon and pooling on the dirt.

But that wasn't enough. She started swinging the handle of the gun with all her might, smashing the glass and breaking off the necks of more liquor bottles. Then she stepped back and watched.

Cason came up beside her. She gave him the gun.

A lanky man came running out of the saloon. "Shit, what happened? Who shot up my whiskey?" He looked over and saw Rosellen and Cason. "What the hell are you doing?"

Cason quickly reloaded the gun. It pleased her that he stood ready to defend her if necessary.

Rosellen looked around and saw Mr. Wilkins and Mr. Carmichael standing in the doorways of their store. Mr. Vestly came bounding down the walkway, and so did several other townspeople, but not a one of them stepped into the street.

"She shot my whiskey bottles! Did you see her?" Alford Clark yelled to no one in particular."

"Is that you, Rosellen? In a Sunday dress?" Mr. Vestly asked.

"Never mind that," the irate whiskey salesman shouted. "Look what she did. My liquor is running into the street. She must have broken two dozen bottles of my finest whiskey."

"That's right, Mr. Clark," Rosellen said. "Think twice the next time you want to repeat saloon gossip for money. Everybody repeats gossip, but it's not right to profit from it."

"You're the mayor," Clark said to Mr. Vestly. "Arrest her. Make her pay for this."

"Nobody has ever been able to make her do anything," Mr. Vestly replied.

"This is an outrage," the frantic man exclaimed, running from one side of his wagon to the other. "Where's the sheriff?"

"You know we don't have one," Mr. Vestly said.

"Then I demand that you arrest her and make her pay for this."

"Won't do any good. She always has been and always will be a hellion."

Cason shoved his gun down into his holster and started toward the mayor, but Rosellen touched his arm and stopped him. "Don't."

He frowned. "I'm not going to let him get away with calling you that name."

She kept her hand on his arm and laughed lightly. "It's okay, Cason. It doesn't matter anymore."

"She needs a man who can handle her," someone called from the other side of the street.

"She'll never change," came another voice.

Rosellen looked into Cason's eyes. "They're right, you know. Are you sorry you married me?"

"Hell, no. I love you, Rosellen. You couldn't do anything to change that."

She looked adoringly into his eyes. "I love you, too, Cason. So very much."

He smiled down at her. "In fact, I think we should give the people of Poppy something to talk about for a long time after we leave."

"What's that?"

"This."

He pulled her into his arms and kissed her with all the love he was feeling.

Let
Andrea Kane
romance you tonight!

Dream Castle 73585-3/$5.99

My Heart's Desire 73584-5/$5.50

Masque of Betrayal 75532-3/$4.99

Echoes In the Mist 75533-1/$5.99

Samantha 86507-2/$5.50

The Last Duke 86508-0/$5.99

Emerald Garden 86509-9/$5.99

Wishes In the Wind 53483-1/$5.99

Legacy of the Diamond 53485-8/$5.99

The Black Diamond 53482-3/$5.99

The Music Box 53484-X/$6.50

Available from Pocket Books